Three Women in November

An incredible true love story

Jim SHOMOS

Three Women in November first published in 2021. New edition published in 2023.

Copyright © Jim Shomos

ISBN Paperback: 987-0-645458-5-7

ISBN Ebook: 987-0-645458-4-0

ISBN Large Print Edition: 987-0-645458-6-4

This story is based on my recollection of shared moments with three special women between 2006-2009. Names, locations, and venues have been changed. Many venues and official events have been invented. Dialogue has been drafted from memory and/or created for dramatic purposes. Some scenes have been composited or invented for entertainment purposes. All emails and messages have been written or substantially re-imagined by the author.

I thank the three women portrayed in this book for letting me into their lives and hearts. I recognize that their memories of the events described in this book may be different than my own. They are each smart, decent, and hard-working people. The book is not intended to hurt them or anyone they care about.

Cover Design: Lisa Messegee

Editor: Carolyn Depew

Proofreader: Shannon Lanham Marshall

Layout and typesetting: Irish Ink Publishing

Screen rights enquiries: Screenrights@JimShomos.com

ALSO BY JIM SHOMOS

Leo's romantic adventure continues in, Kissing Scars

Leads your heart to a festival of love. A romantic comedy novella inspired by a true story.

www.JimShomos.com/kissing-scars

Intoxicating, organic, and simply breathtaking. The Never Ending Bookshelf, 5*

Don't miss Jim's debut novel, Up Here

When you've had two dream marriages, choosing your eternal soulmate in heaven is one hell of a dilemma.

www.JimShomos.com/up-here

The most original romantic-comedy this century. Artisan Book Reviews, 5*

Up Here touched my soul, a beautiful romantic comedy about love, hope and courage. Alli, 5*

Jim Shomos must have written this with a twinkle in his eyes, as moving, as it is funny. Ella, 5*

Jim's latest novel, More Text Than Sex

A relationship comedy-drama drowning in the music biz.

www.JimShomos.com/more-text-than-sex

Deeper than an edgy contemporary romance, More Text Than Sex is a slow dance with the very soul of music. Tanya Doko, award winning singer/songwriter.

What a treat to dive into this insatiable story. Shomos is a literary rock star! Marcelle, singer/songwriter.

Get VIP release news about Jim's coming books at:

www.JimShomos.com/contact

Dedicated to
The spirits that endlessly feed my romantic soul.

This love story happened between 2006-2009
Despite being set in Australia, this book is edited in USA English.

1

I'LL LINE YOUR PALMS WITH SILVER

HER SOUL-MAMMA LAUGH BURST THROUGH LEO'S FOGGY HEAD; DEEP, physical soundwaves pulling him into a virtual group hug with everyone else in hearing range across the hotel's expansive lounge area. Leo shifted in his seat towards the epicenter.

A few yards behind, the focal point amongst a group of women in armchairs, her huge cheeks and shoulder-length wavy black hair danced to the rhythm of her laugh.

His soul scrambled for its dancing shoes.

Who is she?

Pumped with antibiotics and flu tablets, he'd skipped the official Digi-Lab introductions, as he needed to crash after arriving in Batemans Bay. He shouldn't have flown up from Melbourne. Shouldn't have been on the three-hour bus ride to the resort. Shouldn't be buzzing from a once-in-a-lifetime laugh.

Who is she?

She wasn't one of the other mentors. He'd read up on the four international digital media gurus and knew his three Aussie colleagues. Wouldn't have missed her photo amongst the eight creative teams participating from film, TV, theater, and publishing.

As the laughter settled, her gaze drifted across the room. Not great timing. With the green, feminine scarf he'd wrapped over his head and the trinkets arranged on the table in front of him, he must have looked like a bedraggled gypsy at a Middle Eastern bazaar.

"I'll line your palms with silver," she said, deep and husky, how a cheeky grin would sound in silk lingerie.

"Come here and say that."

For a moment, Mystery Woman seemed surprised by their mutual cheekiness, then unleashed her smile. As big and warm as her laugh, it wrapped around his heart in a nanosecond.

I have to meet her. Get up now, stroll over and—

"Ahoy there, Gypsy, we've come to loot your bounty."

He wrenched his eyes from Mystery Woman as Raf and his teammates dropped plastic gold medallions onto his table. They had been quick. Too quick.

Digi-Lab leader, Giga, had given Leo the low-energy role of 'seller' in his traditional ice-breaker game. The eight project teams and seven other mentors had to solve riddles in the virtual and real world to collect medallions hidden outside Suzella Cliff Resort, then exchange them for trinkets, which each team would use in a short play after dinner.

By the time Leo had sold his merchandise to all the teams, exhaustion and achy bones set up camp in his body again. His mission was Survival Sunday, Manage Monday, Flying by Friday. He needed another round of legal chemicals, or he wouldn't survive Sunday. Or maybe that smile. He turned around as casually as he could towards Mystery Woman... but she'd left. Left a massive void in the lounge area and a ton of curiosity in his heart.

Who is she?

Zoya Orlenko.

Leo had extracted some info out of Giga. As the CEO of shiny new government body, Digital Media Australia, Zoya was a major VIP. Despite only being in the Canberra-based role just two weeks, she'd already invested DMA funds to cover all food and drinks for the Digi-Lab, including the Friday night party. She'd obviously done her research on Giga and the six-day residential workshops he created before she started the role.

A burst of her laugh tested the restaurant's floor-to-ceiling windows and triggered his smile. Zoya mingled among the tables while participants and mentors gobbled their breakfast before the five intensive days of the lab kicked off.

"They promised six megabits but we're not even getting one," said Giga, who didn't earn his nickname by accident.

He nodded while sneaking glances over Giga's shoulder.

Zoya Orlenko.

A strength to the name and definitely European ancestry, eastern or Baltic. Late thirties, maybe forty. A high forehead added to her regal air.

"I'll have to redesign half my presentation if the hotel doesn't get their act together," said Giga.

"Yeah, frustrating. Will she be here all week? Do you have her making a presentation?"

"No idea. Zoya did her intro yesterday while you were napping. We bring in experts from all over the world to talk about new media and we can't even give them a decent internet connection. In 2006!"

"That's ironic. Eating the muffin?"

Trimmed bacon rinds were the only remaining evidence on Giga's main plate. Three pastries and a blueberry muffin crammed his other plate. He wasn't overweight, just a huge guy with an uncanny likeness to the actor who played Ray's brother in the TV show, 'Everybody Loves Raymond'.

Giga shook his head.

Leo put the muffin on his plate and cut it in half, then cut the bottom section into four pieces, then the juicier top into four, which he always left for last. He enjoyed it from memory because his taste buds were one of the casualties of the flu.

Zoya headed to their table. He'd taken another bucket of meds earlier but her approach blasted him past 'Managing Monday' to buzzing again. *Maybe I should just stand and introduce myself…*

Zoya answered for him. She stopped at their table, dropped to her knees and threw a short, business-like half-smile at him. "Sorry, I just need a quick word with Giga." She turned to Giga before he could think of a response. Keep her attention. Hold onto those eyes.

"I was hoping we could plan our strategy for the dinner on Thursday." Her tone could tame tigers.

Thump-a-thump, thump-a-thump… went the jungle drums in his heart.

"Are you here tomorrow?" asked Giga.

She shook her head. "Any time this morning?"

"Now's good," Giga waved across to him. "Have you met Leo? Leo, this is Zoya."

Zoya offered her hand. She held on a bit longer than a normal business greeting, a strong grip but welcoming skin.

Thump-a-thump, thump-a-thump, thump-a-thump.

His mind scrambled for something funny or romantic. Clever— he could work with clever.

"You look different without the scarf," she said.

He'd settle for mildly interesting. All he could do was grin.

Zoya unleashed her full, light-up-a-village smile.

Their window table overlooked a shimmering Batemans Bay, but the magnified spring sun couldn't match the warmth she launched through him or the light sparkling from her brown eyes.

"Look at that smile. What a perfect way to start the day." His romantic muse and ego high-fived.

The light in her eyes intensified, like she was trying to shine more understanding on what this stranger dared to say. "What a charmer." Her tone wasn't dismissive, a light cadence. Attention-seeking cheeks were crimson moons to her sun smile. Zoya turned back to Giga and the sun spun away to another universe.

"Do you want to do it here?" she asked.

Despite being left in the cold in this corporate conversation, Leo could only admire. She was comfortable interrupting breakfast between two men for her agenda. By kneeling, she showed a non-corporate, almost girlish friendliness, yet she was on a mission. Zoya lost nothing for being on her knees. Not many women could have pulled that off.

"Sure. Do you mind if Zoya takes your seat?" asked Giga.

Bastardo. Why can't he invite me to stay? I could find another chair for her.

"No, of course not." Smiling at Zoya, he got up and as she sat down, he squinted hard at Giga, snatched his last pastry, then let them be.

Zoya Orlenko... I've got to find a way to meet you properly.

2

MELBOURNE, NEW YORK, SYDNEY, CANBERRA… LEO

Leo was mesmerized by the waves crashing against rocks at the bottom of the cliff. He hadn't had time to soak up the resort's spectacular location, high on a small peninsula of the bay. He wasn't a surfer or into fishing, but loved the waves. There was something intoxicating about their relentless persistence. He'd tried to 'bump' into Zoya on Thursday night after the power dinner with Giga and her Government Department head, but never got the opportunity.

Tonight was his last chance.

He turned around and leaned back on the timber balustrade. The large balcony hummed with mentors and participants high on adrenaline, lubricated with alcohol. Giga had not only created an innovative six-day lab, he'd also structured it to mirror the real world. The participants start the week curious or skeptical, then move into a creative high as they embrace the new digital playing field. By Friday, emotions range from anxious to frantic because the teams had to pitch their revamped, digitized, and interactive projects to a VIP industry panel.

The presentations were a success, releasing a monster wave of tension, leading to Friday evening party time before everyone headed home the next morning.

6

Sitting at one of the long timber tables, Zoya's intensity focused on Juancho, a zany Canadian mentor and kindred Leo-spirit. She was safe with him, the only person he'd mentioned his Zoya-interest to. On her right, there was a gap on the bench seat and then Janey, another fun mentor and Giga's right-hand in the workshops.

Perfect.

He slid into the space and joined in with Janey's conversation. There was some fun banter with her and the others to his right. He was angled towards them and physically reacting to them, yet his soul was contorted in the opposite direction, watching Zoya. He felt her lean back and forward, heard her chuckle, followed her expressive hands. He sometimes felt he had a sixth sense but right there it was a Zoya-sense. His soul enjoyed every second of being that close.

Time to test the love skies, see if their clouds connected. He turned and slid over towards Zoya, but Janey grabbed his arm.

"Hey, Yoyo, would you mind getting me another wine, please?"

Janey was the only person in his life who had tagged him with a nickname. At the first of these workshops, she yelled *"Hey, Yoyo"* across the room and later explained he just looked like a yo-yo to her, like he was always going to bounce back up. It made her an instant friend.

At that moment, he could have killed her, all primed for his approach to Zoya, but he couldn't refuse Janey.

She slapped his back as she swung off the bench seat.

"Just kidding I'm going to the bar. Want another?"

"I'm good, thanks." He held up his half-full glass of Pinot Gris.

Janey patted Zoya's shoulder. "Since you're our host, can I get you another drink?"

"Thank you, Janey. Another Pinot Gris, please."

Same wine. Good sign. Last woman he met who liked the same drink, he married. Although that didn't turn out so well, so maybe it wasn't such a good sign.

"You remember our Melbourne star, Leo?"

Bless Janey's socks.

Zoya turned towards him, "Of course."

"Can you believe he's forty-six? Without make-up too." Janey ran her hand over his smooth head, which he shaved when specs of grey started appearing a few years ago. "If I wasn't happily married, I'd take those chocolate biscuit eyes home myself."

Maybe she'd gone too far.

"Immaturity used to work against me and now it's working for me," he said straight at Zoya.

Her smile made his stomach yo-yo.

"I've got some questions for you." She slid along the bench seat towards him.

Six days of waiting to get this close. Close enough to kiss her natural, artisan-sculptured lips.

Zoya flicked to a blank page on her black notebook, thick, shiny pen poised.

"You want my number for your black book?"

She jerked her head up, the setting sun behind her. It could have been setting in her eyes, her big cheeks tinged with crimson.

"You really are cheeky with a capital CH."

His Judas muscles broke out. She hadn't forgotten their ever-so-fleeting encounters. He *had* registered on her radar.

"Thank you."

Crimson cheeks turned red. She tapped the notebook with her pen. "This is my work buddy. Ideas, goals, meeting notes." A 'she-doth-glare-too-much' glint shined in her eyes. "And these are work questions." The slightest of smiles broke on her lips, yet the slightest smile on Zoya still showered him with a mega dose of vitamin D.

She morphed into work-mode in an instant, probably her comfort zone. So many members in that modern sisterhood.

"Congratulations on the Cannes award."

It still sounded weird three weeks later. Winning a Cannes Inter-active Award for the prototype iPhone game he'd created, '8-Crocs', ages before the phone was to be released in Australia. "Thanks. I was lucky the two tech dudes I stumbled across came on board and made my crazy idea even crazier." Leo didn't mention he felt like a forty-six-year-old phony in the cool-kids playground.

She rattled off the usual questions about 8-Crocs: funding models, revenue streams, marketing, and distribution. He could answer them on autopilot, but from Zoya they had a melody, and he was a sucker for a sweet tune.

He wasn't technical or an academic. And the biggest crime of all, he wasn't even a gamer. He wanted to write humorous, clever pieces for magazines. Maybe write a book one day. Frustrated with his inability to get any articles published, he turned up at a digital media seminar a year earlier. New online magazines and self-publishing opportunities intrigued him. The technology and process behind all of it scared him.

He'd almost drowned with boredom from all the digital terms and acronyms. But one speaker, Mark Pesce, connected in non-tech English, and inspired an idea for a game.

Through most of the other seminar geeky gobbledygook, he feverishly scribbled out his idea.

While at the networking lunch, he met Jason.

Jason lived for games and devoured technology, washing it down with gallons of Coke. At twenty-five, he and his first cousin-come-business-partner, Nicholas, had already built up a niche animation and digital technology company, 'Pirate Bunnies'. Introverted and totally non-business savvy, Jason and Nicholas created clever interactive animations for ad agencies.

8-Crocs was a silly game with eight different jungle locations —'levels' in game-speak. To successfully achieve each level, you had to navigate increasingly bizarre crocodiles. Being so early in the evolution of the iPhone, it wasn't difficult to break through as an Australian 'first'. The Cannes success was a bonus, and they became the darlings of Victoria's Digital Media Fund.

Success was a very relative term. In the ten years since Leo had walked away from a lucrative sports marketing career, he'd never earned half of his old salary in a year, cash-flowing his larger creative dreams with freelance copywriting for magazine, radio and online ads. After paying for his kids' private school fees and other support, he often had more month than money. Being broke in your forties wasn't fun, but it was for his kids and his dreams, and you can't beat that for a double mission.

Zoya filled pages of her book with his ramblings. He respected this was still an important work function for her, yet that night was the last chance for them to connect before he flew back to Melbourne, and she was swamped in Canberra. It wasn't something to rush but they didn't have much choice. Raw desire wanted to lead the way, but his heart kept fighting for the driver's seat.

Was she grappling with the same dilemma? Was he even in her thoughts beyond professional curiosity?

She put her pen down and picked up her wine.

He picked up the pen and slid her notebook across, flicked to a clean page. "Enough about me. Tell me your story."

Question marks flared in Zoya's eyes. He wasn't surprised she focused on her career journey. After an arts degree at Melbourne Uni, she packed her bags and headed to New York for an intern role with an ad agency. Flourishing in the never-sleep competitiveness, she worked her way up to senior TVC producer. Homesickness led her to Sydney as general manager of a large production company. His arithmetic as she dropped unintended clues suggested she was around forty or forty-one.

"At first, you're seduced by the big personalities. Then you get worn out by the egos, greed, bullies, and more egos."

"So, you took the Canberra gig for bit of a retreat?"

"Hardly. I'm over my head with admin and politics. But at least this job brings me closer to true artists. I admire people who create something from nothing."

And for nothing, he almost added. Most so-called true artists had a perennial choice: starve our stomach or starve our soul.

Zoya was distracted by her assistant. "Excuse me a sec." She got up.

He stared at the blank page on Zoya's notebook then summarized her journey:

Melbourne... New York... Sydney... Canberra... Leo.

He almost drew a heart around his name but tossed the idea.

That was too much at this stage, even for him. He closed the black book, slid it across to Zoya's spot and placed her pen on top.

Maybe she won't see that till first thing Monday. It will put a smile on her face. Lucky colleagues that get to see that smile every day.

"Sorry, Leo. I've got to sort out some things with Bec before she leaves." With warm eyes, yet her mouth arched with genuine disappointment.

He swung his legs around and joined her. "Will you sit with me at dinner?" Her perfume held a fruity scent. His nose was useless with details but the fragrance and being that close made him tipsy.

She shuffled back a half-step, eyes sensually massaging his body. "Do you even eat? You're sooo slim."

He stepped close again. "You have something against stamina?"

Her cheeks inflated into red balloons, a glimpse of tongue between lips. "Maybe you can save me a seat." Zoya spun and glided after Bec.

His heart glided after Zoya, and it wasn't the only part of his anatomy heading after her. Leo had to sit before the effect in his jeans was spotted by anyone.

3

ROYAL DINNER

Zoya waltzed into the dining room wearing black flared pants over brown leather boots. Her black blouse was covered by a sprawling black shawl with splashes of deep burgundy and pink. For the first time Leo noticed she stretched the definition of voluptuous by a couple of pounds. He'd never been addicted to stick-figure women and something about Zoya made petty things like that irrelevant. The woman was both comfortable in her own body and radiant.

Leo wasn't a big drinker, but he forced himself to stop staring by topping up his glass and a couple of glasses across the table. He took a sip of his wine and when he looked back towards Zoya, she was in his aisle squeezing towards him.

"Is that seat reserved for someone?" she asked.

"Yes, the Queen of Canberra. You have no idea how many battles I fought to save this humble bit of furniture." He jumped up and pulled the chair back for her.

"No queen here."

"Tell that to your loyal subjects." He waved across the table.

Zoya was popular at their table, and she gave everyone her full attention right through the first course. She didn't turn to him till she'd finished her shrimps. Their faces close, her perfume fluttered down his throat and into his lungs like spring butterflies. Cinnamon? Caramel? Red lipstick silently teased him.

"I take it you haven't found a prince in your new kingdom yet?"

"I haven't had time to even think about it. The first three weeks in Canberra have been crazy."

"It's not the thinking that matters." His disloyal mouth and facial muscles lifted into a grin.

"You are cheeky. Is there a special woman in your life?"

"Yes, two."

"Two! Why am I not surprised? Is one serious and the other a mistress?"

"Both serious."

Zoya's eyes dulled, brow furrowed, and she shifted back in her seat. "Do they know

about each other?"

"Of course." He nodded. "My mum and baby sister are very close."

Zoya slapped his arm below his rolled-up sleeve. Red lips, perfume and heat from her touch brewed an inner cocktail, fueled his growing confidence.

"You like teasing, don't you? But tomorrow you'll be back in Melbourne and forget about me. Plus, I've got a million priorities on my desk." She presented it like a mathematical equation, which led to the answer of zero romance. Nil sex.

Understandable for her to question where anything could lead. He wasn't into one-night stands either but romance never popped up as a neat piece of algebra.

"Yet here we are."

"I'm enjoying our chat but there's no point staking your territory." She patted his jacket, draped over her seat. The protective tone set up her defensive trenches, anti-romance tanks, and no-flying-over-the-sex zone missiles.

"I was just saving the last seat at the romantic table."

He'd taken the risk and thrown a pebble across her moat, but only she could lower the drawbridge to her castle. As her eyes scanned back and forth between his left eye to right, he was a kid on a swing, intoxicated by sweet g-forces.

Zoya was saved by the waiters and main meal.

Temporary diversion.

In any new romantic connection, there was always a break-through moment. Words or a gesture that confirmed they'd crossed the line. Juicy anticipation was part of the fun.

The definitive moment came with dessert.

While Zoya talked with the couple across the table, she placed her right hand on his left thigh. It seemed subconscious, and she didn't acknowledge it in any other way. Not an overtly sexual gesture; her hand wasn't high up his thigh, or in the more sensual inner-thigh zone. He couldn't focus on anything else. Heat raged from her skin through his jeans and over his body.

Naturally tactile, he had consciously held back his hands from Zoya but now unleashed them, placing his left hand on top of hers. From what little he knew of this woman, there was no turning back now. Something was going to happen.

"Nothing's going to happen, Leo." Zoya furrowed her brow and angled her head towards him a touch. "I'm serious."

"Define 'nothing'," said Leo.

"You know exactly what I mean."

"So, you've been thinking about it too." He fought hard not to grin and might've won the battle for a second. He was in hyper-cheeky, romantic-sexual, pursuit zone. It had been a few months since his last fling and as much as he liked Zoya, the more he'd thought about it, the more their logistics made it all about that one night.

Zoya avoided his eyes, wrapping her shawl tightly as she hesitated before the big sliding doors.

Earlier, Zoya had a responsibility to do some final mingling at the post dinner party. He enjoyed the downtime with some of the gang as well, but there was no doubt what he would've enjoyed more. Just before midnight, Zoya had hovered back to the couch where her shawl and handbag were thrown amongst other jackets and bags.

Cinderella time.

"Thanks for the royal dinner," said Leo.

"It was fun."

"Yeah, for a queen you're not bad company."

Zoya shook her head. "I'm an exhausted peasant after a long day on the farm." She fluttered her lips as she blew out a noisy sigh.

"Maybe I should walk you back to your room, just in case you collapse?" Blood pounded through his heart and loins.

"Would you carry me if I collapsed?"

"No, but I could run for help."

Zoya's laugh hadn't lost anything for her tiredness. The sparkle in her eyes certainly suggested hidden reserves of energy. She settled, with her head tilted on an angle, tip of her tongue loitered between red lips.

"Okay."

Leo's heart, loins, lungs, and tummy danced to a calypso beat. It took all his self-control to not pick her up and swing her around, kiss her right there in front of the whole party.

He gestured with a sweeping arm and slight bow for Zoya to take the first step towards the wide stairs. Side by side, they climbed their first mountain. By the time they got to the top, he had heart vertigo. It was a pity this had to be just one night of sex rather than something deeper, but he didn't create the circumstances.

The air at the top of the stairs must have cooled Zoya. Her '*nothing's going to happen*' line hadn't cooled Leo. Not one degree. She probably thought she'd launched a nuclear mood-breaker. He saw it as gorgeous fireworks.

"Nothing's going to happen that you don't want to happen." He stuffed his hands into the pockets of his black jeans, thumbs caressing the belt loop.

She couldn't hide her crimson cheeks or the two other tell-tale signs before she tightened the shawl over her chest. Zoya's brow morphed from a rough ocean to a serene pond.

She nodded and they headed outside.

The big glass doors slid open like covers of a picture book revealing a galaxy of sequins twinkling against a flowing black gown. The salty breeze off the bay was fresh but not cold. The instant they stepped onto the driveway, without a word or look, they both leaned in and wrapped an arm around each other's waist, like they'd walked that way for decades. After a few yards, he faced Zoya, and she looked up at him.

They burst into laughter. Didn't miss a step, didn't let go, roared in harmony from deep in their bellies for ages.

Sense of humor well and truly consummated.

One down, one to go...

4

BEDS ARE OVERRATED

AT THE DOOR TO ZOYA'S CABIN, LEO SWUNG HIS OTHER ARM AROUND, both hands resting on her waist. She didn't step away.

"That was sweet of you... to walk me here."

"The pleasure was mutual."

"I'm not inviting you in."

"I'll try to not jump off the cliff."

Zoya half-smiled, pecked him on the cheek and stepped back, yet she didn't turn away. One hand clutched her handbag to her stomach, the other bending a strap with her thumb.

He stepped close and took both her hands.

She stared down at their physical bond. "You have small hands."

"Small hands, small feet and biiiiiiig..." He swayed his hips in an arc. "Biiiig sense of humor."

Her laugh skimmed across the bay, echoed across the South Pacific Ocean, possibly all the way to New Zealand. The golden glow from the porch light turned her dancing cheeks and hair into a carnival.

There wasn't a part of him she didn't electrify.

"You're so beautiful, Zoya. If you were in Melbourne, I'd walk anywhere to feel your smile, bathe in your laugh."

Her eyes were like marshmallow stars, sweet and soft and shiny.

He stepped in and hugged her. Zoya dropped her bag and wrapped her arms around him, their bodies melding into one. Her strong hands felt familiar through the back of his shirt. A homecoming, his heart taking over from the rogue testosterone. As she nuzzled into his chest, the aroma of her hair took him to childhood holidays when picking berries was fun and warm and sweet.

Zoya let go a marathon sigh, melting deeper into him. Softening his breathing. Two clouds connected, floating together.

Laughter crashed up the pathway, sounding like some of the gang were going to continue the party in a nearby cabin.

Zoya stepped away, frowned down the path then back at Leo. "You can come in but we're not going to bed."

"Beds are overrated."

She picked up her bag and searched for her key.

"I'm serious. No sex."

"Okay, I swear on your gorgeous body."

"Huh." Zoya opened the door, stepping in.

He squeezed her butt cheeks. "Gorgeous, gorgeous body."

Zoya slapped his hands off as she scurried inside.

LEO LIKED HER CABIN, A LARGE SUITE ACROSS THREE LEVELS, DESIGNED around amorous activities. To the left you could step down to the large, triangular spa bath with a view across the treetops to the bay or step up to the king size bed. He gave a silent nod to the mates that designed the Suzella Resort, Suzanne and Stella. To the right, the kitchenette where Zoya had retreated for safety. He was an enchanted audience across the small table, in the alcove seat.

"So...chamomile." She shuffled through the individually wrapped tea bags in a small basket.

"Peppermint."

"Right."

Zoya was ten times busier than she needed to be for two teas. He doubted she would be this inefficient at her office.

"How long were you a DJ?" she asked, continuing the backwards journey through his CV.

"Four years full time. Slowed down a bit when I got married in eighty-six, then gave it away when James was born in eighty-nine."

"The eighties were fun, but you chose the wrong era. DJs are superstars now."

"I had a ball. DJing and writing lyrics was the only way I could dabble in music." Lyrics were his first creative passion. He loved the magic of collaborating with a musician. A couple of songs had won minor contests, but nothing had ever broken through commercially.

She brought over the mugs of tea and squeezed next to him on the bench seat, keeping the interrogation flowing about his Calabrese parents, and baby sister. Then she rambled about her dad and younger sister.

The Form-Filling stage, general information you provided as part of an application for any new relationship. One moment Zoya strayed into the Intimate-Journal-Sharing stage when she'd mentioned her mother had died. The shadow of that memory dulled her eyes before she quickly changed the subject to Giga and the mentors at the workshop.

"You're just talking now because you're nervous."

Zoya stopped mid-sentence, mouth open.

"It's cute how nervous you are. I'm honored."

"Are you always this cocky?"

"I knew we'd get there eventually."

"We're not going there." Zoya placed both her hands flat on the table.

"Maybe not, but I do want to go here." He gently caressed her right cheek with the back of his hand.

Both her cheeks flushed crimson. She wedged her inverted palms between her closed thighs and turned her body towards him, calves touching. Electric.

"And here..." He traced one finger underneath her mouth.

Her lips parted. He ran the back of his forefinger slowly across them.

She closed her eyes and shuddered.

"And here..." Leo traced his right hand over her left cheek, sliding his fingers through her hair.

Zoya's eyes opened with fire, her breathing so heavy he could surf her bosom. She shifted closer.

His own heat unbearable, lips the pressure valve, he moved closer. She met him halfway. Her mouth burned and soothed, spicy and sweet, like the chili-chocolate she magically poured through his veins. Her tongue both rough and smooth, their bodies edged tighter, hands frantic. Everything was spinning fast, yet every sensation lingered in slow motion.

When he gently pulled back, he saw the same wonderment in her eyes. Zoya snaked her arms around him and snuggled into his chest, their teas cold and neglected on the table.

"Wow."

"Mmmmmnnn..." purred Zoya.

"I never imagined this at the beginning of the week."

She snuggled tighter into him. "Me, neither. I feel so comfortable with you."

"We'd be more comfortable on your bed."

Zoya jolted, untangling herself. "You're so smooth."

"This bench is very narrow and my butt's numb. I want to hold you properly." His brain pleaded with his rogue facial muscles. *Don't grin. Don't grin. Don't grin.*

"Or maybe it's time for you to leave, walk some blood into your butt."

"That's one option," he said with a little confidence. She hadn't gotten up to show him the door, and he couldn't get out unless she moved.

"We stay on the bed, not under the sheets. And we keep our clothes on."

He nodded. *Don't grin, don't grin.*

She pinched his chin and shook it. "And wipe that cocky grin off your face."

Traitors.

IN ALL OF LEO'S EXPERIENCE, FIRST-TIME SEX WAS NEVER PRECEDED with a formal request and official response. It evolved from a moment, or moments... gestures, a look, a touch... until the mutual passion meter red lined. He was determined not to break his promise to Zoya, but he couldn't help pushing the boundaries of that promise to the extreme end of the meter.

They red-lined early, but Zoya pushed him back and rolled away.

"It's two a.m." Her voice was so steamy and husky it almost sent him over the edge. "You... have... to... go." Each syllable punctuated by deep breaths.

He rolled onto his back. *Go? Now? Seriously?*

Zoya looked down at his erection pushing through the denim. "You definitely have to go. Now." She rearranged her blouse, covering most of the cleavage.

"Shit."

"What?"

"I left my leather jacket in the bar lounge."

"So?"

"My key is in the pocket and reception closes at 1a.m."

"You are so, so smooth." She prodded his chest.

"I swear, Zoya, this wasn't planned." He propped himself on an elbow. "I totally forgot about my jacket the moment I saw you were free in there."

"Aha..." She didn't sound convinced, but there was a glint in her eye. "I don't want people to know you were here. I've got clients and colleagues out there. I haven't even settled into this job yet."

"Sorry. I could wake Juancho, crash on his floor."

She checked the bedside clock again. "You can stay here."

"Here, in your bed?"

"I was thinking in the spa with the spare blankets."

He wasn't as excited by that idea.

"Unless you promise to—"

"I promise," he snapped, before she changed her mind.

They set the alarm for seven-thirty a.m. to give him time to sneak out before gossipy eyes started peering over their hangovers. Zoya came out of the bathroom in her brown flannelette PJs and an orange t-shirt underneath. He called it The Royal Armor. He kept his boxers and t-shirt on. She put pillows along the middle of the bed for extra safety. They lasted about nine seconds, then she threw them on the floor. He opened his arms, Zoya slid in and fell asleep on his shoulder before he remembered to ask about the scent of her perfume.

ZOYA'S EYES SHINED OVER HIM BEFORE HIS PHONE ALARM. HE WASN'T sure if they were questioning or adoring, but waking up underneath them was like a ten-stack pancake breakfast with blueberries piled to the ceiling, drowning in pure maple syrup, with a big bucket of strong black coffee on the side. Giddy on a Zoya-sugar-and-caffeine-high, he tried to come up with something romantic or funny.

Zoya rolled onto her back and pumped her fists like she'd just scored a World Cup winning goal, "Yes, yes, yes. I did it. No sex. Yes!" she yelled.

"I think that's a compliment."

"You didn't even try. You just slept," she said with child-like surprise wrapped in adult admiration.

"Please don't let that rumor get out." He reached for his phone and turned off the unnecessary alarm.

He rolled out an arm and Zoya rolled in. He played with her hair. Sunlight tried to sneak around the closed curtains, distant bellbird whistles from the forest providing a sweet counter melody to the attention-seeking seagulls over the bay. Somehow, they created a peaceful soundtrack.

"I've never been with a guy who's so comfortable lying here like this... with his eyes open."

"I'm trying to memorize every gorgeous bit of you."

Her eyes sparked up a level in wattage doing that swing-thing between his eyes. She rolled on top and pinned his arms, raw passion streaming out of every pore on her skin. He'd never been driven so erotically insane and mesmerized into a dreamy stupor at the same time.

She kissed him hard, his head almost bursting through the mattress. His hands found a warm playground under the back of her armor. Zoya murmured and groaned with every caress. Her goose bumps trailed his fingers down her spine, and when he slipped them under the elastic of her pajama pants to her coccyx, she shuddered and ground her pelvis into his thigh. His other hand slid to the base of her breast.

Zoya rolled onto her back, gulping air.

He didn't dare follow because he doubted he could stop next time. Stop. Why? Two single adults over forty. Was it the work thing? Too close to her stakeholders? It was Saturday. The Zoya sugar-caffeine-adrenaline-endorphins-pheromone-testosterone cocktail raged through him with no sign of slowing down, no control, no release. He needed an irresistible Plan D, or was he up to Plan D-twelve?

He rolled on his side, and she did the same, pulling the sheet up over their waists.

"My flight doesn't leave till five p.m. tonight and our bus hits the airport around two. Would you like to give me a quick tour of Canberra?"

The tiniest of angles furrowed on her brow pointing towards her nose. Her hand spread across her tummy as if searching for her gut feeling.

Before they'd fallen asleep, Zoya insisted he would have to go back to Canberra airport on the official bus at eleven a.m. with the other interstate mentors and participants. She was driving a Sydney friend, one of the participants, to the airport and had stayed on the *keeping this private* theme.

"Sure. But I meet you after I've dropped off the others and away from your bus gang."

Yes, Sergeant-Major. Zoya's safe zone, all business. Plan D-twelve was a go.

They'd extended their nine a.m. deadline to nine-thirty but that zipped by. Lying side by side, holding hands, soaking in the bird choir, he couldn't find a pinch of motivation to move. Zoya glanced at the digital clock on the bedside table and fluttered her lips with a long sigh.

"Thirty more minutes, my gorgeous Canberra virgin."

Zoya shook her head and angled a grin at him. "Ten a.m. is the absolute final limit."

He raised his arms, pumped his fists. "Yes, yes, thirty more minutes without sex. Yes!"

Slap. Zoya landed a flat hand on his bare thigh.

"Hey!" He rubbed his skin. "All right, we'll have sex."

"Arrgh!" Zoya rolled away, pulling the sheet over her shoulder.

"You're the best sex I've never had."

No reaction.

"You're smiling, aren't you? I can tell."

"Huh? You can't see a thing."

"No, but the room temperature went up twenty degrees and the wall is shining."

She covered her head with the sheet.

"Ten second warning. I'm coming for a spooning."

With Zoya on her side, he couldn't see the clock, so he picked up his phone to set the '*Ten a.m. absolutely final limit alarm.*'

"Shit."

"What now?" asked Zoya from under the sheet.

"The bed clock was never changed after daylight savings ended last weekend, it's actually ten-forty."

"Fuck," said Zoya.

"Now you want to—"

"Get out." Prison guard shrill, Zoya jumped out of bed like there was a mass escape, sheet flying off the bed.

He scrambled to pull on his jeans and boots. Zoya pecked him on the cheek and pushed him out, slamming the door.

5

FOURTEEN HOURS AND TWENTY-THREE MINUTES

Zoya had eased her SUV into a parking space at the Canberra Yacht Club, possibly with the intention of walking him around the postcard location, but she didn't take her seatbelt off.

"This is beautiful, Zoya. I didn't realize Lake Burley Griffin was this big, but we've only got a couple of hours. Don't you want to show off your place?"

Little angled furrows on her brow pointed at him. Yacht masts bobbed behind her, up and down, a little left, a little right. He focused hard on holding down the traitor-muscles that wanted to push through with a moment-killing-grin.

She straightened, hands wedged between jeaned thighs. Turned her head to the moored yachts, masts bobbing up and down, a little left a little right. She started the car and headed out. Shortest Canberra tour in the history of Canberra tours.

Plan D-twelve on track.

The tour of her modern apartment was quicker than the Canberra sights. Holding his hand, Zoya took only seconds to sweep through the large, open space with galley kitchen, dining, and lounge area. Unopened and half-full boxes scattered between homey knick-knacks, pictures, and rugs.

Zoya led them down a hall, pointing at open doors.

"Spare room, bathroom, study... and this is my room." She led him inside.

White pillows and duvet cover against the blue sky through the balcony sliding doors made her bed look like a cloud.

"Zoya, if we were based in the same city, I wouldn't have pushed to—"

Zoya kissed him hard, tumbling them onto her bed. Hands, legs, and clothes flew around. After all their sexual tension, there was no way he'd last long inside her and the one thought clinging to his sex-raging brain was to spoil her first.

Nice guys come last.

He worked his mouth and tongue down her body...

THERE WAS NO FAKING ZOYA'S ECSTASY, AN AMAZONIAN-JUNGLE-warrior scream. Leo had never heard anything like it, wondering if anyone in the other three apartments of the block could hear. Hell, half of Canberra must have heard.

Both of them heaved for air, Zoya between murmurs, Leo between little kisses on her inner thighs and navel. He moved up from Zoya's epicenter and held her tightly. She nuzzled into his shoulder. Every few seconds, her body trembled. It seemed to take ages before her muscles relaxed.

She shifted her head back and opened her eyes.

"Welcome back."

"You're amazing." Zoya's whisper was husky, dripping in sensuality, almost caressing him to an orgasm.

"You're amazing. The way you let go."

"No one's ever made me come like that before."

"Really? That intensely or that way?"

"Both."

"Wow. It was probably the fourteen hours of foreplay."

She smiled, kissing his hand. "You were so patient."

Thank the stars for all the impatient men out there.

"I wanted to spoil you."

"You have permission to spoil me anytime."

Zoya kissed him and worked her way down to his hyper-ready penis, but he pulled her back. She didn't need a second invitation and straddled him slowly.

LEO COLLAPSED ON HER AND ZOYA HELD HIM TIGHTLY. THEY STAYED like that for a few minutes, no words passing between them. Hearts pumping like an AC/DC drum solo on a stadium stage, fast, deep, and loud as hell. Her messy hair, red cheeks, purple lips, and fiery eyes branded in his mind. Dreamy, hypnotic, a purring poster of wild jungle passion.

"That was the sweetest, most delicious..." he mumbled into her neck.

"I'm sure it was just the fourteen hours and twenty-three minutes of foreplay," said Zoya.

He rolled onto his back. She snuggled into him, draping a leg over his.

"I'm not getting sentimental, just avoiding the wet spot." She stroked his chest hair.

He smiled. It wasn't who you went to bed with that mattered, it was who you woke up with. Would it be fun? Could you actually have a conversation? Did you want to run?

Not running anywhere. This kind of sexual connection is rare. And she's a full-on bucket of fun-buzz.

"What time did you want to be back at the airport?"

"Four-twenty. Have to check in by four-thirty."

Zoya looked across to her clock radio. "Fuck."

"Not again."

"It's ten past four."

"Shit. I promised the boys I'd pick them up by eight."

6

HI, HONEY, I'M HOME

"I'VE NEVER MISSED A WEEKEND WITH THE BOYS SINCE I LEFT MICHELE, apart from work stuff like the Cannes trip." He'd lost half the weekend for this workshop, but it was work and unavoidable, easier on the conscience and explainable to the boys.

"Couldn't you just swap weekends with her?" Zoya was checking alternative flights on her computer in the study.

Sitting on a large exercise ball, he turned to the window, watching as the trees swayed wildly on the wide grass strip next to the road. This wasn't the time to get into the dysfunctionality with his ex-wife. "Didn't work out for her this time."

"Next available flight is nine."

"I won't get them to my place till midnight." His hands clasped, fingers intertwined, rocking at the wrists, facing the double barrel shotgun of guilt with his boys and vitriol from Michele. James was seventeen, so he could squeeze in some time with him. Thomas just turned thirteen and little Jake ten. Being a Saturday, they'd want to party late too, but Leo would be exhausted. Not exactly quality time.

"You may as well stay the night, catch the first flight tomorrow morning." Eyes sprinkled with a touch of hope and glint of mischief. "Leaves seven-thirty a.m."

He placed his palm on her cheek. "You think we could possibly get our act together that early in the morning? With our track record?"

"Third time lucky." She winked and grinned.

"Are you the bi-polar twin of the 'yes, yes, no sex' woman?"

Crimson cheek-moons came into orbit.

"Okay," he whispered into her ear. Zoya pushed him back, turned back to the computer. He almost fell off the exercise ball, then steadied himself. "I do one-on-one nights with James on Mondays and the other two stay over every Wednesday. I'll take them out for pizza as an apology." He swallowed his logical words, but they were lumpy in his gut.

"Aha." Zoya focused on the screen. After maneuvering and clicking the mouse through the process, she faced him.

"One thing you should know before I hit confirm. I've got a dinner with my boss and his wife tonight."

"You want to take me to—"

"No!"

He reeled back on the ball. She helped steady him with her hands on his knees.

"Sorry, it's a 'welcome to Canberra' dinner at their place. I have to go but I'll be home by nine-thirty at the latest."

The lumpy guilt in his gut hardened. Being with his boys had always been sacred and he cherished it. When he was with them, he was fully with them. Now he was limiting precious family time for limited time with Zoya. But it had been almost five years. Surely, they wouldn't crucify him for one blemish?

He nodded. "Book it. I'll get some takeaway and have a nap so I can be all charged up when you get back."

Zoya hit the enter key. Confirmation flashed through. "Speaking of third time lucky..." She grabbed his hand and dragged him back to her bed.

Leo woke before the five a.m. alarm to Zoya's adoring eyes.

"Good morning, gorgeous."

"Good morning, mystery man in my bed."

"No mystery here, just me."

"Do you want to see the breakfast menu, or would you prefer to help yourself to the buffet?" Zoya pulled back the sheet and glided a hand over her curvy naked body.

"I feel like a little kid in the Zoya shop."

She kissed him and they made love again. Truly made love. His Zoya-sense extended to every touch and taste. Such a joy to spoil someone who let go so completely; spiritual and rare. She'd sung *"Hi, honey, I'm home."* when she'd got back from her work dinner the night before. Buzzing about her boss and his wife. It took a marathon session in bed before she finally crashed.

Zoya's mood was heavier after her morning shower, a towel wrapped around her chest, watching him pack.

"Got everything?" Monotone. Her usual expressive face turned into a blank shield, eyes neutral. Any more Switzerland and they'd be sipping hot chocolates watching the Matterhorn. But a cold mist was part of their one-night-only package.

"Yep."

His bag wheels rolled easily enough on the polished floorboards, yet an invisible anchor made it difficult to leave her room.

The mood didn't improve on the drive to the airport. As they crossed the bridge over Lake Burley Griffin, Canberra already felt like a second home.

"I can see why you like it here."

"It's picturesque and peaceful," she said.

He nodded and turned back to Zoya. "We'll always have Batemans Bay."

"And Manuka." She tried to make it more positive, but it wasn't her light-up-a-city smile. Yesterday she'd explained the locals pronounce it *Maneeka*. From what he could see that morning, it was a leafy upmarket suburb but not pretentious.

The orange glow from the sunrise wasn't that bright behind clouds either, but Zoya put on her big sunglasses.

"We have a special connection," said Leo.

"You really think so?" More light in her tone, her smile.

"Yes. If we were in the same city, we'd obviously…"

"Aha." Total eclipse of the smile.

He'd led them into a quicksand conversation. How could they explore a romance when he was committed to living close to his boys in Melbourne and Zoya was three weeks into a five-year contract in Canberra?

He guessed Zoya had been running the question around her busy head too. The sunglasses couldn't hide her furrowed brow, or how tightly she was squeezing the steering wheel despite barely any traffic.

Weird, but he felt like he was leaving home, not heading there. He'd been presented with a three-hat romantic menu and only had time to sample the appetizer. It was eating at Leo. The closer they got to the airport, the warmer the sun shone on the windshield, the colder the anchor-knot in his stomach. Not anchored to her bedroom, it was anchored to Zoya.

She turned the car off the highway at the sign proudly beaming 'Canberra Airport'. They made it with plenty of time, but she seemed to be cruising way below the speed limit.

She doesn't want this moment to end either.

Zoya eased into a parking spot and turned off the engine. He took off her sunglasses and placed them on the dash, holding her hands. *"Never afraid to miss,"* a philosophy he'd read from one of his early Arsenal heroes, Malcolm McDonald, and quickly found it relevant beyond soccer. Most regrets in life didn't come from missing, they came from not having a shot when you had the opportunity.

"I'm just putting this out there. No pressure or expectations. Next weekend I don't have the boys. I know this might sound crazy but if you want to come over... to explore this thing..." he waved their hands between them.

"And what, exactly, would this thing be?" Zoya mimicked his hand motions.

"I don't know, Zoya. I just feel it's worth exploring."

On that beautiful swing again, as her eyes scanned his, deep furrows on her brow. "Don't answer now. Think about it. But don't over think it." Where were his Judas muscles when he needed a smile to counteract his tight lips?

At check-in neither of them knew how to say goodbye.

"I'll call you."

Zoya nodded. "Safe travels." A tight smile, no light in her eyes.

Maybe he was overthinking it. Maybe she wasn't as keen on them as he thought. She hugged him like she didn't want to let go, or like she wasn't going to see him again.

7

RUSTIC & RETRO

"You didn't think I'd call did you?" asked Leo.

"You didn't think I'd answer."

"Never had a doubt."

"Does your ego ever rest?"

"It was resting peacefully in your arms a couple of nights ago." He resisted filling the space. Her reaction to his line would say a lot. He muted his TV to make the call but now she'd answered, he clicked it off with the remote and curled his right leg onto the futon under his left thigh.

"I found some words in my notebook this morning. A cheeky intruder must've scribbled them."

"Oh? What words?"

"You know exactly what words, Mr. Cocky."

"I love the way you say *that* word."

"Mister?"

He laughed. Such a relief to be with someone that made him laugh, even if she was making fun of him. So many relationships he'd been the solo clown. He wasn't sure about cocky, but when 'Zoya' popped up on his phone screen, it did launch a helium mood balloon, light and happy and a little tipsy. Crazy. "Did your assistant ask why you were smiling?"

"I'm not saying that C word again, but you are. Anyway, I'm probably one of many women you're swimming around with right now." She threw the line out with a huge fishing net, ready to catch the slightest slippery excuse to end things before they really started.

"I thought I cleared that up Friday night. I'm a one-fish-in-the-ocean kinda guy."

Music in the background from her end, something folksy.

"Nice music," he said, changing the subject.

"Music? Oh, Eric Bibb. He often keeps me company. Do you know his work?"

"No, but speaking of company, have you thought about my suggestion for this weekend?"

"Too busy."

Helium mood punctured, he straightened up on the futon. "Too busy to come over, or too busy to think about it?"

"I had a thousand emails waiting for me this morning and a big presentation to create for this Thursday."

"So, too busy to think about anything other than work."

"Yes. Plus, this is all a bit surreal, isn't it?"

He could work with surreal. "Yeah, eight days ago we didn't even know each other."

"We still don't know each other." Zoya said it like a school principal.

"Let's chip away at that now."

Eric Bibb's gravelly mumbles and guitar echoed in the distance.

"Zoya?"

"Okay, but this has to be short. I have a seven a.m. breakfast meeting tomorrow."

By one a.m. she'd opened up her 'intimate journal.' Her Ukrainian Gypsy parents had separated when she was twelve. Her mother was a colorful, unpredictable woman, with a gift for painting and piano but also a paranoid schizophrenic. Her father moved out when Zoya was twelve, leaving her and her younger sister with a mother who wasn't up to joint parenting, let alone being a single mom.

They moved around Victoria. At seventeen, Zoya moved out of the family home in Bendigo and lived with her aunty in Melbourne while she did her VCE and subsequent college degree. Their mother died two years later from unknown causes. Her sister moved in with their dad in South Australia. It sounded like her sister had never really forgiven Zoya for *abandoning* her.

It felt like a confession. *"Here's my baggage, beware."*

He respected her more for being able to carve out a successful life from such a tough upbringing. His own issues with ultra-conservative Italian parents were a holiday in comparison. Leo had a functional relationship with his younger brother and was very close with his baby sister.

"You probably just want to run now," she said.

"Run to the airport, pick you up and swing you around."

"You're crazy. I'd wreck your knees."

"So, you're coming?" He said it as gently as he could, but he punched his thigh in annoyance because his high inflection probably made him sound nervous, or worse—needy.

"I don't know yet."

"Okay."

"Okay."

He could work with okay. "Zoya, what's the worst that could happen? Look at how much fun we had last weekend and that was under all kinds of time pressure after an exhausting week. We owe it to ourselves to enjoy some unrushed time."

"An unrushed dirty weekend."

"You just want me for my body."

"I guess I asked for that."

His spare hand squeezed his thigh, clamping his silence to the futon.

"I'll see how much work I can plough through next couple of days. Let you know by lunchtime Thursday."

Not a no is half a yes. He could work with half a yes.

LEO WAS LATE—TYPICAL—AND THE PLANE RIGHT ON SCHEDULE, frustrating. He'd planned to surprise Zoya at the gate but had to settle for the escalators leading down to the exits. She hadn't confirmed she was coming until late afternoon the day before. He'd dropped everything to get the condo extra shiny. The Friday evening frenzy of corporates on mobile phones and party weekenders on alcohol bustled past. He saw her dawdling about thirty yards away, dragging her red travel bag.

She wore a flowing black skirt with overlapping material in angles, black blouse, and her favorite shawl. Plus, those high brown boots he'd unzipped once. She unleashed her smile. All his tension—the planning, special food shopping, cleaning, nerves about whether she might pull out at the last minute—dissolved. He handed her a bouquet of native flowers.

"That's blush pink and burgundy protea, silvery gumnuts and some tiny red berry thing."

She inhaled slowly and studied every petal, every leaf. She balanced the bouquet carefully on her bag, wrapped her arms around him and kissed him.

"Get a room!" some young guy yelled, and his cricket fan mates laughed.

His lower body not-so-secretly agreed with them, happy to run to the airport hotel with Zoya and test the strength of a room. Their lips and tongues had their own schedules. He surrendered to her taste, her texture, her fire.

Zoya pulled back, eyes flaming. "Okay, that was worth it," she whispered.

"DON'T KNOW WHY YOU'RE SO HARD ON THIS PLACE. IT'S GOT A NICE, rustic feel," said Zoya.

Tension eased out of Leo's upper back and neck muscles. Between his divorce, supporting three kids—two in private high schools—and pursuit of a creative career, there was often more month left at the end of the money. He had been conscious of his average car, rented old-but-presentable detached condo, and even older furniture. Especially after seeing Zoya's modern apartment with quality bits and pieces.

Zoya ran her fingers over the small brown tiles on the kitchen countertops. "This is handy."

True, they were handy. You could leave hot plates or pans on any counter. *Strong enough to hold a sexy Zoya while—*

"And I love the light." She stepped over to the glass sliding doors next to the eating area.

"That's what hooked me. The view was a nice surprise."

On a Templestowe hill, his condo was the bottom of four. The house behind had a flat roof, so the lounge room, meals area and kitchen looked out to Westerfolds Park and further in the background to Plenty Hills. Zoya sauntered into the lounge room.

He pulled out an antipasto platter he'd prepared from the fridge and laid it on the counter.

"The retro furniture is cool."

"I'm glad my eighties-furniture is now retro. Lucky I hung onto it." He kissed her cheek. "I should name this place Rustic and Retro."

"Sounds like a comedy."

"We could write it together." He nuzzled up behind Zoya and wrapped his arms around her waist. Standing in front of the two-seater that backed onto the rear floor-to-ceiling window, sun slipping behind the gum trees in the distant park.

"You think you're strong enough to work with me?"

"*Squawk-squawk, squawk-squawk.*" A flock of white cockatoos from the jacaranda tree in the neighbor's yard made their presence known.

"Even the cockatoos are scared," she said.

"They're still there, and you don't scare me. I know underneath your tough exterior, there's a really tough interior."

"Huh." She postured with an exaggerated *you're in trouble mister* face.

"But deep under that, there's this cheeky little girl who loves to have fun," he said.

"So now you're a pedophile?"

He laughed. "For that mission, I send out the cheeky little boy in me."

She squeezed his butt cheeks, pressing her navel into his thigh. Her face transformed from Alice-in-Leo-Land to Jungle-Warrior. "And who do you send for this mission?"

"For this mission," he kissed Zoya's neck, "for this mission I send..." He worked his lips and hint of tongue to her ear. "This is a mission for Rustic and Retrohhh."

Zoya exploded with laughter. Glorious, contagious laughter. They collapsed onto the couch in harmonious hysterics.

When they'd settled down, Zoya's skirt was scrunched up her thighs. He dropped to his knees between her legs, slid his hands lightly over her inner thighs, locked on Zoya's eyes.

"I have permission, right? Anytime?"

Zoya nodded. She probably been thinking about this the whole trip, maybe all week.

He certainly had.

Zoya's screamagasm had the cockatoos outside screeching in a wild chorus. He joined her on the couch and she held him so tightly, he was struggling for air again but he wouldn't have moved for anything, enjoying the little aftershock tremors rippling through her body.

She opened her eyes, loving and fiery, gentle and strong.

"You let go so completely, it's like a different person takes over your body. A sexorcism," said Leo.

"There's only one devil who makes that happen."

"Right now, he's one horny devil."

Zoya ran a fingernail over his erection through his jeans, making his whole body rock-hard, invincible.

"Corny devil, maybe. But I do owe you some spoiling."

"Lose the blouse, leave the boots."

Zoya's blouse was flying through the room before he'd finished the sentence. She mounted him, skirt scrunched up. He flicked her bra strap with his left hand.

"You are good at that."

He had to think about the cockatoos and jacaranda tree with the purple flowers, otherwise he was going to bloom straight away.

Purple flowers, cockatoos, purple flowers, cockatoos, purple cockatoos. Fuck the cockatoos.

THEY'D BEEN SPOONING ON THE COUCH FOR AGES, AFRAID TO MOVE OR speak in case it broke the afterglow magic. A tinge of purple sunset washed through the window onto the wall.

"You always say my name." Zoya raised his hand, kissing it.

"Couldn't remember the name of the woman I was thinking about."

She bit his hand.

"Just kidding. I love your name. Only two syllables, yet it has a strong, mythical beginning, like Zorro or Zeus. Zoy, Zoy Zoy...then a friendly agreeable ending. Zoyaaa," he whispered in her ear.

She wrapped his arm tightly around her waist, snuggling her back deeper into him.

He'd never forget her face in the moment—ferocious, warrior-in-battle-frenzy wild. In any other context she'd be scary. During their lovemaking it was raw, powerful, erotic.

"*Squawk, squawk.*" The cockatoos were back.

He chuckled.

"What?" said Zoya.

"Nothing."

8

NUMBER FORTY-THREE

LEO TURNED OFF THE HEAT UNDER THE BOILING POT OF LINGUINE AND gave the marinara sauce a final stir.

Such a delicate thing, seafood, a bit like the early days of a relationship. If it's rushed you want to spit it out, push the plate away. Overcook it, and every mouthful is hard work. Get it right, the texture surprises and taste lingers, always leaving you wanting more.

A risky dish for a first home dinner date but he had fun choosing the fresh seafood and pasta from Preston Market and nothing seemed a risk with Zoya. Or every risk was worth it. Never afraid to miss.

He sprinkled the chopped parsley over their bowls and brought them to the table.

"This is beautiful, Leo."

"You haven't even tasted it yet."

Zoya waved her hands around slowly. "It's all beautiful. The music, the candles, the flowers. It's perfect."

He lifted his glass of Pinot Gris for a toast. "To your courage."

"To our madness," said Zoya as she clinked his glass.

It had been perfect. Last night they'd devoured the antipasto platter he'd already prepared then made love in his bed before crash-ing. Saturday morning, he woke with Zoya staring at him again. Beyond perfect. They made love then walked down to Harry's Café in Templestowe Village for breakfast. An afternoon walk to his favorite spot on the Yarra River. A short nap, then he made dinner while Zoya read on her new favorite couch, with sunlight beaming through the window.

"This *is* delicious. Not easy getting it right with olive oil, that's why I always do the tomato-based version."

"Thanks. I'm no chef, just do some basic things well. This is my trickiest dish."

"So how many women have you cooked for?"

His upper body tightened as he focused on spinning the linguine with a scallop.

"Ten? Fifteen?" Her voice played good cop, strong stare, bad cop.

There were major dangers in talking about exes, but she'd kept pushing the interrogation down that slippery lane. Resting his fork, he leaned back. "In the first year after the separation I dated fourteen women."

"You slept with fourteen in one year!" she said, waving her fork, making some of the candles flicker. "What are you up to now, eighty, ninety?

"I only slept with ten of them."

"Huh. Only ten one-night stands." All bad cop.

"They weren't one-night stands."

Her bad cop blinding-lamp-glare made him turn away, reach for his wine. Took a sip, held onto the glass.

"I'd been with the same woman over seventeen years. I didn't want another relationship straight away. Plus, it was easier than when I was young and single."

"Really?"

He nodded. "Maybe by the time women hit mid-thirties they're over the pure physical aesthetic thing. Or maybe most men behave so badly it helps me look good."

"Probably both, but you are cute, Leo. You don't think I date ugly guys?" She squeezed his hand, her glare dimmed to a warm glow. "So, what happened after a year?"

The conversation thread was wound up tight. He took a long sip of his wine.

Zoya topped up her glass.

"I met Mia. We were together for three months then she decided to give her ex-husband a second chance."

"Did you love her?"

"I liked her a lot. I was falling for her, and I never expected she'd scamper back to that arsehole after everything she'd told me about him." He stabbed a scallop, brought it to his mouth and chewed.

Zoya watched, sipped her wine, right eye distorted through the fishbowl effect of the glass.

"With Mia, I confirmed I like being in a relationship."

"Aha. So, I must be forty-three."

The romantic Gypsy Kings CD ended, and the lack of music amplified the tense atmosphere. He got up.

"Excuse me a sec, need to change the music."

He gravitated to his vinyl collection, needing some comfort music. Pulled Stevie Wonder's *'Original Musiquarium'* from the shelf, slipped record one out and flipped it between his hands a couple of times—old DJing habit—then set it on the turntable to side two. Gentle, romantic, perfect background support. If things weren't flowing smoothly again with Zoya by the end of track four, *Ribbon in the Sky*, they never would be.

Zoya took his hand and kissed the back of his palm. "Sorry about the numbers thing. I don't want to spoil tonight."

Inner tension uncoiled like linguine off a drooping fork. Stevie Wonder does it again.

"That's okay." He kissed her hand. "And for the record, I think you'll make a great number forty-three."

"Huh!" She slapped his arm. "And you're full of number two."

AFTER DINNER, HE LIT A FIRE IN A DRUM IN HIS SMALL COURTYARD. THEY laid back on angled banana lounges side by side, under a blanket. Typical spring Melbourne, warm afternoon flowed into a cool, clear night.

"We used to lie down in the backyard and Mum would make up silly stories about the stars and the moon." Zoya smiled.

"We go water skiing at Torrumbarry Weir on the Murray. Sky's amazing up there. Boys love sitting around the campfire and counting all the satellites crisscrossing the sky."

"Have you ever thought about having more children?"

The hairs on his arms and back shot up like antennas. Emergency alarms buzzed through his veins. Leo's brain lit up with a million warning lights. Not wanting more children had already cost him two relationships with women he could have ended up marrying.

The most recent, Elly, was thirty-seven and had never dreamed of having children until she'd spent time with him and his boys. A sad, frustrating ending two years ago. The first, Maria, was a thirty-five-year-old bio scientist who knew exactly how many children she wanted. He'd met her soon after his separation, and their connection was instant, deep, and fun. Which is why Maria had to end it six weeks in. Maria went back to her previous boyfriend, they married, and she had her two children. Of all his ex-girlfriends, Maria was the only one he'd count as a friend. He was delighted for her, and at least she was absolutely clear from the beginning.

Despite his discomfort and anxiety with Zoya's baby question, better the topic came up early. He didn't want things with her to stall on the runway, but it wasn't something he could control. He never fudged it.

"I had a vasectomy before I left Michele. Technically, it's reversible but I only went with that to keep her happy." He studied Zoya but she stared up into the stars, no discernible reaction. No verbal response either, he needed to fill the void. "We were living in Sydney at the time, and just by luck I got referred to Professor Earl Owen. He's an international pioneer in microsurgery. I don't care who might need to operate on my brain or heart, but down there, I only wanted the best."

"Typical man. Was it painful?"

"I was on a plane to Melbourne for an event the next day. No trace of it after a few days."

"So, you wouldn't be afraid of the reversal procedure?"

His ears weren't perfect, but he could hear a biological clock ticking from a hundred yards away. He would never stand in the way of a woman who wanted a child. Primal need. Once it kicked in, the woman had little control herself.

He rolled to his side to face Zoya and waited till she mirrored him. "You've probably guessed by now I'm a natural romantic. Falling in love and marrying again, no problem. But I've been clear for a long time I don't want more children. I love my boys and can't imagine my life without them, but I've had that part of my life."

"That's an interesting way to put it, 'I've had that part of my life.'"

"Had plenty of time to think about it. It's difficult enough being the best dad I can be to the three I have. Jake, the youngest, is going to be eighteen in less than eight years and I don't want to start at the beginning again. It's a stage that—"

"Okay, I get it." Crisp as the air, she shifted back to the stars.

He almost asked, "*Do you want children?*" Almost. They still had a day together this weekend. More importantly, he'd been clear. If she wanted a child, it was up to her to take the issue further. Zoya was about to turn forty-two. Surely, it wasn't a real option?

As the clock ticked past six p.m. on Sunday, Zoya's requested time to head for the airport, her bag was at the door, but she didn't move. Spooning into Leo on the futon in the lounge room, she tightened her arms around his.

"You don't want to go, do you?" asked Leo.

She wriggled her body deeper into him.

"It's been fun," he said.

An *I agree* sound squeezed out of her throat.

The day had flown by. She always managed to wake before him, her eyes his new sunrise. Their lovemaking was back in form. The sex, post baby chat, was good but not at their usual celestial level. In the Sunday morning light, he'd discovered a new angle on the missionary position and Zoya was born again.

He'd cooked scrambled eggs for brunch with toasted Turkish bread. They enjoyed a stroll and coffee in Warrandyte, a crafty suburb nearby that had retained some old-world charm. Zoya loved it, even checking out the houses advertised on a realtor's window. She also enjoyed beating him in Scrabble. He thought they'd end up with one more lovemaking session, but time and melancholy had snuck up on them.

"But where does it go now?" asked Zoya, grieving.

"We get to spend three nights together on the Sunshine Coast."

The third annual Digi-Tent conference focused on professional digital media content, kicked-off on Tuesday night with a cocktail party and ended Friday. Leo was presenting on a panel about mobile phone games on Thursday morning, and Zoya was attending the conference in her new role for the first time.

"I don't want people to know about us yet. There isn't an 'us' yet." She emphasized *us* with her two forefingers.

"Right, no us. I'll wear a mask."

"I'm serious. We have to keep this underground."

"I can do underground. In Chinese astrology I'm a Rat."

"I can't do Tuesday night. After the opening drinks, I'm having dinner with girlfriends from Sydney, and I've got a breakfast meeting early Wednesday."

"Wednesday night we can crash in my room."

She stiffened in his arms. "I'm taking a bunch of Tasmanian creative folk to dinner

Wednesday night. Tassies always feel left out, so I want to start this role on the front foot. Probably be a late finish."

"I'll wait. If you're okay with it, I'll need a room for Thursday night, otherwise I'll head back that afternoon."

She shifted around onto her back and faced him, angled furrowed brow. "I don't know..."

"Zoya, listen to yourself. Do you really think we could be in the same space in two days' time and ignore each other?"

She swung off the couch, slipped into her boots and yanked the extended handle up on her small suitcase. "We have to go."

THE WAY ZOYA KNEADED HER HANDBAG STRAP, IT WOULD BECOME THE softest leather known to man, or fall apart before they reached the airport. The silence formed a physical ball lodged high in Leo's gut. As he drove under the airport exit sign on the freeway, he struggled for a way to break the tension.

"Maybe Wednesday night," said Zoya to her handbag, "but you don't tell a soul about us."

He smiled, the ball in his tummy becoming a balloon. "Not a soul. What if I bump into a zombie? Can I tell my new zombie mate all about this amazing woman I've met? About her gorgeous smile and sense of humor and the wild sounds she makes when—"

"No. That place will be full of zombies. But you are charming." She took his left hand and kissed it, then placed it on her thigh with her hand on top.

She could rattle off ten major decisions at work without blinking, yet in something so sweet and personal – and to him incredibly obvious – she had needed time. He'd met a few women like that: industry dynamos, romance dynamite. Push them and they explode, destroying any remnant of a relationship. A valuable lesson moving forward. He might light the fuse, but Zoya needed to control the length of it.

She stared out the window at the long-term car park, endless rows of empty, dusty cars. "Maybe we can have dinner and crash at my room Thursday as well... but no promises."

I can work with maybe. Maybe is half a yes.

As they neared the terminal building, a Qantas jumbo soared on take-off. He was still in awe of the technology. Heavy, cumbersome machinery, full of hundreds of people and tons of luggage, piercing gravity against all logic and gliding up through the sky.

This crazy thing with Zoya might work after all.

9

TWENTY GOOD REASONS

Naked.

Naked with bathrobe?

Fully clothed?

Leo had vacillated on the best way to greet Zoya in his hotel room. He chose jeans, t-shirt, and bare feet. Didn't want to appear like he was assuming anything, or make it look like he was only interested in her body. Plus, she was coming from a work dinner, probably needing a few minutes to transition. Lying on the king-sized bed, hands behind his head with legs crossed at the ankles, he glanced at the radio clock.

Eleven. Surely, she hasn't changed her mind?

He rolled off the bed and shuffled into the bathroom, splashed some water on his face and patted dry. Two things highlighted the quality of a hotel for Leo: fluffiness of the towels, and comfort of the pillows. This room passed with distinction. Still found it difficult to believe the organizers had paid for his flight and a room like this just so he could share what little he knew about the game and interactive media landscape.

Crazy.

He couldn't lie down again. Decided on some stretches, a habit

49

from his soccer days that helped him prepare for any meeting or public presentation. Started with calf lean and hip lunge, three each calf. Then threw his leg up on the desk and worked his hamstrings, three each leg, finishing with thigh muscles. He was standing on one leg, stretching his right quad when—

Knock, knock, knock. An urgency to the rhythm.

His instinct was to rush to the door, forgetting he was on one leg. Luckily, he fell onto the bed, had a little chuckle, and bounced up again.

He swung the door open.

"Hey, Zoy—"

She sidestepped him and tramped to the middle of the room, stood with feet wide, hands clenched tight, and game face as intense as he'd ever seen it. Wouldn't have surprised him if she stomped and screamed the New Zealand rugby haka.

Something must have gone wrong at the dinner with the Tassie creative folk. Maybe they bombarded her with complaints and demands? So many creative people felt entitled to government funding for their 'important' work. Tinges of anger in his belly, he wanted to go and set those lazy idiots straight.

"What happened?" he said.

"We can't do this. It's madness. I like you but I'm in Canberra for at least five years with this job. It's everything I've worked for my whole career, and I need to make the most of the opportunity." Her hands alternated at emphasizing every point. "I want to buy a house there and you're... you're stuck in Melbourne." Sparks spat out with the last three words.

He shuffled closer but not too close. He recognized the fight or flight mode with a little surprise. He picked her as a fighter.

Fight. Fight for time, fight for something.

"We knew this was crazy from the first moment we were alone. You're in the middle of your first major industry event. It's natural you'd question the whole thing. I have been, too."

"Just proves we should end it now, before someone gets hurt."

His inner-romantic pointed towards the glimmer of hope hidden inside her fear: *Before someone gets hurt.* She must like him as much as he was already falling for her. "That's one way of looking at it."

"There's no other way."

"There's two of us here, Zoya, so there are at least two perspectives. Even if there's no way forward, you can't just barge in here, dump your decision on me and walk out."

"Why not?"

"Because you're not that cruel."

Her game face softened. A glimpse of pain, maybe confusion. She pointed at the king-size bed.

"I'm not staying." But she wasn't leaving either.

"That's okay. As much as you drive me wild sexually, this is more than a fling for me. My hunch is that it's more than sexual for you too."

"That's why we have to end it now."

Confirmation he was craving, his upper back and neck relaxed, but she was hanging onto her flight ticket.

"I can't force you to stay, but nothing about this has been forced, has it?"

Zoya's eyes searched the floor, and she shook her head a fraction each way in agreement.

"As crazy as it is, it's been beautifully, naturally easy." He waved his hand back and forth between them. "This thing is really rare."

"You'd know." Threw it with a playful tone, like a beach ball, a grin winning over her game face.

Winning over his insides. "There are advantages to a king size bed."

Zoya squinted, angled brow sharp as an arrow.

He sat on the bed with his back to the wall. He turned two pillows into a border in the middle and fluffed another one up against the wall on the other side.

"Please sit down wayyyy over there. Let's make a list of all the reasons why we should end this thing now. At midnight, you do a Cinderella. No matter how we feel at the end of this list, you leave, and we don't make love."

"You are so smooth. Do you really think that—"

"I swear on my boys' lives. No sex and you walk out that door at midnight." He pointed to the radio clock on 'her side' of the bed. Eleven-seventeen.

Zoya stared at the black radio clock, put her handbag on the table behind the clock, sat on the bed cross-legged, back to wall, then re-wrapped her light, silky scarf around her neck tightly. "You start."

"You're committed to working in Canberra for five years, and I don't want to leave Melbourne for over seven years. Until Jake turns eighteen."

"This job will take most, if not all my energy."

"I'm not in great financial shape, so flying back and forth will be a challenge." His ribs constricted as his lungs and throat pulled each other tight. He studied Zoya because this was the first time he'd opened up about his embarrassing weakness. Always expected to be in much stronger financial shape by this stage of his life, not a potential obstacle to love.

She didn't blink. "You have projects with teams we might fund and that will create a conflict of interest."

Air flowed in, and his ribcage expanded back to normal. He hadn't thought of the conflict angle. The two projects were with teams from the Batemans Bay workshop where he'd met Zoya. Both projects still in early concept stage but it could be an issue later. Minor issue.

"We both have strong personalities and that could lead to many clashes."

"I have Ukrainian Gypsy background so will win most of those clashes, and your Calabrese ego won't handle that."

He smiled and nodded, Zoya grinning. He didn't want to destroy the good mood building, but no point going through this ritual if they didn't clear out the baby elephant in the room. "I don't want more children, and you're not really sure about that." His chest and lungs dived into water too cold and deep for a human heart. Everything froze.

Her smile lost wattage, her eyes some sparkle.

"Your boys might hate me."

Blood rushed back through his heart, took a deep breath. The baby elephant was out of the room and stomping back to the jungle. The boys' reaction to her was another angle he'd never considered, but the fact it was something she'd thought about was another good sign. A beautiful sign.

"No way, you'll get on great with them...but my ex-wife will hate you, try to make things ugly for us."

Zoya dismissed the threat with a wave of her hand. "My family is insane and will scare *YOU* away."

"My parents will probably never accept you because they still haven't accepted me leaving Michele."

"I'm..." She waved her hand over her body. "And you're so...so fit. You'll get bored with me and go for a skinny young thing."

He'd never predicted all these insecurities. She had seemed so confident, majestic, powerful. He leaned across the border pillow and squeezed her hand.

"If I ever left you, it wouldn't be for that. You have no idea how sexy you are." He kissed her hand.

She unraveled her reddish scarf. "I have a thick neck."

He threw the border pillows on the floor, shuffled across and kissed her neck.

Her whole body softened with a long exhale.

When he pulled up, she bent forward and kissed him on the lips. Hot and sweet with hints of Pinot Gris.

She straightened but stayed close, her breath warm, eyes softer, doing that swing thing.

He raised his arm and she snuggled into to his chest.

"So...all the logic says you're right."

"Always right." She patted his thigh.

"We should end it right now. Send out a press release."

"Immediately, but—" She slapped his thigh. "No media."

"Yet I feel like I never want to let you go."

"Me, too."

He kissed the top of her head, tasting her hair three times, enjoying a waft of strawberry or raspberry... something berry.

"Let's not make any decisions tonight. Sleep on it. If you still feel the same way tomorrow as you did earlier, just call me. I'll accept your choice and go home."

Zoya nodded gently along his chest.

"But if you decide to keep exploring this thing, let's see where the madventure takes us."

"Huh. Madventure. Perfect."

They stayed curled up for a while, wrapped in a blanket of silence. He wasn't sure whether they were out of words or afraid of more. Reluctantly, he squeezed Zoya's arm and pointed at the clock. Midnight.

At the door, he kissed her forehead.

A hint of a smile rose over the wall of her melancholy.

"Goodnight, Signor Leo." She kissed him on the cheek and shuffled out the door.

"Goodnight, Signorina Zoya."

*Goodnight, Signor Leo...*Playful, good sign. He could work with Signor Leo.

10

READY BUT NOT PREPARED

"You resisted longer than I thought you would," said Leo. His phone displayed two-thirty-three p.m. when it buzzed with Zoya's name on the screen.

"Hah. How do you know I'm not calling to say goodbye?"

He'd been confident all morning. The late call was part of her MO. Seemed she had to grapple every romantic step to the deadline or beyond. He could tell from her tone it was good news but asked as a courtesy, "Are you saying goodbye?"

Silence. A hum of conversations and energy in the background. She must've been in the hub between the conference rooms and main lounge.

"There's a VIP cocktail thingy between five and six. I put your name on the guest list. We can meet there and then get out of this dump."

"So, I need to delay my flight till morning?"

"Maybe."

"Zoya, I need to know so that I can book—"

"Yes, you can stay with me tonight. Bye." She hung up.

Words were so fluid. 'Good' was usually a positive. But he'd take 'bye' ahead of 'goodbye' any day. He checked the time on his phone again. No rush. One more meeting at three and he'd prepared well. Running from meeting to meeting was for amateurs. No hurry to head back inside. Glitzy hotels were ninety percent the same anywhere he'd been in the world. They had a tendency to heighten glitzy behavior and hollow conversations.

He leaned back, his hands resting on the couch grass, a front row ocean view under the palm tree shade, taking in a deep breath of thick salty air. Waves, even the shallow white caps, captivated him.

ZOYA CRIED FOR AT LEAST THREE MINUTES, MAYBE FIVE.

Her feet back on the bed, legs bent at her knees. Leo held her tight, lying on top, his forehead on the pillow next to her trembling head and neck. He had a woman cry post-orgasm before, but they were gentle sobs, an emotional release after years without sexual relief due to a neglectful ex-husband. Understandable. Zoya's came out of the blue, and it was like grieving agony from a wailing widow at an Italian funeral.

She'd been relaxed and funny as they took their time with dinner after a lazy swim in the hotel pool. He wondered if Zoya had chosen this hotel, a thirty-minute drive from the conference resort venue, so she didn't have to stress about who might see them.

She opened her eyes, stared straight up at the ceiling, placing the back of her right hand over her mouth. "Sorry," she whispered.

"Don't be silly. It was the most amazing thing watching you let go like that."

"Letting go? That was a bungee jump into a black hole of...I don't know where. Don't know who I was...how I got back."

He kissed her shoulder.

Zoya shifted onto her side, resting a leg over his. She spread her hand over his cheek and kissed him, her pure affection tingling all the way to his toes. She caressed his face then rested her hand on his hip. They stared into each other's eyes for a long time before she snuggled into his arms. She fell asleep first. No idea how long he enjoyed her sleeping smile.

He had no doubt he was in love with her.

Body exhausted but his heart laid out a bunch of the softest pillows, handcrafted by

Zoya. There was nowhere else he wanted to rest.

11

CRUISING WITH ZOYA

"You made me cry again," said Zoya.

Her croaky voice on the phone hinted she might still be dropping tears on her always-white sheets. Sitting on his own bed, Leo held a printed version of the poem he'd emailed in one hand, his mobile in the other.

FOUND US
Raw tears from the deepest well
Wild waves in a secret cave
Answers to questions we never asked
Destination we dared not search
Found us ready but not prepared
Through the emotional jungle
This blissful stillness found us

The words had flown into Leo's head while he was flying back from Noosa. He hadn't written a poem since his twenties. He'd dabbled with song lyrics when he needed a creative outlet for his sanity, but poetry was beyond him. He'd never studied the craft and didn't care what English poetry professors might think, Zoya inspired it and all he cared about was her reaction. He'd waited till Tuesday morning to send it and she called the same night.

"It's beautiful," she said. "Really, really beautiful."

He closed his eyes and held the poem to his chest.

"I didn't know you were a poet."

"I'm not...but you inspired it, so thank you."

Silence, some rustling then a muffled blowing of her nose.

"Sorry," she said. "I love *'found us ready but not prepared'*, so perceptive and...elegant."

Probably the only decent line. They were both at a stage of their lives where they were ready for love, for a truly special relationship, but they weren't prepared for the way their connection came. Both the timing and logistical challenges. Was any couple ever fully prepared for that moment? Weren't there always obstacles to commitment? Adjustments that need to be accepted, before love could settle in?

"I've never done a long-distance relationship before, have you?" she asked.

"No. Luckily I've got some frequent flyer miles left."

"Me too, but I was saving them for something important." Her inflection teased.

"There's the spirited Zoya I like." He'd nearly said love. What a disaster that could have been so early.

"I've got the boys this weekend. But I can come to your place next Wednesday and stay for five days."

"I'll be working." Her tone bounced straight into work zone, like she'd been beamed into her office.

"Me too, but I can work at your place. We'll have Wednesday to Friday nights together and all the weekend. Work as much as you need, then come home to my world-famous hug."

"Mmmmmm."

He could work with *Mmmmmm*. The sexiest 'yes' he'd ever heard.

His first five-day stay in Canberra was perfect. Zoya was excited to show off her new town, and an excited Zoya was a unique micro-universe he could orbit forever.

They bookended the weekend sauntering through Kingston Foreshore Market on Saturday morning, and a lazy drive to Lanyon Homestead on Sunday afternoon. But mostly they enjoyed hanging at her place eating delicacies they'd bought at the market, silly banter, dancing with lots of laughter, and making love. All lubricated with Zoya's new favorite wine, Trampanillo from the Mount Majura vineyard, about twenty minutes from her place.

No melancholy at the end of their first extended Canberra time because now that she'd released the anchor in her heart—even if she wouldn't verbalize it—they always had a rendezvous to look forward to.

Zoya travelled regularly, so in between official trips to Perth, Adelaide and Hobart, she'd swing by Melbourne early or late in the week, creating four-day stays. She'd work from his place Friday and Monday but insisted no one know she was there on the 'school days', with strict orders he had to be deadly silent when she was on her phone.

They mostly hung at or near Leo's place because Zoya was usually exhausted from work and every minute together was precious. Canberra or Melbourne, they were happy and comfortable cocooning in their romantic bubble.

In early December, Zoya was invited on a Batemans Bay cruise by a prominent supporter of the arts in the ACT, Damon Normski. She insisted Leo join her, not that he needed any encouragement for the major step, the first time she had been willing to flaunt his existence outside her close friends and family. She even paid for his flights that trip.

Leo recognized two other alpha males in the ten-person cruise group, but it was Damon that raised his snake-alert, immediately super flirty and slithering around Zoya, ignoring the other seven guests, including him. Leo hated snakes.

Showing off his boat, Damon had encouraged Zoya to step down into the bedroom with his left hand all over her bare arm and back as he pointed out the features, while Leo had to bend down behind them, peering over her shoulder. When they came back up the steps, he watched Damon ogle Zoya's bum, courtesy of her cotton floral dress that became almost invisible from the sun catching it at just the right angle.

She had her black one-piece swimming suit underneath, but a cold python coiled around his stomach, squeezing venom into his gut. It didn't uncoil until he heard Zoya refuse Damon's encouragement to join him up behind the steering wheel.

They pushed off from the marina about two p.m., a humid, high-twenties day in early summer with a few light clouds. Damon steered the cruiser out of the bay then headed north, hugging the coastline. About an hour after they'd departed, he anchored near Richmond Beach. For a moment, the whole group was as calm as the ocean, soaking up the spectacular view of the tiny, secluded beach surrounded by lush forest and a rocky point. Then the game, or tipsy ones—as the wine and champagne had been flowing—decided it was time to brave the water.

First one to dive in was Zoya with barely a splash. She came up again twenty yards towards the rocks. A few others dived in, but he just admired Zoya as she glided back towards the boat. Until he saw Damon leering at her, in ridiculously tight Speedos that nearly made Leo puke. So, he ripped of his t-shirt and jumped in. Leo was an okay swimmer but not that comfortable in the ocean, but Damon dived in, so Leo swam over to Zoya. He was going to say something about Damon, but she was like a baby dolphin in an ocean playground, and he didn't want to spoil her innocent joy.

Zoya was the last back on the boat. She'd swum all the way to the rocks, at least one hundred yards, stood up to wave to him, then swam back. When he helped her back on board, her foot was bleeding. Must've cut it on the rocks. Damon, suddenly a compassionate nurse, offered to patch it up but his wife was quickly back from the cabin with a first aid kit and led Zoya into the covered area.

That thing about sharks being attracted to blood seemed to apply to a certain snake over the next hour. Zoya had perched herself on a padded bench in a corner of the cabin, leaning against the end, one foot on the floor, her bandaged foot spread across the bench. Demon, much more appropriate than Damon, had been circling for a while. Leo saw him offering to refill her glass or get a snack a couple of times, always a glass or snack behind him. The longer the boat party continued, the less he enjoyed it.

Zoya's laughter dragged his eyes away from a boring conversation about politics or literary books. Demon had plonked himself on the bench seat close to Zoya, who had bent her sore leg to make space for him.

He was laughing. She was laughing.

Leo cringed, the invisible python colder, tighter.

Demon's smarmy dentist-smile beamed while his hand kept tapping her knee. He'd thought Zoya looked sexy with her dress split at her thigh but with her leg bent up on the bench, her dress had scrunched around her waist, and it looked sleazy. Especially with the frontal view Demon was obviously making the most of.

Zoya fully stretched her leg to show Demon her sore foot. He shuffled back a little, held her calf and heel. The dress had scrunched up so much Leo could see a glimpse of her pink panties from the right angle he was on. He could tell where Demon's snake eyes were focused.

Leo tensed up so much he almost dropped his wine.

He balanced the glass on the fold-up table and took a step towards them then stopped when Demon's wife trooped over. Demon pointed to Zoya's foot, and his wife nodded as she checked it out then patted Zoya on the shoulder, said something to Demon and came out to the deck. He kind of heard her announce that Demon was going to start the engine soon and head back. But he was stuck on Demon, who lowered Zoya's leg back onto the bench, sliding his hand from her calf to the back of her knee.

Super, super sleazy, yet Zoya didn't flinch. Not one negative reaction from her. When Demon got up, he kissed her on the forehead. It was after four and cooling down quickly with a fresh breeze, but Leo's blood boiled into a feverish cesspool. The intimate kiss was bad enough, but Demon's hand was on her neck.

Calf and heel crossed boundaries, but her neck was Leo's territory. Intimate territory. No other man's territory.

LEO HAD SNAPPED A QUICK *'NO THANKS'* WHEN DEMON INVITED THEM TO stay on the boat for dinner. A cool breeze and grey clouds had followed them into the harbor and a cold shoulder fitted his mood more than a cold dinner with that snake.

He could wrap his food up with his port and starboard and shove it up his aft.

"What a great day," said Zoya, as warm as her car, which had been sitting in the sun all day.

Leo glared out the passenger window as they crossed over the Clyde River a second time.

"The swim was sublime," she said.

He bit his bottom lip, needing time to process and line up the best words before mentioning her flirting. Getting this right with Zoya would be delicate.

"And isn't Damon a funny guy?"

"He's a sleazebag. How could you let him lech all over you like that?"

The temperature inside was like instant air conditioning. He sensed her glance and kept his focus outside at the small town they were passing, but all he could see was Demon's hand on her neck.

"You had your dress around your waist."

"It was not around my waist."

"You really don't remember raising your foot in his face while his hand was all over your leg?"

"Jesus, where did this come from? He was just concerned about my cut."

"He certainly wasn't looking at your cut. You missed a letter."

"Fuck off."

Thump.

He jumped in his seat and turned to her.

Thump. She banged the console again.

"We had a fun day thanks to a generous couple and now you call me a slut?"

Somewhere deep in his heart he knew he should answer quickly and with caring reassurance. But her flippancy didn't help, and images of Zoya and Demon were chewing up his gut. He wasn't innocent when it came to flirting but there was a line, and Zoya had crossed that line with an Olympic record long jump. If she flirted this much while he was around, what was she like when he was in Melbourne?

"Fuck you, Leo."

Zoya swerved to avoid a puppy waddling across the road. He turned back. The dog made it across safely, but their six-week honeymoon was roadkill.

12

FLIRTING WITH DISASTER

If slamming doors was an extreme sport, they were ready for the World Championship.

Car doors, house doors, wardrobe doors, bathroom doors all shook in their wake. Zoya showered in her ensuite, Leo in the main bathroom. The steamy water fogged up the glass and his head wasn't any clearer. He couldn't believe she was trying to take the high ground on Mount Anger when her flirting was so blatant. Maybe he could've avoided the *'cut/missing letter'* line or waited till they'd gotten home to raise his feelings. At least she hadn't thrown him out. Once they'd talked it through, she would surely recognize her ugly behavior.

Zoya was in the kitchen preparing dinner. Almost went in to help and talk, but the way she was chopping the red capsicum with a huge knife screamed *"Fuck. Off. Leo."* The red juice soaking into the wooden cutting board didn't encourage him. Luckily, Zoya had most of her smaller intestine removed a few years ago due to some medical complications. It meant she couldn't leave long gaps between meals, otherwise she might've stayed in her room.

They ate in clear and present silence.

They always sat opposite each other at her dining table, which he had more time to study during that meal. Chunky, dark timber and wide enough for a comfortable dinner party of eight. Probably hand-crafted as the edges were straight but not perfect. He stole glances at Zoya and matched his eating timing to hers, not wanting her to finish early and leave him alone at the table, or finish before her and hang around with nothing to chew. She didn't meet his eyes, and he never felt hers when he focused on his chicken breast.

Zoya fiddled longer than usual lining up her knife and fork on the empty plate, like she was lining up her words. He gave her the space to apologize.

When she looked up, her angled brow pointed a through-line across her nose and raised chin. "I'm sorry for swearing at you. There's no excuse for that."

He was about to respond but she raised a flat hand.

"But I cannot accept being called a slut by anyone, especially you."

He shook his head, trying to shake 'slut' out. "I never said the word. I'm sorry if it came across that way. It's not what I meant."

"What did you mean?" Her tone might've frozen Lake Burley Griffin.

Almost froze his throat. He needed a sip of wine. Two sips. "Please let me explain exactly what I saw and how it made me feel. Without interruption or reaction. Then I'm all ears."

She shifted forward in her chair, opened her mouth, closed it. Leaned back, arms crossed like two MK-17 assault rifles with a grenade-eyes-glare any sergeant major would have been proud of.

His hands gripped the edge of the table, a corner of his brain screaming to push off, walk away. He gripped harder.

She nodded.

By the time he'd finished painting the undisputable picture, Zoya was on the edge of her seat again, cheeks red, obviously embarrassed by her behavior. A pang of guilt rippled through him. Wasn't easy helping her understand how badly she'd behaved. It was a no win.

"I was having a good time. If you can't handle me flirting, too bad."

"It wasn't just flirting—"

"I've watched you flirt your little butt off. You're a world champion."

"Yes, but there's a line."

"Where did I cross the line?"

He shifted sideways in his chair, leaned back, and raised his leg high as he could. "Way up there. That's why your dress disappeared."

"My leg wasn't that high."

"You're more flexible than me. It was high enough for him to..."

"You have a jealousy issue."

He dropped his leg, studied his socks. He did have a jealousy moment back with Elly and she helped him see it, grow from it. This was different, this was provoked. Justified. He spun back and faced Zoya.

"Why do you think his wife came and interrupted your little tête-à-tête? I bet she was the one who suggested we head back, then."

If he could have videoed the moment, she would have seen how her eyes flashed from grenades to confusion. How she dropped her head a little and stared at her plate, chin tucked in. How the slump of her shoulders lost maybe three inches in height. Damon's wife had wrapped a whole new frame around the harbor picture.

He didn't enjoy watching her morph into a ball of embarrassment. He'd never seen her so vulnerable.

"I'm sorry," she mumbled to her plate.

"It's okay, Zoya. It was probably just the sea air and alcohol."

"But I only had three, maybe four drinks." More questioning than defensive.

Four wines in four hours weren't excessive.

She looked up with teary eyes. "I'm really sorry, Leo."

He moved around the table then dropped to his knees, holding her hands.

"Hey, you gorgeous thing. It's okay. If I didn't like you so much, it wouldn't matter. But I do like you... and I love your beautiful neck and I'm selfish... I want to be the only one to spoil it. To spoil you."

He kissed her hands. She pushed her chair back, dropped to her knees and hugged him tightly.

"Are you sure?" asked Zoya. Her eyes did that swing thing between his eyes but faster. "Isn't it a bit soon?"

Leo shook his head. "No, I'm comfortable with it."

She pulled up another pillow from the stack on the floor and stuffed it behind her, like she needed more support to make a decision. He readjusted his position on her bed so that he was back at eye level.

"They're probably used to the female merry-go-round at your place."

He smiled, sensing she was deflecting the decision, showing a hint of the vulnerable terrain under the surface of Mount Zoya.

"Since I left their mother five years ago, I've only introduced one woman to the boys, Elly."

"Really? Just Elly?"

Her swing-eyes slowed to a gentle sway.

"Yes. We dated three months before she met them."

More light beamed out. She seemed chuffed about breaking the record, meeting my boys after just seven weeks.

"Next weekend..." She turned towards the soft clouds and blue sky through her bedroom window, maybe imagining flying to Melbourne to be greeted by Leo and three mini Leos. Well, three boys with very individual personalities and tastes.

He'd have to hit the Monday sky soon for a work meeting in Melbourne. If they could survive their first real fight the way they had, he had no doubt they could survive anything. They made love on her rug and polished timber floor after their kneeling hug next to the dining table the previous night. Then in bed, they both collapsed with emotional and physical exhaustion.

When he woke under her eyes again it was early, five-thirty, and he was sure he wanted his boys to meet Zoya and he knew they were curious, too.

Zoya turned back from the window "Okay, have to do it some time." She whacked him in the face with a pillow.

"Hey, what was that for?"

"Early practice for next weekend's pillow fights." She whacked him again.

"This is war!" He grabbed a pillow and swung gently but she got another whack in.

13

IT'S A BOY THING

Their first date as a 'family unit' was a soccer match. The boys, particularly his younger two, were much more comfortable talking and interacting while they were watching or doing something else. It also took the pressure off Zoya, as she didn't end up being the constant center of attention. Besides, there was no way they could miss that Friday night game between Melbourne Victory and Sydney, Zoya or no Zoya.

He'd watched his favorite sport struggle for success and acceptance in the Aussie sporting landscape since he was four. When the A-League launched the previous season, the signs were good. The fifty-thousand-plus attendance that night at Docklands Stadium created history for a club match. Zoya loved the atmosphere, a combination of English and European chants with South American rhythm, and a twist of Australian humor. She even bought a Victory scarf and screamed and cheered like a founding member.

Bless her socks.

At a city café after the game, James, Tommy, and Jake were wedged into the opposite side of the booth. Their built-up curiosity and game buzz had spilled out with a sugar burst from cakes and milkshakes as they vied for Zoya's attention. Leo loved how she took it all in stride, never condescending or patronizing, balancing evenly between the three.

DRIVING THE BOYS BACK ON SUNDAY NIGHT, THE CAR WAS QUIET. TOO quiet. They were in that strange zone of ending a fun weekend with their dad but heading back to their delicate mum. Maybe their guilt compounded for enjoying Zoya so much. When it comes to handling divorce, the kids are generally okay if the adults are okay. But deep down, he knew they missed being part of a family unit. Initially, they hoped their parents would get back together. Later, they just craved the fun family stuff in any unit.

"I'm proud of all of you the way you made it easy for Zoya."

"She's funny," said little Jake.

Leo caught his grin in the rear-view mirror.

"She's okay." For thirteen-year-old Tommy, more an action man than talker, the understated compliment was a major tick.

"I like her, Dad. I'm happy for you," said James.

"Thanks, James." Leo wasn't surprised by his empathy.

"Does she like us, Dad?" asked Jake.

He hadn't even considered that angle. Kids fly the thought kite on a tight string, close to their little universe.

"She likes you all very much, except when you beat her in Monopoly, Jake."

"She should've swapped Bond Street for Strand when I gave her the chance."

"Shut up, Jake. You just fluked it with the dice today," said Tommy.

"Sore loser," said Jake.

Tommy pushed Jake, who pushed him back. In the front passenger seat, James rolled his eyes. Luckily, they were almost there.

It was a boy thing.

BACK HOME, HE FOUND ZOYA ON HER FAVORITE COUCH BY THE WINDOW, feet curled up underneath, writing in her journal, bright yellow and larger than her business black books. She put it on the little table, smiled and patted the couch.

"Congratulations, you survived." He slumped next to her.

She flopped out her tongue and puffed like a worn-out puppy. "So much energy in their skinny little bodies. But they're really good boys, Leo. You should be proud."

"Thanks, I am." He kissed her cheek.

"James is smart and easy to talk to," she said.

"Yeah, sometimes I think he's more mature than me."

"Just sometimes?" She poked his tummy.

"Tommy is a charmer. He's got bit of a swagger."

He nodded. "Yeah, he'll always land on his feet."

"And Jake's so funny. He's adorable."

"He's the creative one. I wouldn't be surprised if he ends up an architect or joins a circus." He kissed her hand. "You were terrific with them."

"I had a ball."

"Favorite moment? Soccer? Sunday pancakes? Warrandyte Bakery and playground? I know it wasn't Monopoly." He poked her tummy.

Her eyes snapped alive. "The Christmas lights. That was beautiful and..." She glanced at her journal. "It was all so beautiful."

A few minutes' drive from Leo's house in Templestowe, Antonio, the owner of a corner one-acre property put on a fabulous display each year. Some of the neighbors were following his lead, turning the street into a must-see destination every season.

Zoya's face shined in pure childish joy as she spotted every single decoration, reindeer, and glowing Santa. James and Tommy, her two escorts, walked either side. Attention-seeking Jake ran ahead, dived and rolled on the nature strip, then bounced up like a commando shooting the lights and reindeer with an imaginary gun.

The only time Zoya took her eyes away from the lights or his boys, she stared at an excited little girl riding her dad's shoulders.

Zoya had turned to Leo and smiled, tears in her eyes. Maybe she'd missed this in her own childhood, or it could have been her craving her own little girl.

A chord tightened between his stomach and heart. Is that what she was writing about in her journal? He pushed the thought deep into the bottom of the weekend's candy jar and let the sweeter memories fill the top.

14

HAPPY FAMILIES

"RIGHT AT THE ROUNDABOUT," SAID ZOYA.

The first words from any of them for almost an hour. Leo had been driving down a double-edged highway. On one side, he was proud of the boys' behavior. But after seven hours of car claustrophobia, Tommy and Jake had a fight in the back about the portable DVD player. Zoya had been fidgety for a while, with legs squashed by a bag on the floor that wouldn't fit in the trunk of his mid-sized Vectra.

She was probably regretting inviting him and the boys to her dad's place for a five-day break. *"Dad's got plenty of room. They'll love it there. We'll walk to the beach every day. He'll take them fishing on his boat. There's a table tennis table."* If she had a tail, it would have been wagging a hundred miles an hour. But now he could sense her tension building. Zoya's universe spun in mysterious ways.

He tried to settle the boys but may as well have been pouring napalm on a fire. The mayhem jumped decibels.

Until Zoya banged the dashboard.

"Just let me out here!" she yelled.

Jake and Tommy froze. In the rear mirror, James's eyes darted from me to Zoya and back. Zoya was behind enemy lines and unsure of the rules of engagement as the father's girlfriend. While she hadn't attacked the boys directly, her aggression shocked him and the boys.

Driving down the main street of Beachport, timber houses gave way to a short commercial section, including an auto mechanic shop, large general store, fish and chip shop, bakery and a hotel clinging to its glory days. None of the people on the sidewalks were in a hurry. With little sign of modern development, it was more of a sleepy fishing village than tourist hot spot. Leo liked it straight away. He just needed to navigate Zoya's mind. There would be enough natural tension meeting her dad and stepmom, they'd have no hope of a fun few days if they dragged the car drama in with them. He pulled into a parking spot near the beach.

Leo and Zoya sat down on the grass. Half a dozen kids were playing cricket to the right. The beach at the end of the grass was tiny, maybe forty yards wide, packed with young families having fun in the sand or shallows.

He followed her gaze to his boys on the long timber jetty. Tommy had one arm around Jake's shoulder near the edge, pointing at something in the water. You'd never know those two were at war six minutes ago. James hovered near them, probably tempted to push them in for a joke. They were all good swimmers, so Leo wasn't worried about their safety, but he didn't want them arriving wet and messy for a first impression with Zoya's dad.

"Are you okay?" she asked.

"Must be the salt air. I was about to ask you the same thing." He was aiming for idling in neutral, but his tone came out a bit more revved up.

"Fair enough. I stuffed up in the car, I'm sorry. I shouldn't have exploded in front of your boys."

"I appreciate the apology, but you need to apologize to them also."

She nodded. "This was a big mistake."

A pang of fear ripped through Leo. As much as he hated her reaction in the car, deep down he didn't want to accept the possibility that his boys might end their relationship. She must have seen it in his face.

"I don't mean your kids. *Myyy* family. I should never have put you through this."

"We'll be fine, Zoya. Your dad and stepmom will—"

She placed her finger on his lips. Shook her head then waved her arm in arc.

"I love it here. I hate it here." Her bare feet rubbed back and forth on the grass. "You have no idea the landmine I'm leading you into."

It all fell into place. Zoya had lashed out because she was on edge about seeing her family. This silly season was aptly nicknamed when it came to many families, including his occasionally. His sister had often joked about cancelling Christmas. Fear and embarrassment clouded Zoya's eyes.

He stroked her cheek with the back of his fingers then held her head between his hands. "We'll be okay because we'll be together this time."

He kissed her lips, which started harder than usual but quickly became mushy, just how he liked them. When he pulled back, her eyes had softened, a hint of a smile too.

"Worst case scenario, we let Jake and Tommy loose in the house," he said.

Zoya chuckled. "James can be mission control. He'll be a good leader."

"He's no angel. Nearly burned our house down when he was seven."

"Perfect. We'll wait for them in the getaway car."

"With long sticks and marshmallows."

She exploded in laughter. He was sure the boys could hear her four hundred yards over the ocean.

15

HAPPY NEW YEAR

No consummating their first road trip that night.

Zoya fluttered the white sheet over them, pulling a curtain down on a long day. Lying on their backs, they held hands above the sheet, fingers intertwined. It was only just after ten, on an old double bed with an old, stiff mattress, but relative to their exhaustion level, the mattress was heaven.

The white linen seemed out of place. All the downstairs rooms featured old brown brick on at least one side and yellowy-beige paint on the other walls. The boys were spread across the rumpus room floor, down the hall, on blow-up mattresses. Tommy and Jake had protested going to bed at all and he heard them whispering in excitement for a few minutes, but they flaked out quickly. James was watching TV with Zoya's dad, Anton, and her sister, Dana, who'd arrived a day earlier.

"Your family isn't that weird."

"We've still got three days. Wait," said Zoya.

"I like your dad."

"He was good with the boys." A tinge of surprise in her voice.

"I don't think he cooked enough food for dinner."

Zoya chuckled. He'd whipped up enough chicken and steaks on the barbie to feed a football team.

After the introductions and unloading bags, they'd thrown on swimming gear, grabbed towels, and Zoya had led them to the beach. A five-minute walk from the house, it was an unsupervised stretch from the boat ramp to a rocky point. The drive was worth it just for that hour. Shallow waves didn't stop the boys from catching plenty of rides on their boogie boards, Zoya body surfing after them.

Water was good for Zoya.

Later, while Zoya and Dana helped Anton prepare dinner, the boys dragged Leo into the garage to play table tennis. After dinner, Anton showed his skill with the little bat, slaughtering Leo. The boys didn't want to stop.

Long day.

"Maja's struggling. It puts a lot of pressure on Dad out here." Guilt dripped off her words.

Anton had been with Zoya's stepmum for almost twenty-five years. Maja had a couple of successful surgeries in recent years but her hips and knees on both legs were struggling. Combined with arthritis of her hands and toes, she was becoming increasingly dependent. Leo's parents were younger and relatively healthy, but he'd seen the same guilt eat at friends with aging parents. The struggle between living their lives versus being around to support the people that gave them life.

"Your dad is so good with her. He obviously loves her."

"Tomorrow, I'll give her a foot massage. That's the only thing she ever likes about me, my foot massage."

He kissed her hand.

Muffled voices and a bouncing ping pong ball drifted from the garage that adjoined the rumpus room.

"Cheeky little buggers must've pretended to fall asleep." He sighed and let go of Zoya's hand to get out of bed, but she pulled him back.

"Let me," she whispered.

She rolled off the bed wearing panties and a sheer nighty.

"Not dressed like that you're not."

She threw on a gown and tip-toed out.

"Right, you're all grounded. Especially you, old man!" Zoya's voice boomed down the hallway.

She came back smiling. "Bloody Dad." She dropped the gown on a chair and slipped back under the sheet. "He's playing doubles with little Jake against James and Tommy."

"I think bringing the boys was genius." He patted her thigh.

"Maybe that's why everyone's so mellow."

"Maybe you're the mellow one this time because you've got this sexy man by your side."

He moved his hand up her inner thigh. She pushed it away.

"They're just down the hall. Awake."

"Not the only thing awake." He rolled on top of her, kissed her neck.

She caught her breath. "If you make me scream, I'll kill you."

"Better grab a pillow," he whispered between her cleavage, then worked his way lower...

Zoya dragged his pillow over her face.

New Year's Eve at the Bowling Club was the most boring Leo could have forced upon his boys. Especially for James, who at seventeen, had plenty of partying options back in Melbourne. Throughout the grilling by Zoya and the boys, Anton insisted the event wouldn't be filled with old bowlers in 'white ghost-clothes' as Jake called them. They gave up grumbling when Anton told them there'd be fireworks.

But dessert was served by nine, which created a three-hour boredom minefield for the kids. Plus, the pyrotechnic wiz, James, had done his reconnaissance and the fireworks were only a few spinning wheels and a couple of lame rockets.

So, they were home by ten. Anton saved Leo from winning 'Worst Dad of the Year' in the closing hours of 2006, by creating a fun vibe with laugh-a-minute table tennis, ice creams, crisps, and coke. Plus, his secret weapon—a dozen packets of sparklers and some illegal firecrackers.

As it ticked towards midnight, the boys were busy on the front lawn and insisted everyone go up to the balcony on the second level. Leo and Anton carried an armchair out so Maja could watch. Dana had left the night before, after a heated argument with Zoya.

"Ten, nine, eight..." the radio announcer counted down.

Led by James, the boys raced around lighting sparklers they'd stuck in the ground.

"... three, two, one," everyone joined in with the radio announcer.

The boys stood back to reveal their sparkling sparklers spelled out: *Thanks A & Z*

"A and Z?" said Zoya to Leo.

"Anton and Zoya."

Tears swelled in Zoya's eyes, sparklers reflecting off them. She might've been afraid she had blown her relationship with the boys—and therefore him—in the car, but the last few days her inner-girl had a ball. She was a natural with the boys. Plus, letting go and moving on is a child's superpower, which somehow gets eroded as we become adults.

"See that, Dad?" Zoya hugged Anton. "They like you."

"Of course, they like me, I don't understand why they like you," he said with a glint in his eye. He kissed her on the cheek and pushed her towards Leo.

"Happy New Year, gorgeous."

"Happy New Year, Leo. Your boys are pretty special and so are you."

Fireworks in his heart, a cluster of sparklers in Zoya's eyes. He moved in to kiss her—

Bang, bang, bang, tat-a-tat, tat-a-tat...

He and Zoya jumped at the loud firecrackers.

The boys burst out laughing.

Anton knelt down to Maja. "Happy New Year, my darling."

"What's so new about it?" she yelled.

Everyone exploded in laughter.

"Since Dad moved down here fifteen years ago, this is where I've come to...to..."

"Touch earth?"

Zoya nodded.

At the end of Anton's street, bushland covered the tip of the point like the bottom of a 'V'. The boat ramp beach pointed northeast, back towards the town. A more secluded beach headed northwest. Near the very tip, a little to the west side, Zoya sat cross legged on the sand beside him. Bushes formed a mini curve around them. He took in the spectacular view, arms wrapped around his shins. A rocky outcrop was walkable in low tide, Penguin Island behind it, but not visible sitting down.

Despite being only eight in the morning, the heat shimmered off the ocean. A few lazy clouds drifted above. Tiny waves lapped against sand to their right in between larger waves hitting the rocks ahead. Every now and then screeching seagulls pierced the serene ocean soundtrack.

Zoya scooped up sand in her right hand and tilted it, studying the grains as they poured off.

"I've been doing therapy for nearly seven years." She turned, her head on an angle, maybe fear in her eyes, a fragile tone.

"Every week with my psychologist. Started in Sydney and now we do it by phone."

"Good for you, Zoya. Most people aren't brave enough."

Since leaving Michele, he seemed to be attracted to, or attracted women that needed counseling. But they were women that didn't seek it, didn't acknowledge any issues, let alone own them like Zoya.

Michele went to two psychologists and one psychiatrist while they were married and walked out each time after just two or three sessions. The third time was the final straw for Leo. She'd continued the pattern after their separation and divorce, walking out on another three. Not accepting your own issues is like leaving your baggage on an airport carousel. No matter how much you ignore it, your baggage keeps coming round and around and around, haunting you. Until you acknowledge it's yours, you can't pick it up and move on.

"You're going to stop calling me," said Zoya.

He shook his head. "I respect and admire you more. And I'm honored you've told me."

She squinted intensely, like she was trying to drill into his head to see if he was just making it up. Then her eyes softened, and a half smile sneaked out. "I trust your eyes. You have the most beautiful, big bear eyes."

His inner warmth matched the heating sun. He kissed her cheek. "I'm a big believer in personal development. We can all become better at understanding and handling stuff. Therapy or counseling is just another way. Says a lot about your character that you've stuck it out this long."

"Yeah, says I'm a nutcase."

He wrapped an arm around her. The roar of the waves crashing on the rocks threw a soothing blanket over them. It always amazed him how such a violent bit of nature sounded so relaxing, almost meditative.

"Mum used to wake us up in the middle of the night and drive to the bush, some remote spot up a dirt track. We'd sleep in the car. She'd babble non-stop *'They're coming to take us away. We have to hide.'* Wouldn't stop till sunrise." Zoya uncrossed her legs, leaving them bent up, dug the sand with her left heel. "Frightened the shit out of us. Dana held me so tight she bruised my arms."

"That's rough, Zoya. I can't imagine how..." Any words seemed useless. He kissed the top of her head.

"She attempted suicide twice. Dad left a year after the first time." Her heel stopped digging, ankle buried in the sand. "I found her the second time. In the shed, standing on a wonky chair with a rope around..."

He squeezed her tighter. "Some people would use that experience as an excuse to stuff up their wholes lives."

She lifted her head, smile and wet eyes creating a tropical sun shower, then kissed him, wild, hungry. If he wasn't holding her tightly, she might've swallowed him whole. They made love on the sand, waves crashing against rocks, seagulls screeching.

"WHAT WAS YOURS, ZOYA?" SAID JAMES.

"You too, Dad. What's your bestest?" asked Jake.

Driving home they played their usual game at the end of any adventure: "What was your favorite thing?" Jake rattled off almost every moment, but fishing on Anton's boat was the *Bestest best thing.* Tommy's was boogie boarding at the beach. James copped some ribbing for throwing in his one-on-one lunch with Dana. "Because you two weren't there." He pointed at his brothers.

The energy in Zoya's grin when she turned towards Leo could've fueled the seven-hour drive back.

The way Zoya had shared such raw, fragile pieces of her life puzzle confirmed for Leo she was falling for him, maybe as deeply as he had fallen for her. He held Zoya's hand, resting on her thigh.

"My favorite? Happy New Year!" he yelled.

"Haaappy Newww Yeeear," Zoya sang back.

"What's so new about it?" yelled Jake in a Maja-accent.

Everyone burst out laughing. Even James.

16

NINE DAYS

"Nine days is the magic number," said Leo into his phone earpiece cable, laying on a sunlounge in his courtyard. The DreamWorks moon was out with its buddy, Venus.

"Mmmm... Nine days, huh?" said Zoya.

Cranky phone calls.

Poison seeping into their emails.

Melancholy poems.

He had recognized the withdrawal patterns back in January, around three months in, but *obvious* could slap Leo in the face till he was dizzy, and he still clung to denial when it came to romance, determined to prove they could handle whatever their madventure threw at them.

After staring at the crystal sky for over an hour, the new March moon shined a new light on his Zoya-romance. He loved the simple moments. Spontaneous conversation, unexpected laughs, little touches, making a cup of tea before she asked for one, or simply looking up from a book and sharing a smile.

Tiny specs of intimate gold dust built up so much value, you missed them when they were vacuumed out of your life.

"We need to keep it within nine days because..." He was wary of spooking Zoya... *but it's how I feel, so what the heck.* "Because this thing between us is the best I've ever had." He braced himself for Zoya's flight instinct. Gripped the chair arm.

"Me, too."

Tension oozed out as he relaxed back into the sunlounge. "Kind of ironic, isn't it? That it had to happen with you over there and me based here."

"Mmmm. Is it a sign to run, or a test?"

"Test," he spat out quickly.

Zoya laughed.

But it was true. Being with Zoya was easy. They curled up on the couch like they were custom made. The fun with her was the zaniest fun. The sex wild and soulful. Just being in the same house was nourishing, which made every day without her harder.

"Okay, my beautiful test dummy, your nine-day angel needs her sleep."

"Just two more sleeps," he said. On top of the eleven they'd just missed...

"Beware the Ides of March." This in an exaggerated, spooky voice.

"You don't even know a Brutus."

Zoya laughed.

Made him grin like the early moon and warm as Venus.

Leo liked the energy at Kiraly Catch. In a trendy section of Manuka, just ten minutes' walk from Zoya's place. Noise from the Thursday dinner crowd bounced amongst concrete, chrome and high ceilings. Usually not his kind of place, but it had a friendly, almost family buzz, not an artificial foodie hum. Sitting at right angles at a central table that could've squeezed in four, Zoya faced the large front window while he explored the creative ocean-inspired mural wall.

"Great choice as always, Zoya."

"You haven't eaten yet." Angsty, face buried behind the menu. Her little, solo tummy must've needed food.

He turned back to his menu, still on a high after running a six-hour digital content workshop for emerging creatives at the Canberra Institute. The day before, he had a series of one-on-one sessions, giving feedback and guidance to more experienced practitioners about their projects. A productive couple of days.

"My shout tonight, don't hold back," he said.

"*Humph*. Hardly." She lowered the menu and stared at him with her full brow furrowed.

His confusion must have spilled over his face.

"What's the matter?" she asked.

A baby snake slithered up his spine. "Every time you ask me 'what's the matter?', or 'am I okay?', there's usually something bothering you."

"Well, it's hardly your shout when DMA flew you up here and paid you good money for three days of your time."

"Two days."

"Threeee." Her eyes narrowed, adding force to her brow.

His battle radar was trying to warn him *beware, there's something not right here,* but the adrenalin and endorphins were still flowing from his workshop. "Oh, yeah." He'd also been paid a day for reading the team's presentations and preparing notes. "Still, it's money I've earned, and I want to shout as a thank you."

The waiter came for their orders. Zoya chose the baked salmon with rocket, pear, and parmesan salad. He went for the Blue Eye and chips. They added a main salt and pepper squid as a shared entree. Zoya lifted her empty glass at the waiter.

"And another Pinot Gris, please"

"We should have gotten a bottle."

"Can you afford it?"

She was speaking to her empty glass, but the jagged words swirled around his gut, washing away his adrenaline and endorphins. He was already sensitive about his limited cashflow and conscious that she'd paid for a couple of his trips and some of their meals out.

But he wasn't a bum. His riskiest crime was investing in his creative career. Zoya, of all people, should respect that.

Leo kept his lips pressed tight in case he said something he'd regret. The thunderous tension between him and Zoya drowned out the restaurant noise. The place seemed hotter too, under his black page boy cap and long scarf. He shucked off his leather jacket, letting it drape over his chair.

He tried hard to get the small-talk wheels rolling during the entrée, but the squid was the only thing Zoya would share. With her one-syllable answers, he may as well have been talking to Jake about school. When the waiter took away the entree stuff, Zoya ordered her third wine, Leo his second.

Zoya examined hers, slowly spinning the glass around by the stem. "Don dragged me into his office today, gave me the third degree about hiring you." Neutral tone.

The way things had been heading that night, neutral was good. He could work with neutral.

"Did you give him the fourth degree?"

She took a swig of her wine, didn't put the glass down.

"Sure. I told him I hired my boyfriend for three days this week and a whole week on a resort in Tasmania next month because I wanted to fuck him on taxpayers' dollars."

The snake moved from his spine and wrapped tightly around his chest. He didn't get why she was so sarcastic, caustic. He still hadn't met Don, but Zoya was always on about him, and the more he heard, the less he liked Bastardo Beanpole.

"They've been paying me to speak or mentor on this stuff all over Australia. Guest lectures at universities, other government agencies. Even been invited to speak at MIPCOM in Cannes this October. I'm the only Australian speaker at the whole conference." Saying it out aloud sounded surreal but it was happening, and he knew Zoya's professional back was covered. "You're hiring the perfect peg for the digital hole at the moment."

"No need to get so defensive, I'm the one that's under pressure on this."

"I'm not being def—". Defensive was exactly what he was being. He didn't have to prove himself to Don Bastardo Beanpole, and he sure as hell had nothing to prove to Zoya. He shuffled back in his seat, picked up his wine and skolled half of it.

When the main meals arrived, the waiter asked if they wanted more wine. He shook his head, Zoya said yes, please. Bad sign. Images skimmed back to the boat trip where she had shipwrecked on four wines.

He was three-quarters of the way through his fish when Zoya tapped her knife on her plate then pointed it at him.

"Fuck you, Leo, you just want me for the money." She glared at him like he'd killed a baby with his bare hands.

His fork stopped mid-air with a speared chip.

In a third person experience he watched himself put his fork down, stand, drop enough cash on the table, put on his jacket, push his chair back in neatly, and walk out.

WHO THE HELL DOES SHE THINK SHE IS? SHE WAS BROKE HERSELF BEFORE this Canberra gig. And what has she got to show for it? Nothing. At least I've got three boys.

He trounced towards Canberra Avenue without a destination in mind other than distance. Distance from Zoya.

She offers me work, then treats it like she's paying out of her own pocket and risking her job for me.

A car horn startled him back to reality. He stopped on a road facing a red light, the front bumper of the sporty black sedan just a foot from his legs. He raised his hand in apology to the remonstrating driver and quickly stepped back to the curb. Music filtered out from the Public Bar across the corner. For a moment he thought about stepping in, then he saw the banner up high:

Ides of March - Thurs 15th - featuring Caesar Rocks

"Beware the ides of March" Zoya had said.

Should've listened, stayed in Melbourne.

The lights turned green, he checked carefully for any other

speedsters, then crossed. Decided against the live music, needing to walk, think. Work out what he was really feeling.

What was she feeling?

At home he was always drawn to the Yarra River for deep contemplation or quiet celebration. The closest water wisdom that night was the Kingston Foreshore. He skipped across Canberra Avenue and headed along Manuka Circuit. But too many Zoya memories floated along that foreshore. Messy gelatos, lingering market walks, zany conversations. If she bothered to come looking for him, that's the first place she'd check. He turned left at the top of Telopea Park. The windchill chopped through him. He zipped up his jacket, tightened his scarf, and shoved his hands as deep as his jacket pockets would let him.

In all his travels, Canberra was the easiest town to navigate, which was just as well as he'd delegated directions to his subconscious. He pounded the pavement while his heart pounded the reality of his time with Zoya. By the time he got to the Canberra Yacht Club, the relationship was over, and he was convinced Zoya wanted it over. Their logistics were always going to be a burden, but her job was the biggest barrier. She would never admit it, but Zoya was driven with a capital D. She found it difficult to let anything else in. A bit of pressure from her boss and she dumped all over him.

He sat down on a bench that had a bit of protection from the wind, the timber slats cold.

Boats bobbled on the shimmering water under the lights. They felt unbalanced, precarious.

Beware the Ides of March.

If Caesar represented their love, Brutus was her boss, Don. Who could blame him? If Leo was in his shiny black shoes, he'd want to protect his latest asset from being distracted away from Canberra too. He empathized with Beanpole, but still didn't like him.

Timber creaked and rubber tires rubbed as boats scraped against each other and the pier.

He could stay in a hotel and book the first morning flight back. She could send his stuff over. Or book a later flight and pick his stuff up after she'd pranced off to her precious office. No. He was not a flight guy. He'd walked out to avoid a fight. Any fight after her attack would have been ugly, public, with left hearts minced up and scattered across their table. She couldn't claim the high ground while he owned the moral turf.

If this thing was going to end, he wanted it to be an adult ending, with some kind of dignity. He shivered, tightening his scarf again. Didn't help. It was nearly midnight and the icy wind had broken through his anger blanket, exposed his tired limbs from the forty-minute walk in stiff, new boots. He ambled back towards the Hyatt Hotel cab rank. The one cab waiting was empty and worn out. Just like his heart.

17

WHEN DO YOU KNOW?

ALL THE LIGHTS IN HER APARTMENT WERE ON.

Probably looking forward to finishing the fight she'd started. He paid the cab driver, unlocked the main door to the building and ignored the elevator. He trundled up the stairs, needing some blood moving, preparing his mind for a battle. His shoulders tensed as he turned the key in her apartment door. He was ready for her hollow attacks, a familiar competitiveness hardening his body, like pre-game in his serious soccer days.

The first surprise was the warm flutter trickling through him, melting some of the tension. Zoya's coats and scarves hanging above two umbrellas, his trainers nuzzled up to hers on the floor, familiar paintings and photos on the wall. He hadn't realized how quickly this had become his second home.

"I was afraid I'd never see you again." Zoya's voice was croaky with care, brittle too, as if she could crack into pieces any moment.

Second surprise.

Angelic, even in her flannelette pajamas with a loose red wool sweater on top, standing behind the couch, silhouetted by the tall burgundy lamp against the back wall.

He'd planned to pack quickly, grab his laptop and head to a hotel. He turned back towards the entrance.

"Don't go, Leo. Please."

He took off his jacket, scarf, and hat, hung them up next to her stuff. Shuffled past the dining table, anchoring himself parallel with the couch. Her yellow journal lay open on the coffee table, big pen across it. Scrunched up tissues floated around a half-empty large box of Rocher Chocolates he'd brought from Melbourne. Her eyes were puffy and red.

She must've been crying. Good.

The venom lingering in his brain dissipated with that one curt thought. Whatever options he'd contemplated after he'd abandoned her at the restaurant, right there, in front of her, every fiber in his body wanted to wrap around Zoya, a powerful muscle memory led by the most potent muscle, his heart. He resisted. Needed to hear whatever her tears had washed up. Wasn't expecting any miracles but deep in his heart, he was hoping for at least a semblance of one.

"I'm sorry, Leo. I had no right to say those things."

Mini miracle.

"I let a whole lot of stuff get to me. Pressure at work's ridiculous and so political. Don called me manipulative today."

One more word about Don and I'm out of here.

"But what really scared me..." she straightened a little, like she was trying to look deeper into his eyes. "Scares the hell out of me, actually."

A hint of a smile, even a glint in her eye.

"Is how much I care about you." She stepped close, hand waving slowly between them. "How important this thing is."

Miracle.

Zoya stepped closer, held his hands. "I didn't mean to hurt you, Leo. I..."

He couldn't wait any longer, he wasn't hurt. Seeing and feeling her this close, this vulnerable, he could barely remember what triggered the anger a few hours ago.

"It's okay—"

She put a hand on his mouth, gentle, warm. He didn't fight it. She moved her hand to his cheek.

"I love you, Leo Devecchio. I'm in love with you, and it scares the hell out of me because I've never loved anyone like I love you. That's why I was pushing you away."

Major-gorgeous-amazing-spin-round-the-universe-in-a-heart-swing miracle.

Droplets from heaven filled her eyes.

His eyes.

"I love you, Zoya Orlenko. I'm in love with you and never want to lose you."

He kissed her. She tasted of chocolate nuts and salty from the tears, and it was the sweetest cocktail he'd never forget.

Curled up in her bed after making love, they should have passed out from exhaustion but were still wired.

"When did you know?" asked Leo. "Was it on the beach when you told me all that stuff about your mum?"

Zoya got up on one elbow, working her fingers through his chest hair. He liked the way she played with his fur.

"It was after that I really accepted it. You didn't judge me. Didn't blink. But really, it happened earlier, and I was in denial."

"When?" he pressed. "Valentine's Day, when I picked you up at the airport with the huge red heart balloon tied to the car?"

Shaking her head while raising the wattage of her smile was the most beautiful visual contrast he'd ever seen.

"No, but that was sweet." She kissed his chest. "You always bring me something at the airport."

Her breath was warm and teasing on his skin.

She pointed to the area between the foot of her bed and the wall. "Here."

"Here?"

"When we danced to Lionel Richie all night... your third stay."

They'd danced naked for the whole of his greatest hits CD, and the dude had a lot of hits.

"I told a couple of girlfriends about it and the way they reacted kind of woke me up. How many guys would dance all night to Lionel Richie? I knew then you weren't just after sex."

"Or money?" he bit his bottom lip.

She pulled a handful of his chest hair. "I've already apologized, mister."

"Okay, okay."

She kissed around his chest. "So, when did you know?"

"I'll line your palms with silver."

She sat up, angled brow aiming her laser eyes.

"I'm not teasing about the money thing. Honest. But how ironic is that? Those were the first words you said to me."

"Really? You were a goner way back then?"

"It was such a cheeky thing to say to a stranger. Totally left field. It inspired something crazy from me."

"Come here and say that," she said.

"You remember."

She nodded, a grin setting up camp on her face.

"Then your smile wrapped it all up... and yes, I was a goner, way back then."

Zoya's grin turned into a carnival.

"Now who's cocky?" he said, slapping her thigh.

They wrestled and giggled their way to making love.

18

KNOCKOUT HONEYMOON

As far as Leo was concerned, this was their mini honeymoon post the '*I love you*' magic.

The next Digi-Lab residential workshop at Freycinet Lodge in Tasmania was Zoya's first major baby in her new role. Fully funded by the federal government, thanks to her tireless maneuvering within her role as CEO of Digital Media Australia, plus a program and mentors she'd carved out with Giga. This time Leo and Zoya were openly sharing a room and staying through Sunday night, long after everyone else would be bussed away on Saturday morning.

Zoya's job honeymoon was well and truly over as she drowned in preparing her first annual budget submission. Teams desperate for funding, bosses nodding in meetings with her about getting more funds, then nodding in meetings with the government razor gang about cutting her funds. It took the entire three-hour drive for her to scratch the surface of unwinding, her car suspension lifting as she dumped one stress bag after another out the window.

As soon as Leo ended his team mentor duties in Giga's traditional icebreaker game, he scampered back to their room to consummate their 'honeymoon.'

"Move one of those and you're dead," Zoya said, without looking up, scrunched over her laptop on the desk, notes and spreadsheets scattered all over the floor.

He zigzagged the minefield and massaged her shoulders.

"I couldn't have done this without you." She patted his hand, focused on the computer screen. "The three trenches thing is clever."

He'd been taught that negotiating tip by Marvin, the best MD he'd ever had a lifetime ago in a day job as sales manager. What's in your trench that you'd take a bullet for? Throw other stuff in a trench you'd fight for, and a dream trench of stuff you'd love to win, but won't lose any sleep over because it's just business.

Her shoulders remained concrete, but he was still hopeful of getting amorous.

"Sorry, hon, I need this first draft in by tomorrow. No time for fooling around."

Damn.

Leo kissed the top of her head. "Okay, I'm going to have a nap."

Couldn't sleep. Went for a ninety-minute walk instead. Zoya joined him for dinner with his fellow mentors, Giga and Janey, but was quickly back in her room working before a few hours of sleep and her early departure Monday morning.

"Zoya's running late but she'll make it before the VIP presentations," said Giga as he bound past Leo.

Friday afternoon the stressometer was smoking for half the teams, including his. Giga and all the mentors were on high alert as counselors, referees, and firemen. One of Leo's team members had insisted on changing a key element of their project the day before the VIP pitch. She'd put in an all-nighter, then fell asleep through tech rehearsal that morning while her team changed it back again. Matt's team replaced their whole project overnight. No one wanted to officially ask the team members how they were so awake and happy. Alcohol was the only acknowledged substance at the workshop.

"What the fuck have you bastards done to my presentation?" The woman's voice boomed around the venue from a meeting room and bounced him back to Freycinet. The sleeping bear had woken.

He headed in to play Switzerland for the team he was mentoring. There wasn't any time to change their presentation again. Plus, he had a big thing about a team being a TEAM, and there was no *my presentation* in team.

TEAM ZOYA ARRIVED FIVE MINUTES BEFORE THE FIRST PRESENTATION. The way she glided in and greeted Giga and the VIPs, most people wouldn't have believed she was flustered and stressed under her smile. But Leo sensed it in her higher octave voice and lower wattage smile.

He was about to kick off proceedings as MC, so couldn't join her. He peered over his notes as she walked in and sat at the front with the other VIPs. Sitting next to her department head, Don Bastardo Beanpole, she didn't wink or smile or wave. Sat there like he was a stranger.

THE SHOW WENT ON AND AS USUAL, THE TEAMS WERE BRILLIANT, THE VIPs were impressed, and Zoya wrapped up eloquently with a touch of inspiration and humor. Even The Bear starred in her team's presentation, later apologizing like a cuddly koala to her teammates and admitting they were right. It was a nice moment, ending in a group hug that they insisted Leo join.

No Zoya hug.

She was busy making sure Beanpole was having a great time meeting all the mentors. All except him.

He understood her nervousness in introducing him to her boss. The boss who hired her for a job in Canberra, to her partner based in the world's most livable city, Melbourne. Giga and Janey were working him, which was fair enough as he'd funded the workshop and funds weren't easy to access in the creative biz.

He should go outside and have a laugh with Matt, the lanky, smart, hilarious mentor from New York. His laidback vibe was so un-New York, and they connected like they'd known each other for years. Or he could have one last drink with his team.

He walked straight up to Zoya, kissed her on the cheek. "Hey, gorgeous."

Zoya's cheeks flushed. Her head jerked from him to Beanpole and back again.

He stretched out his hand to Beanpole, concentrating hard under his smile not to call him Beanpole.

"Hi, you must be Don. Zoya's told me nothing about you." He often got a chuckle with that line, but the gag came out with an unintended edge. *At least I didn't call him Beanpole.*

They shook hands.

"This is Leo," said Zoya, regaining her composure.

"Wonderful to meet you, Leo. Nice job out there. I much prefer being in the background."

I bet.

"I hope you're planning a hefty pay raise for this amazing woman." He wrapped an arm around Zoya's waist. "She's put in a year's work just on your budget."

"Yes, I'm afraid we're all a bit under the hammer at the moment. Difficult to compete with schools and hospitals under the umbrella of record budget deficits." Slow and measured, like a school principal teaching a grade-three pupil.

Leo wanted to drag him out to the back of the shelter-sheds and kick his butt, even though he'd never done that at school. He matched Beanpole's glare and felt Zoya tense under his arm.

"Don, have you met Paul? He's our London star," said Janey. She guided Beanpole away.

Bless her socks.

"Good job," said Giga as he patted Leo's back and disappeared.

Good job? With his team? As MC? Potentially pissing off Beanpole, their latest financier?

He swung round to wrap his other arm around Zoya, but she caught it and wriggled free, holding his hands like strangers at their first dance class.

"What the fuck," she said through gritted teeth. "You trying to get me fired?" Her smile would have been convincing to anyone watching from a distance. They couldn't see the spears in her eyes.

"Just making sure he knew how val—"

"I know what I'm doing. He's my boss, not yours. We'll talk later." She flung two spears and let go of his hands. As she scanned the room, her face transformed into full work-charm zone.

"Do you have to sit with him at dinner?"

Zoya shook her head. "He's not staying for dinner." She took off towards a Hobart theater team at the bar.

Schemo.

What kind of childish rubbish was that, Schemo?

"It's so good to see you and Yoyo together. Everyone saw the sparks flying at Batemans Bay," said Janey across the table to Zoya.

Zoya left her fork with the last bit of the chocolate dessert on the plate and for the first time since she'd arrived that day, really looked at Leo. Poker face. But that was a step up from spears and disdain.

He could work with poker face.

She turned to Janey. "Really? You could tell then?" The melody was back in her voice.

Janey nodded and drew a large heart shape with her hands.

Zoya's cheeks caved under the pressure and matched the Bream Creek Rose in her glass.

I have to buy a present for Janey.

He raised his glass halfway between her and Janey.

"To Batemans Bay."

Janey clinked his first then Zoya's.

"To Batemans Bay," both women said.

Zoya brought her glass to his slowly, clinked then they sipped their wine with eyes locked on each other. He had no doubt they were back on track. Their track. Get through the after-party early. Get in their room. Get naked.

Honeymoon time at last.

LEO CHECKED HIS WATCH AGAIN. ONE-OH-FIVE A.M.

"An hour, maybe ninety minutes," she'd said, two and a half hours earlier. Just like on the boat with sleazebag Damon, Zoya was flirting with a wet sail through the after-party. Difficult to watch. It wasn't jealousy. He had no doubt there was a hyper-link between her drinking and extreme flirting. Her drinking and extreme anger. He'd worked out why and would flag his theory as soon as he could find her and get back to their room.

When he coasted around the bar, his body froze. Zoya was on a couch under the stair wall with one of the VIPs, Stefan 'Hoppy', hop into bed with as many women his CEO job could seduce, Hoppy. Zoya's legs were crossed as she leaned close while rubbing her shin, long skirt crumpled above her knee. Hoppy had both his hands on her other arm as he prattled some story, probably made up.

The intensity of Zoya's stare on Hoppy burned Leo's stomach. He unclenched his fists, took a deep breath and strode over.

"Hey, Zoya, I'm beat. See you in our room."

She patted the couch. "Join us. Stefan's telling this hilarious story about an actor he worked with in LA."

"Sorry, Hoppy, these workshops are draining. I'm sure Zoya will be enough audience for both of us." The tiniest crumb of pleasure when Hoppy's smile dulled as he called him Hoppy. He gave Zoya a quick wave, turned and bound up the long stairs.

At the top, he slowed down and shuffled to the external doors with slumped shoulders, eyes watching his feet.

Schemo, you said no more childish rubbish, and you act like that?

"Leo, wait," said Zoya, a little breathless, but familiar icicles.

He didn't turn around, just straightened his back, and strode through the doors.

"Leo!" It was a muffled yell, probably wanting to scream at him but not attract attention. Ms. High-profile-public-CEO straining to hang onto her precious privacy.

He heard the doors slide closed behind him, zipped his jacket against the cold wind and headed up the path to their cabin.

ZOYA'S BAG HIT THE DESK HARD, KNOCKING THE COMPLIMENTARY HOTEL pen and pad onto the floor. Leo turned back to the wardrobe, hung his jacket, and closed the door gently, a volcano building inside him. He'd never ever erupted physically with a woman, his lava usually made up of scorching words. But all live volcanos are dangerous.

Zoya dropped her jacket and scarf on the armchair then prowled the wall between the desk and door.

He stood in front of the bed. She stopped a yard in front of him, glared with fists clenched at the end of slightly bent arms, leaning forward on the balls of her feet. Reminded him of that documentary he'd watched recently on how thousands of years of evolution had tuned human bodies to fight, to defend, to survive.

"You want to explain that childish shit back there?"

"The irony is killing me. You're so hyper-conscious of public affection with me at a work function, yet you flirt like you're at a desperate singles party." It was time to give her his theory about her drinking and flirting problem. He was sure once he explained his theory that—

Zoya lunged and pushed him with both hands, just under his ribs.

The force of the blow knocked him back onto the bed, air whooshing out of his lungs. He clutched his body in shock.

Lungs wheezing, specs zipping around the ceiling.

The emotional right side of his brain couldn't register what logistics on the left were trying to tell him. *Zoya just slammed you.*

The realization was like a second blow. He wanted to slap Zoya. Smash her against the wall then throw her across the room, crushing her Luis Vuitton bags.

As air filled his lungs, blood rushed back to his brain, pushing out the fleeting violent instincts. He'd only ever hit three guys and they were pathetic, one-punch affairs that his mates had to finish. This was Zoya, who'd said she loved him.

Zoya.

Zoya shoved him. Hard.

He sat up on the end of the bed. Zoya stood stunned, mouth open, lips moving but silent. She shuffled back to the wall and slid down to the floor, wrapped her arms around her knees, and closed her eyes tight.

He slid down the bed's footboard to the floor, seated the same way opposite her. The polished floor between them may as well have been the Bass Straight. Leo hated the riptide churning inside him, yet his heart was desperate to throw her a life buoy. Drag her into a hug and hold tightly until the nightmare few seconds drowned in the distance.

"Well, that's a first. I've never been attacked by a woman."

She opened her eyes. "I'm sorry. I...I don't...there's no excuse. I'm sorry." Her voice was a half whisper through a coarse throat.

"The desperate singles line deserved a beating." He tried to push a smile out as his body came out of shock, but his skin felt tight, and probably ended up a creepy grin.

"Are you all right?" she asked, pointing to his torso.

He nodded. "Like Ali."

She closed her eyes, nodded.

"Zoya, this might not be the best time, but I have a theory I want to share. It's kind of relevant... but you have to stay there until I finish, or a referee turns up."

19

SWIMMING NAKED

Zoya looked across to where their bags lay side by side, lids open, black t-shirt hanging out of Leo's, her black and burgundy-pink shawl draped across both, her boots and his sneakers acting as sentries. When she turned back, her eyes were softer. She nodded then rested her head back against the wall.

"This is just a theory, okay?" He waited for acknowledgement, getting the barest of nods. "You only have one stomach, because your small intestine was taken out years ago. So, when you have a drink, the alcohol flies through to your head quicker...much quicker. Probably one drink for you is like two for anyone else."

Her eyes focused on the ceiling between them.

"You have three drinks, and you naturally reckon you're in full control, like you were before your stomach operation. But for you, because of your solo tummy, that's six drinks, maybe more. I know I don't trust myself after five drinks. I think I'm a fun drunk...but by five, I'm an obnoxious joker."

Zoya met his gaze.

He nodded. "Yeah, a couple of times someone put me in my place. I was never a big drinker and four seems to be my limit."

She'd let go of her legs and sat with them crossed, color in her cheeks, light back in her eyes. Maybe this resonated. Maybe no one had noticed or had the courage to tell her before, and she respected his bravery and honesty?

"You don't flirt because you're a...a tart or something. It's just too much alcohol and everyone goes too far one way or another if they've had seven or eight drinks. Which is just three or four for you." It felt good getting that out. His shoulders relaxed and he stretched his legs out. "Well, that's my theory. If I didn't love you, I wouldn't have mentioned it."

Something brewed in her eyes. Love? Appreciation?

"So, you think I'm an alcoholic." She stood up, walked into the bathroom.

SLAM.

MAYBE MY TIMING WASN'T GREAT. MAYBE THE MESSENGER ON THAT ONE WAS always going to get slaughtered.

Leo lay under the duvet in his blue, long sleeve t-shirt and boxers.

Maybe it's just a dumb theory. What do I know about that shit anyway? I didn't even Google it.

He checked the clock on her side of the bed again, the empty side. Almost an hour since she'd fled to the bath-cave. He'd heard the shower running but that stopped ages ago.

Rincoglionito! Resident specialist, Dr. Fool.

Then two opposing forces invaded his thinking. On one hand, it wasn't just the flirting, she did push him. Hard. That wasn't normal behavior. He'd never been attacked by a woman. Such an unexpected and weird sensation.

There'd been feisty fury in a few arguments but never any physical lashing out. Not even close. Not even with his ex-wife.

Yet his heart wasn't cowering, it expanded, pushing through his chest towards the bathroom. As crazy as it looked, he wanted them to work their way through this.

The door opened. Wrapped in a bath sheet, Zoya stomped to her bag, flung a few items around, and went back to the bath cave carrying her pajamas. Door closed.

Not a good sign. Then again, she didn't dress to drive home, or take any bedding with her.

After a couple of minutes, she emerged in her PJs, standing in the doorway a few seconds.

He couldn't make out her eyes, but her chin was up, and a Pilates instructor would have been impressed with her posture.

"We'll talk about this after breakfast." She slipped under the duvet without eye contact and switched off the lamp.

He wasn't enamored with the idea. His former father-in-law, Al, wasn't much of a talker, but before the wedding to his daughter, he shared the only bit of advice he believed in. "Never end a day angry with each other." He'd seen the benefit of that advice in his own marriage and the ugly consequences of not following it.

Staring at Zoya's shape as she lay curled away from him, he found a candle of light that flickered some hope. Technically, the day was only beginning. All the madness happened after midnight. So, while they were going to bed angry, there was still hope of not ending the day angry.

He could work with that.

He flicked off the lamp, closed his eyes and fell asleep listening to the rhythm of Zoya's breathing.

LIKE MANY WOMEN LEO HAD MET POST-DIVORCE, ZOYA SUFFERED FROM the modern morning syndrome, CWC: Cranky Without Coffee. Proper coffee. When he'd woken that morning, her eyes weren't hovering above him like he'd grown to love. They were beaming *hurry up* from the armchair as she sat dressed, with feet tapping alternative beats, arms on the side, ready to push off. She hadn't snuck off to the restaurant on her own. Good sign.

"Still up for exploring Wineglass Bay?" He'd aimed for casual, but the words slipped out schoolboy falsetto.

She shrugged.

A shrug isn't a no.

"I need caffeine," she said.

He showered and dressed in record time.

Walking through the trees onto the pristine sand, Leo caught his breath as he stopped next to Zoya. The shimmering sun off the turquoise water was blinding even with sunglasses. The curved beach was the whitest and most beautiful he'd ever seen, much longer and wider than he imagined from the mountain lookout. Without another soul in sight, Wine Glass Bay was their giant private beach, the benefit of starting their ninety-minute hike over the mountain early.

They hadn't spoken throughout the hike, and he didn't dare disturb her.

"About your alcohol theory..." said Zoya, pointing at her tummy.

He faced her.

"It kind of makes sense. I'll check it out with my specialist."

"Cool." He nodded.

"Do you forgive me for..."

"I forgave you before I landed on the bed."

Zoya smiled then headed for the seawater, throwing off clothing. Her spontaneity infectious, he dumped his t-shirt, shorts, and boxers next to her shorts then raced her into the shallows.

Both naked.

Both stopped after a couple of steps into the water.

"It's freezing," he said.

Zoya's arms were wrapped tightly against her chest. "I've got instant goose pimples on my goose pimples." Then she shrieked like she'd won the lotto, grabbed his arm, and pointed about forty yards out.

Dolphins.

Three sleek, grey miracles gliding in and out of the water towards the shore. Her joyous face made him fall in love all over again.

Zoya waded towards them, he followed. They waited with the water lapping at their waists, crystal clear, not a shell or rock on the sandy bed. The dolphins had circled back towards the sea. Zoya's face saddened, but they kept circling and then headed back to where they were standing. The larger dolphin, maybe one and a half yards long, headed straight for them like a torpedo.

For a horrible moment he was afraid it would hurt Zoya's legs, and he almost pushed her aside. At the very last split-second, the dolphin swerved around just a couple of inches from her bare skin. Breathtaking agility at such speed.

Zoya's gasp was as big as her Wine Glass Bay smile. "Look, Leo, look." She was trying to whisper but her excitement boosted the decibels, pointing at the two smaller dolphins following the larger one back towards them.

The three dolphins swam close for a while then got cheekier, diving in and out between him and Zoya. Every now and then they swam slower and brushed against Zoya's legs. Not his. A dolphin-to-dolphin thing. She stroked them as they passed. After a minute or two, they glided out to sea.

Zoya raised herself as much as she could on the soft sandy floor, pining after her cousins. She wiped tears with the back of her hand. "That was...the most amazing thing...amazing." She shook her head. "Amazing."

An overused word these days but he struggled for better. "You're amazing."

Zoya kissed him passionately. Salty seawater, big, soft lips, and pirate tongue. When she pulled back, he had well and truly un-shriveled. She grinned, grabbed his hand, and dragged him to the beach.

By the time Zoya had finished with him, half his body was buried in the sand, along with her knees and feet. When she stopped panting next to his ear, he heard voices from the trees, but it was impossible to tell how close they were. There was at least one excited, high-pitched child's voice.

"Shit." Zoya pushed off him and ran to the water. He followed and they splashed sand off each other, then sprinted back to their clothes. Leo had his shorts and t-shirt on, and Zoya was just pulling her tank over her unfastened bra as the family broke through the trees. Leo waved to mum, dad, a boy, and girl about five and seven. They waved back and continued around the beach.

Zoya turned and stared at her spiritual home, the sea. "Thank you, Leo. I'll never forget this...ever."

"It's not like I ordered the dolphins. They came for you."

"But if it wasn't for your patience and persistence after...after my explosion, we never would have been here this morning."

He wrapped his arms around her waist, nuzzled her neck, soaking up the view with her. "I love you," he said.

She squeezed his arms tighter. "I love you."

20

DAVINCI EASTER BUNNY CODE

"Zoya uses this first thing in the morning, otherwise she's grumpy and yawning." Jake read the clue on the thin strip of paper and looked up at Zoya.

She broke out her smile. "I know! This way." She ran with Jake into the kitchen.

Tommy and I followed her out of the lounge room, James loping behind us.

She opened the cupboard next to the oven and pointed.

"Oh, yeah," said Jake. He pulled out the bronze Italian coffee pot, removed the lid and broke out his adorable crooked-toothed smile. He scooped up five solid little Easter eggs and dropped them into his collection bucket. Then he pulled out another thin strip of rolled up paper. Jake started to unravel it with wide-eyed Zoya looking over his shoulder.

"Hang on, Tommy's next. Everyone does one clue at a time." Leo gave Tommy his first clue.

He unraveled the paper and squinted as he read it silently.

"Out loud," said Leo.

"Listen carefully for musical sounds, watch a movie and hear it surround." He stared at the paper, then grinned and shook his head.

"That's lame, Dad." He walked back to the lounge room, straight to the TV unit and looked behind the sound system. Picked up his five little eggs and the next clue.

"Your turn, James," said Zoya, excited as young Jake with the adventure.

Leo had started the Da Vinci Easter Bunny Code the previous Easter and the boys loved it, even the too-mature James. He'd written five clues in rhyme for each boy. Starting easy and getting more cryptic, each clue would lead to bigger eggs and another clue until they got to their giant chocolate bunny. This year he'd thrown in a couple of harder ones for Jake at the end of his trail because Zoya wanted to team up with him.

His original spin on the traditional Easter egg hunt was the most joy he'd ever had from anything he'd written. Zoya's delight as she skipped around the house with Jake made his heart skip.

Zoya was still smiling in his bed that night, facing the ceiling, holding his hand under the covers.

"That was my favorite Easter ever," she said.

Pride sloshed around Leo's tummy and heart like a warm puddle of the sweetest, purest honey. He squeezed her hand.

"You were like a little girl with the eggs and clues."

She nodded. "I can just see a little girl running around behind Jake."

The honey-ball in Leo's stomach froze into a rock of toffee. Jagged. Brittle.

Zoya rolled onto her elbow. "I didn't mean that the way it…"

He placed his hand on her cheek. "I had my kids with the wrong woman."

Dark clouds deep in her eyes. Tears.

It was the deepest, most loving compliment he could give her, laid out on his raw heart, but the futility whipped his soul. Must have been torture for Zoya.

"Then they wouldn't be the boys they are," she said, wiping her tears.

"And I can't imagine my life without them." The modern paradox. Their mother wasn't his soulmate—far from it—yet they'd created three beautiful boys together.

Zoya kissed him on the forehead and lay back, taking his hand again.

"I like Maria. The whole family, actually."

He was grateful for the subject detour. His sister, brother-in-law, Giovanni, and their kids, fifteen-year-old Mateo, and eleven going on twenty-one Natalie, dropped in after the lunch feast. Maria had an impeccable peoplemeter and Leo knew within five minutes she liked Zoya.

"Natalie's special. She's going to shake the world a bit."

He nodded. "She liked you, so does Maria."

"I'm looking forward to hanging out with both of them. Maybe the three of us girls can go shopping next time."

He lifted his arm and Zoya snuggled into his shoulder, resting her leg over his. He kissed her hair. Her shampoo teased with an apple scent, reminding him of the apple trees at the big red-brick Preston house he grew up in.

"I love you, Zoya Orlenko."

"I love you, Leo Devecchio."

He had no doubt his close friends would love Zoya. The two big ones that mattered had worked out: Kids, tick; Maria, tick. Maria would help smooth out any potential bumps with his parents. They'd survived their own Ides of March and now he couldn't imagine a future without this crazy, gorgeous woman.

SEVENTEEN DAYS. EIGHT INCENDIARY DAYS AND NIGHTS LONGER THAN their souls could handle apart.

"Is Mark going to be there?" Leo had asked during their heated phone call the night before, but Zoya ignored the question.

"Can't talk long, cab's almost there." Sounded like she was juggling the phone with her shoulder while shuffling through her bag. Sounded like she was avoiding the subject. Again.

He barely sat on his couch, hunched and leaning, elbows on knees. "It's a simple question." He didn't plan the edge, but he was trying to do the right thing—raise something that concerned him, rather than leave it to fester and explode later in anger. He pressed the mobile tighter against his ear.

"A lot of my old Sydney colleagues will be there. Gotta go. Have a good night, Leo. Call you tomorrow. Bye."

"I'll wait up, call me as late as—"

Her phone cut out. He glared at his screen then flicked the phone onto the couch.

One of the days that Leo had been working in Zoya's study, he sifted through the trays stacked on her desk looking for a writing pad as he'd forgotten to pack his. He found a birthday card, an expensive, arty design on thick, soft crinkled cardboard. Something he'd be proud to give Zoya.

Simple handwriting in a thick black pen:

Dear Z, Hope you have a special birthday in your new home. Look forward to seeing you down there soon. Love, Mark.

Big heart drawn on the left side.

Zoya's birthday was in November last year, a couple of weeks after she first stayed at his place. He didn't make it down for her first celebration in Canberra because he had the boys that weekend, and Michele wouldn't budge.

The longer he looked at the card, the more he wanted to tear it up. It fired him up so much, he was surprised the paper didn't combust in his hand. She had told him it had been a couple of years since she'd had a relationship. But this felt fresh. Lipstick-still-on-the-collar fresh.

When Zoya got home from work she sang, "Hi, honey, I'm home," like she always did when he was there.

She bubbled into the study and gave him a sloppy kiss on the cheek as he faced his laptop on the desk.

"Have a fun day in mia casa?"

Leo turned, and her smile and eyes dulled.

"What happened? The boys okay?"

Normally he'd take heart with her immediate care about his sons. He wasn't in normal mode. He pointed to the birthday card he'd left on the corner of the desk, about to question her but she jumped in first.

"You're snooping around my stuff now?" Verbal venom. Eyes tight under her furrowed brow.

"I was looking for a writing pad. You said you haven't had a relationship in over two years."

"I haven't."

He tapped near the card, didn't want to touch it again. "That sure looks like a relationship. Who's Mark?"

"I don't have to explain my whole love life before we met." She dropped her handbag on the floor and sat on the exercise ball.

"What a hypocrite. You dragged me through the coals about—" He raised his pointing fingers to emphasize "—all my other women."

She opened the card. A smile crept back to her lips.

He hated Mark.

"That's over...and it was never really a relationship, anyway. It was just a sexual thing. He's just twenty-eight."

He despised Mark. It took all his willpower to stay silent, muscles hardening, veins boiling.

"I didn't tell you about him because we worked together. It was secret. Only one friend knew. No one at work."

Toy-boy and illicit. Leo wanted to murder the bastardo. "When was the last time you saw him?"

Zoya put the card back on the desk, squeezed her hands under her legs and stared down.

"My last night in Sydney," she told her red shoes.

Three weeks before we met.

"Did you...do you love him?"

Zoya raised her head, only love in her eyes and if it was about Toy-Boy, he didn't know how he'd react.

"I'm fond of him."

He dropped his gaze to his white socks, brushed some fluff off his blue Adidas track pants, afraid to speak.

Zoya dropped to her knees, hands on his thighs.

"I'm fond of him like I'm sure you're still fond of Elly. Mark was a thing in another world in another life. You made him superfluous. I love you."

He let out the breath he'd been holding in a long, slow sigh. He ran his hands through her hair, held her head.

"I'm sorry, Zoya. Seeing the timing with the card and the intimacy...I just had to know."

"It's okay. This time your jealousy is kind of cute." She squeezed his thighs.

He smiled and nodded. Copped that one on the chin.

But now she was at an industry function in Sydney. In the same space as Mark, *and* alcohol. Seventeen days since Leo had seen Zoya. Kissed Zoya. Touched Zoya. She'd refused to stop in Melbourne for a night or two before Sydney or on the way back. Too many work pressures. School fees and unexpected extra-curricular expenses for the boys left him temporarily broke, so he hadn't been able to fly to Canberra.

He swung over to the other side of the futon, thrashed the pillows, then lay down again to watch the DVD on the TV. Might've been the fifteenth position he'd tried during the first hour of the movie. It wasn't the best thriller he'd ever watched. Wasn't the worst, but it had no chance of competing with the big screen in his head, where a French film was starring Zoya and an opportunistic young Sydney gigolo.

As much as he tried to resist, his fingers somehow sent off three text messages, aiming as usual to make them funny or romantic.

No response. Eleven-fifty-three, ticking down to danger time. He always remembered a sticker in the toilets at a nightclub he'd seen back in his early twenties: *Nobody's ugly after two a.m.* Taking into account Zoya's stomach-drinking thing, Leo figured midnight was her two a.m. He grabbed the remote, paused the DVD and sat up. Dialed her number. After four rings he was about to hang up, but she answered.

"Hello, who's this?" A loud voice, fighting the music and hum of humans partying in the background.

"Who were you expecting at this time?"

"Leo? Seriously, you're checking up on me now?"

"You cut me off before."

"I was in a cab and...hang on."

Rubbing on the phone, then the party noise muffled. A couple of women talking with a slight echo. She must have walked into the bathroom. A door shut and a lid slammed down.

"You still there?" she asked.

"Where else would I be?

"Are you on the toilet? Do you want me to call back?"

"I want you to back off and trust me."

"I trust you, it's the alcohol inside you I'm worried about."
Silence.
Then giggling in the background as at least two women left the toilets, a noisy burst when they opened the door, then quiet.

"Zoya?"

"I'm tired of you making me feel like a slut and alcoholic."

"Even your doctor confirmed the alcohol thing was likely."

"Maybe you're used to cheating and that's why you're afraid but—"

"You're the one drinking and partying with Mark. You're the one—"

"Shut up, Leo. Just shut up." Within her anger, there was a desperation laced with care.

It stilled him.

"You know your black undies, the ones I found under my bed?"

"Yeah, but what have they got to—"

"I'm wearing them. I missed you and wanted a part of you with me tonight, so I put them on."

His eyes, heart and soul cringed so tight, the reverberations pound into his skull.

Ricoglinito, stupid fool. Schemo.

He needed to apologize. Send a million roses. Hug her till she remembered how much he loved her.

"Now I'm taking them off and dumping in the bin. Fuck off, Leo. You and your cheesy texts and your medical theories can all fuck off."

Silence. Cold, phone-shut-off silence.

Acid flooded his stomach and heart. He wished he could hit a reverse button on his phone like a DVD player. He picked up the remote and turned off the TV. Stared at his dark reflection on the black screen, hunched on a cheap futon.

Alone.

LEO STIRRED AWAKE, ROLLING HIS JAW TO RELIEVE THE DESERT MOUTH and sandpaper tongue. He slumped his feet off the futon and stared at the black TV screen. The three wines he knocked back after the black-undies phone disaster helped him doze off for a few hours, but it made him sleepier, the back of his eyes carrying the weight of his dumb brain.

Schemo. Water and coffee. I need some coffee then work out how to make up with Zoya. Stupid, bloody schemo.

As he sipped his muddy coffee, he leaned against the kitchen cupboards, staring at the bronze brewer Zoya had given him. The round bottom curved in. The top was a series of straight sides that fanned up and out. He could see his tiny reflection in three different angles.

Different angles, same schemo.

He took a long sip. He was no connoisseur but had to hand it to Zoya. The brand she chose and this old Italian engineering she'd gifted him made a decent coffee.

Can't lose her over this. It's scary how much I already miss her.

The realization, the fear, sparked him more than the caffeine. He zipped over to his desk and fired up the laptop.

Ten minutes later his cup was empty, and the cursor hovered over the send button on the email.

SUBJECT: *I'm sorry. I'm an idiot who loves you & I'm sorry.*

He'd resisted writing anything in the body of the email except the lyric she'd inspired:

Please Come Home
Didn't mean to hurt you
Put a monkey on your back
Words don't travel that well
Wish I could take them back
You always admired my courage
How I turn darkness into light
But there's a shadow in my soul
That I just can't fight
Chorus
And I know this might scare you
It sure as hell scares me
I'm surprised how much I miss you
Do you miss me

Now I don't want to lose you
Don't want to live alone
I'm showing how much I love you
Will you please come home
I respect your independence
Love the spirit in your soul
I know you need the distance
To chase your own goals
Chorus
And I know this might scare you

It sure as hell scares me
I'm surprised how much I miss you
Do you miss me
Now I don't want to lose you
Don't want to live alone
I'm showing how much I love you
Will you please come home
Please come home
Didn't mean to hurt you
Put a monkey on your back
Words don't travel that well
Wish I could take them back

He hit send.

THE MELODIC GUITAR SOLO CHIRPED FROM HIS PHONE WITH ZOYA'S name on the screen, Monday night, eight-forty-seven p.m. She didn't have her private email hooked up to her work-supplied mobile so he knew she wouldn't have seen the lyric till she'd got home Sunday night at the earliest. Some distance from the Friday night fight was probably a good thing, anyway.

"Hey, gorgeous." He winced as the instinctive greeting slipped though.

"Now I'm gorgeous."

Couldn't identify the tone, or her mood. Maybe business zone. Could be worse. He could work with business zone.

He got off the futon and sat at the smaller couch near the window. Even though it was dark outside, he felt some comfort sitting on her favorite spot in his home.

"You're always gorgeous, even when I stupidly make you angry."

"Before I forget, that was a nice lyric."

A good sign, he loosened his grip on the phone. "You inspired it."

"I did miss you and I do love you. More than I've loved any man." Voice softer, croaky, like she was crying.

Her words took the edge off his fear, tension oozing through his muscles like he'd been injected with a mega-dose of magnesium. Only then did he realize he'd been a borderline blubbering mess. He collapsed back, closed his eyes, and rested his head on the top of the couch.

"I love you too, Zoya, and—"

"I have to end this, Leo. I'm sorry to do it on the phone but I have to end it now."

He snapped up, icy fear driving a rod in his back. "Zoya, I fucked up Friday. It won't happen again. I trust you unconditionally."

"It's not Friday night, Leo. That phone call simply helped me shine a spotlight on something I've shoved into a deep corner of my soul."

His brain was way ahead of him, warning his gut to harden up, his heart to brace itself, but his heart wouldn't listen. "We've been through the hardest part. We can make this work. I know we can."

Sobbing from Zoya's end. These tears weren't the type he could collect in his pride jar.

She blew her nose. "I want my own little girl. I deserve the joy you have with your kids. I want to experience all of that."

Relationship kryptonite.

Zoya catastrophe.

His heart slumped all the way to the floor, rolled under the couch and curled up in the dusty darkness. There was no way back.

"That's a beautiful dream, Zoya and...and you'll be an amazing mum." On autopilot, he meant the words, but every syllable was scratched into his soul with sharp fingernails.

Her sobbing became louder, deep, husky.

Triggered his tears.

"I'm sorry. It's so crazy. The world finally throws a man in my path I love..." She blew her nose. "But he has three boys and doesn't want any more children...do you?"

Hope dripped off her last two words. She was throwing him a lifeline for their love, but he couldn't grasp it. Leo just watched it swing in the air above, while he drifted in a sea of frustration.

"No, I'm sorry. I can't, not even with you. If I could with anyone…"

He'd thought about it a lot in the last few months. Especially since Easter. Tried to imagine becoming a father again at forty-eight or forty-nine, running around with a little munchkin in his fifties, the emotional energy for a teenager in his sixties. He just couldn't see it, wasn't him.

"I'm glad we met," she said in between more sobs.

"Me, too. I'm proud of us, our courage." Didn't want it to end. Not like this. Not after a stupid act from him a couple of days ago. Not on the bloody phone.

Too sudden, too distant, too cold.

He was desperate to keep the call going, clinging to the cliff of their relationship with the tip of his heart.

Silence broken by her sobs.

Silence was still a connection, her breath at the end of his ear. He could work with silence.

His elbows drilled into his knees, hunched, one hand holding up his head, the other pressing the phone to his ear. She was probably sitting in her bed, knees scrunched up under the white duvet. Silence on the phone with Zoya was better than any silence he could imagine.

"Take care my, beautiful man. Ciao."

Tears snaked around the fingers on his cheek. "Ciao, gorgeous. Ciao." Leo couldn't hang up. "I'm going to miss you," he whispered.

Sobs for a second, maybe two, then Zoya let out the beginning of a raw wail.

The phone went dead.

Cold silence echoed down the black hole in his mind, spiraling down through his bones, dragging him off the couch.

Thud.

He crashed to the floor, sitting with his back to the couch. A shell, a zombie, couldn't feel or hear anything, except for the sledge-hammer pounding his heart.

21

EPIC

LEO DRAGGED DARK CLOUDS AROUND LIKE GIANT BLACK BALLOONS FROM a doomed fate fete.

His closest friend, Bruce, who lived in Sydney, and his sister, Maria, were the only two he'd blabbered to about the break-up. He and Bruce were unusual as men as they could talk about anything. A few years older, decades wiser and a lot funnier, Bruce had survived two divorces, and together with his second ex-wife, helped guide two children into high-achieving adults. He listened to every word and tear Leo dumped on him during the three or four calls within the first two days.

He hadn't been ready to share the news with the boys yet, knowing they'd also miss her. Maybe trigger some emotions from when he divorced their mum as well. Shock and denial only moved aside for moments of torture.

Zoya lasted two days.

Almost exactly forty-eight hours after the heartbreaking call, she sent an email Wednesday night. At first, he thought it may just be a goodbye note until he read the greeting: *My Dearest Leo*. His heart took off like a dog chasing birds in a park, his brain couldn't hang onto the leash.

Huge difference between *My Dearest Leo* and *Dear Leo*. Massive difference.

Didn't want to read it on his phone, this email, their love, deserved a bigger screen. He zipped over to the dining table, turned on the laptop. Pointer finger and middle finger tapped the wood as the system took an eternity to fire up. Clicked on his email server... clicked on Zoya's email.

My Dearest Leo,
I never thought I would have a relationship as lovely as ours. You
have become one of the most beautiful things in my life. Ever. Yet it
has thrown up challenges that keep sneaking up on me.
On Monday night it became obvious there isn't a way forward
for us.
To survive my past, I've chiseled out a very independent life. I'm not
one to be controlled or told what to do. Even when your intentions
may be based in kindness, a relationship where there is no chance
for negotiation or compromise is not a relationship for me.
The way you project your jealousy and anger whenever you feel
insecure, like last Friday when I was in Sydney and you were
angry that I didn't call, and back on the boat last year, made me
more than anxious. You scare me.

He jolted back from the screen. No woman had ever said that to him. *You scare me.* His heart shriveled up. Hate is the logical opposite of love, but to scare someone you love, that has to be worse, the extreme opposite of love and kindness. *You scare me.* He'd triggered her emotional fear with some super schemo behavior. He dragged his mind back from hindsight to the screen. The email so far had been mostly positive. Zoya seemed to be opening a door, rather than changing the locks. He leaned forward and scrolled down.

Over the last eight months I feel that I have gotten to know you a
bit, and through you, gained a bit of understanding into the kind of
relationship you had/have with your ex-wife and her difficult

behavior. I won't deny that her antics at Tommy's soccer game were distressing for me. But I acknowledged my hurt feelings, dealt with them and now I laugh, because I let it go. She doesn't deserve any power between us.

Leo sat back again. Michele had never been to one of Tommy's away games all season yet decided to attend that particular Saturday, after she'd heard Zoya was going. When Zoya found out Michele was also going to be there, she wanted to pull out. Tommy wanted Zoya to come and his mum promised him she wouldn't make a scene. Leo should never have pushed Zoya because her instincts proved correct.

While coaching Tommy's under-fifteen team, Michele started taunting Leo about ten minutes after the game had started. She'd plonked herself on a fold up chair, ten yards from him. Her insults started loud and as Leo ignored her, got louder. His assistant coach, Jimmy, had to speak to Michele before she quieted down.

The boys won 2-0 and Tommy had scored one, set up the other. Tommy and Jake were buzzing when they got into their mum's car. Then Michele made a scene in the car park, abusing him and Zoya. It took ten-year-old Jake to get out and drag his mum back to her car. The incident triggered a fiery argument between him and Zoya that night.

He should never have pushed her to go, but he and Tommy had done it from a positive place. He unclenched his eyes and continued scrolling.

I don't feel we were aiming too high, because what we have/had is/was so special and lovely.

Have/had is/was? His always half-full heart was filling, then draining, then overflowing with hope. Despite a ton of justification and a bit of finger pointing, it still didn't feel like a goodbye note. He kept reading.

I know I can't continue with the arguments and conflict that we've dragged each other through in recent months. I have been resentful toward you, and you have suffered because of my anger. But I am not an angry person normally. I know myself pretty well. I know my flaws as well as my strengths.

I'm not making excuses for my anger, I have treated you unfairly. I am sure that there were alternative ways to go about things, but I am so far from bloody perfect, as you well know.

One thing I fought internally but now realize you are right—I can manage not having a bab, if I was happy and content in our relationship. But that's only possible if we work out a future together, and to know that we are both open to taking advantage of what life has to offer to us as a couple – and as individuals within.

To be open to discussion and suggestion and ideas doesn't mean losing one another, it means being open to the journey of life together. Would you support me in funding a school for children in Uganda? Would you structure your career with the flexibility to allow us to spend time there?

Which means a relationship based on equality, and mutual respect and trust. This is the only kind of relationship that we should both want for ourselves.

His heart was overflowing again. *I can manage not having a baby*, a major thing for her to think or feel, let alone write. Megasational. He loved the Uganda school idea. She'd envisioned a life without her own children, but still contributing to nurturing children. Perfect.

We could create a life in Canberra, you know. You could get the kids excited about soccer here, the boys could be at Canberra schools for a year or two. Like a student exchange, an adventure. We could have made it work if you were open to considering different options. Sell it to the boys.

Zoya's love laced with naivety. There was no way he'd be able to take the boys away to another state from their mother, just like he'd be devastated if Michele had tried that on him. Despite all the animosity from Michele, she was still their mother. However, it was exciting that Zoya was thinking about him and the boys moving in with her. A good sign.

You say you believe we could work through our stuff. I am still doing therapy, but at least I do own my issues. That chiseling I have done on myself hasn't been easy. You never end up with a perfectly smooth marble version of yourself, you just get better at dealing with all the jagged edges.
My guess is that a lot of your anger isn't anything to do with me. You applaud me for doing therapy, you're frustrated that Michele won't, yet you reject therapy for yourself. Don't you think you are worth caring for? I do.
You admitted being jealous with Elly. I suspect your feelings of jealousy toward me and irrational fear that I will be unfaithful is not really to do with your love for me at all, but a fear of loss of control. But that is just speculation, really. That is for you to work out.
I guess what I'm trying to say is, take responsibility for your own issues rather than projecting your anger onto me. Cut out your passive-aggressive stuff too, because sometimes that rips through me more than our stupid arguments.

His shoulders and neck tensed. He pushed his chair back a little, hands clinging tightly to the end of the table. He acknowledged the jealousy thing, even though he thought it was exacerbated by her drinking problem. But the constant references to his 'anger' surprised him. *His anger?* And he'd never been accused of passive-aggressive before. Not once.

He got up, walked to the lounge room, paced the carpet end to end a couple of times. *Who was she to focus on his anger? If only they could've videoed their arguments and watch how she drove all the—*

He stopped in the middle of the room, looked up at her favorite couch then down at his hands, one wrapped tightly around the fist of the other. She was reaching out, communicating exactly how she felt. Raw and brave. His reaction? Anger. Arguing with her through a laptop screen and his red-misted imagination. Proving her accusations.

He rubbed his hips and thighs over his jeans, then slumped onto the futon. Head heavy, he grabbed a pillow to support it. The coffee table needed wiping. A three-quarter circle from a glass of something, probably Jake's milk before bed, and a few biscuit crumbs stared at him. Dusty, too. The reflection in the old, curved TV screen showed his shape but no details.

He got up, shuffled to the kitchen and poured a glass of water. Leaned back on the counter and took a swig. There must have been some truth in her words, or it wouldn't have thrown him out of the email. Maybe there were a few moments his tone was aggressive, and his timing could have been better a couple of times. He didn't have to work it out now. He was sure they could talk through this.

He headed back to the table, sat down, interlocked fingers and stretched his arms high. Took a couple of deep breaths and then focused on the rest of the email.

I have made some dumb decisions and walked away from relationships because I have been confused or fucked up, or I was going through a self-hate phase, which made it impossible to like anyone else. This is not the case here. I like so much of you. In fact, I adore you, and if there was a sign or a commitment on your part that you were prepared to acknowledge all your issues and do the work to understand them, then there is hope for us.
You're probably angry just reading this as it's pretty stark. It is meant to be. Because I want us to be together in a wonderful and loving relationship. I want to be able to talk about and dream and fantasize about our future together, safe in the knowledge we are able to reach happy compromises.
I want a home. I want to feel a sense of belonging. I felt that was possible in Warrandyte or Templestowe, but equally we could do that here for a bit, or in London or LA, if we we're happy together. I want and need my life to be more than a career. Travel and being fit and making love, playing piano and buying a home and enter-

taining and animals, and getting to know your boys. I do want family and friends around me, but mostly I want you.
I think this epic email is the longest I have ever written.
I don't expect you to respond tonight. Maybe you've already thrown your laptop away. Whatever your response and whatever you decide, please know that I have loved you, and do love you very much.
Zoya

A long sigh escaped. Relief and happiness floated into his lungs with each new breath.

The email was a rollercoaster because it had been her self-therapy, dumping all her thoughts and feelings in an unchartered field until she worked out which path she really wanted.

Leo.

She still loved and wanted him.

22

FAVORITE SPOT

"I found a therapist," said Leo.

Zoya stopped pushing chicken pie onto her fork with her knife, lifting her eyes. "Really?"

He nodded. "I booked four weekly sessions, and assuming I'm comfortable with her, I'll keep going."

She put down her knife and fork and held his hand across the wooden table. The old-world Hamilton Café had safe, sound-soaking acoustics, and he was keen to share this news before they reached Zoya's dad's place for a mid-winter break.

"My anger bucket lately has been almost full with scorching water. One little rattle and it bubbles over the top, burning anyone nearby. Recently, that's been you."

Zoya squeezed his hand then let go and scooped some more pie into her mouth, barely taking her eyes off him.

"But most of my life I've never had more than a few drops simmering in that bucket, if anything."

"So why is it so full now?"

He leaned closer and despite being on opposite corners from the only two other occupied tables, lowering his voice, "Michele. Not because of what she says to me or about me. It's my frustration at how she uses the boys as a weapon...does the opposite of what every book and counsellor advise us...not realizing how she's hurting the boys much more than me...and I can't do anything about it."

Pride and love and respect and delight overlapped her face like posters on an inner-city wall. "That makes a lot of sense, Leo."

"She's really pushed it this year. The longer our relationship has gone, the worse she's been."

"I've seen your love for the boys. They'll be okay. When do you start the therapy?"

"Sounds weird when you say it like that, 'the therapy.' She had a spot available this Friday, but we'll be in Beachport. She's going away for a couple of weeks after that, so my first session isn't till six weeks away."

Old cake and biscuit tins filled the walls from a time before therapy and counselling pervaded the common language.

"I'm proud of you," she said.

"I'm terrified of you."

Her angled stare pinned him.

"Seriously, Zoya, you had the courage to shine a mirror on things I couldn't see. Thank you." He took her hand back, stroking her skin with his thumb. "If we can work through stuff the way we did last week, we can work through anything together."

Zoya studied their hands for a beat, looked up and launched her full weapon-of-mass-construction smile. It lassoed him the first time in Batemans Bay, and it still tied him up in knots.

It had taken two marathon phone calls Thursday and Friday night to work through Zoya's email thesis. Each paragraph. Line. By. Line. Neither of them lost their temper. They just talked and talked till they found common ground, understanding exactly what the other was feeling. Before their mini break-up she was planning a few days at Beachport on her own and then a few days to recover at Leo's. Saturday morning, she called and told him he should pack for the week at Beachport too.

"Coffee and muffins for the road?" he asked. "They've got raspberry and white chocolate."

"You know all my weak spots." Zoya was a raspberry girl.

"Will you sing it for me again? Please?"

Her smile could've launched a hundred rainbows.

Zoya was the first woman who'd ever written a song for him. She was genuinely shocked at creating her first song out of the blue. At her friend's piano in Canberra the day before their trip to Beachport, the words and melody had flowed out. *Ice Queen.* All about the way Leo had broken through when she least expected it, his cheeky grin and loving arms, how she'd been on ice until his eyes melted her. Lots of lyrical clichés, but it was the most beautiful song he'd ever heard.

And Zoya could really sing. She'd begun her surprise with tight, tinny vocal cords about two hours into their drive. As she loosened up, the melody and her dulcet, diva tone hooked into his heart. Didn't need fuel for the car, he could've carried it on his back all the way to Beachport, flying through the sky with Zoya's words fluttering in their wake like a cape.

ANTON WAS PLEASED TO SEE THEM, ESPECIALLY ZOYA, BUT DISAPPOINTED they didn't bring Leo's boys. He must've asked about 'little Jake' three or four times. Maja had noticeably deteriorated, more hunched, slower, limping around. Zoya became her punching bag that week and the tension between the two women grew each day, neither holding back on aggression or octaves. Anton conveniently disappeared outside during most of the battles, probably grateful for Zoya's diversion.

Zoya's release was lots of sex with Leo and long walks on the beach. Sometimes they'd sit at Zoya's favorite secluded spot.

On the second day, Zoya and Leo were digging into their sandwiches at the teak dining table. They'd missed lunch with Maja and Anton, who always ate at noon sharp and were now sitting in their adjoining recliner armchairs watching a movie.

He couldn't see the TV, but he pointed at the cute sight of Anton and Maja holding hands across the little gap between their chairs.

Zoya smiled, then her face scrunched up.

He also noticed the sounds from the TV.

Zoya stood to confirm what they were hearing. She dropped back into her chair, eyes as wide as her open mouth. "Turn off that bloody porno!" she yelled.

"It's not a porno, it's a movie," said Maja without taking her eyes off the screen.

Laughter launched from deep in his belly. He clamped his lips tightly, but it was impossible to disguise his inner hysterics with upper body shaking and air hissing out of his nostrils. A three-way toss-up whether discovering a couple in their late seventies watching a porno was funnier than the crimson-faced embarrassment of their daughter, or Maja's classic retort.

Zoya transferred her glare onto him, which only released his resistance and he exploded with uncontrollable guffaws.

LEO WAS ON A MISSION TO BREAK THEIR FRIDAY NIGHT HOODOO AND had planned an evening Zoya would never forget. His toe tapped to a nervous internal beat as he stood near the entrance of the lounge room, behind Anton and Maja watching TV.

Up the hallway, Zoya stepped out of the bedroom and spun slowly.

"Wow," he said.

Long, knitted black dress to just below her knees met her new black leather boots with red sole and heel. Already wearing her red coat, she had slung a new black shawl spotted with large red roses loosely over her shoulders.

Her dad jumped up from his armchair and together they admired her waltzing down the hallway, her smile highlighted by red lipstick and framed with her wavy black hair.

"You look beautiful my, darling," said Anton.

"Thanks, Dad." She pecked him on the cheek then turned to Leo. "Doesn't my man look handsome too?"

He'd brought his favorite black coat just for this night, combined with his black pageboy cap and a new silvery silk scarf with splashes of golden-brown.

"He looks French, but I forgive him," Anton said, grinning.

"Why do they have to waste money at a hotel just two minutes from here? They're mad!" barked Maja, her eyes on the TV.

"Because they're sick of us," Anton said over his shoulder. "Now go. Have fun." Anton gave him an exaggerated wink.

Zoya noticed and did a double take, raising her eyebrows.

He headed for the door.

"It's left," said Zoya.

As far as she knew, they were simply having dinner and staying the night at the local boutique hotel, Bompas. She loved how the place had retained its heritage charm while incorporating an updated dining room overlooking the water.

"Slight detour." He straightened her car onto Beach Road.

"This is a dead end."

He smiled. "Maybe. Maybe it's a portal." He avoided her stare but had no doubt her brow would be angled over her nose, eyes squinting at him. He slowed into the parking lot and stopped next to the boat ramp. Waves swelled past the mid-level of the concrete ramp, glimmering in the parking lot lights.

"You want to smooch in this freezer? The heater's not even warm yet."

"Trust me." He turned off the engine, jumped out and shut his door. He lifted the rear tailgate, and a gust of icy wind blew in.

"Maja was right, this is madness," said Zoya, trying to wrap her shawl tighter.

He put on his long winter coat, swapped his cap for a wool beanie, grabbed Zoya's warmer coat and woolen gloves that he'd secretly packed earlier, and opened her door.

"Put these on, princess, and jump out of the carriage. The rest of our adventure is on foot." He held his hand to help her out, head slightly bowed like a gentleman of yesteryear.

She stared at him a moment, then took his hand and lowered herself down.

"I didn't miss the axe murderer signs in the last eight months, did I?"

Her smile would have warmed him, but he was already simmering on adrenalin and endorphins. He shut her door and zipped round the back, Zoya zipped up the coat and shuffled after him pulling on her gloves. She took the large flashlight he passed her, then he placed a battery-powered lantern and his large sports bag on the ground. He slammed the tailgate shut and locked the car with the remote.

She pointed at the bag. "Well at least I know that won't fit me, not even chopped up."

He sensed her joke was more curiosity than humor, adventure sparkling in her eyes.

It seemed a longer walk than usual along the short beach. In the windy darkness they could only see the sand about three yards ahead of them, thanks to the flashlight and glimpses of the waves as the Beachport Beacon flashed its rhythmic light from the hill to their right.

The smell of the ocean was crisper in the dark, air saltier.

"I know where we're heading but I hope you aren't planning a bloody picnic," said Zoya.

The simmering inside Leo began to waver between sizzling excitement and icy fear. *What if all this stupid preparation and planning turned out to be the coldest, most uncomfortable and unromantic idea of all time?*

23

SAY IT AGAIN

No matter what happened from that moment, Zoya—at her favorite spot in the world, with the yellow glow of the lantern washing over her beauty and vulnerability—was a painting he wanted to hang on the wall of his memory forever. Stunning. Sitting with legs tucked underneath, in front of 'their log', on one of the blankets he had packed, another wrapped tightly around her shoulders, and a bottle of Moet in front of her with two empty glasses.

He stood between her and the ocean on the other corner of the blanket, barefoot. Not as blustery as the beach but still cold, wind and ocean for a backing track, including the percussion of waves crashing against nearby rocks.

Zoya wiped a tear from her eye. "You're making me cry again." Her mind must've put together his crazy jigsaw.

He took off his coat, then his V-neck sweater together with t-shirt. He undid his belt and dropped his black jeans, slid down his boxers and stood naked.

"This is who I am. This is all I have. I love you, Zoya Orlenko." It came out husky, but he couldn't have planned how the emotions would strangle his vocal cords.

Zoya wiped a tear with the back of her glove.

He dropped to one knee next to his jeans and pulled a ring out of a pocket.

Zoya gasped, a gloved hand across her chest, adoring him with her classic sun shower. She'd almost bought the chunky ring from Dinosaur Designs on a shopping excursion along Chapel Street together. Featuring swirls with sandy beach colors, created from resin. He knew she'd want a pearl engagement ring custom designed by her mate, Henrietta, so the proposal always had to be with a temporary ring.

"Zoya, will you marry me?"

"Say it again," she whispered.

"Zoya, will you marry me?"

"Say it again." Sweetest tune his heart had ever heard.

"This is who I am, this is all I have. Zoya, will you marry me?"

Her smile answered before the words came out. "Yes! Yes, yes, yes."

Relief joined hands with euphoria, and they ran around his heart collecting elation and bliss, and all their positive cousins, for a carnival of dancing and celebration that spilled into every molecule of his body. He dropped to his knees.

Zoya bounced up to her knees, wrapped her blanket around him, ripped off her glove and put out her left hand. He slid the ring onto her finger.

"Oh, Leo, I love you so much."

"Say it again."

"Are you moving to Canberra, Dad?" It was the slowest Leo had ever heard words come out of Jake's mouth. Measured curiosity with a hint of fear.

Leo had been waiting for it. He felt Tommy's and James's eyes branding him with the same question mark.

"No, I'm not moving to Canberra. Zoya will be spending more time here but still keep her place. And we'll all spend time over there together, especially on holidays. There are some nice beach spots not far from Canberra."

"Can we hire a campervan?" asked Tommy.

"Yeah, cool, Tommy. Can we, Dad? Can we?" asked Jake, back to his usual frenzy.

"I'm busy that week," said James. "No way I'm putting up with these two in a bloody campervan."

"We might have to buy a separate tent," said Zoya. "And a motorbike."

James' eyes lit up. He'd been talking about getting a bike.

"Can we have one too, Zoya?" begged Tommy and Jake in stereo.

She'd fallen into the trap of boys and their toys. Endless wants and expecting to be treated equally, the large discrepancy in their ages irrelevant in their myopic minds. Zoya turned to him for a way out.

They were saved by the waiter bringing the heart-shaped cake Leo had prearranged, one half topped with blueberries, the other, raspberries.

"Surprised it's not a soccer ball," said James, smiling at his dad.

"It's perfect," said Zoya, starring at the cake before kissing Leo on the cheek. "Raspberries are my favorite and blueberries are your dad's."

"I hate raspberries. They're sour," said Jake.

Tommy elbowed him.

"But I like you, Zoya," he blurted out loud.

Tommy and James laughed.

Jake lowered his raspberry face, shoving Tommy with his shoulder.

"I like you too, Jake, and Tommy and James," she said.

He lifted his glass. "Here's to brave Zoya joining our cheeky little family." He turned and clinked glasses with her. "Welcome, Zoya."

"Welcome, Zoya," said the three-boy harmony, leaning their glasses towards her.

She clinked glasses with all of them, "Thank you." She took a sip, "I... I really do adore you all." She put her glass down and wiped a tear. Regrouped, picked up the large knife and started carving the cake. "Right, looks like the raspberries are all mine."

"I like raspberries," said James.

"I want both," said Tommy.

Leo never expected any issues with the boys. He knew they'd be happy for him, and happy it was Zoya. He'd never have proposed if there was any danger of her piece of the puzzle knocking one or more of the boys off the table. The Sunday dinner celebration at Carlucci's in Templestowe was fun and cruisy. The romantic carnival that had begun on Zoya's favorite beach spot continued.

LEO SAW ZOYA'S NAME ON HIS PHONE AND HIT THE 'ANSWER' BUTTON. "Hang on a sec, gorgeous, I'm going to pull over."

After the euphoria of their engagement and celebrations, and calling close friends and family, Zoya hit a wall of reality on the eve of returning home, worried about how her bosses would react. She'd decided to speak to her Human Resources director first, get a feel from her.

He turned off the main road into a quiet street, parked and turned off the engine. "How'd it go?"

"As soon as I told Macy we were engaged, she immediately said I should work in Melbourne Monday and Friday and commute three days."

He pumped his fist but held back his celebration. She sounded relieved or excited, but he had to be sure. "How do you feel about that?"

"Well...good. It means Don can't have any problem with it. Macy didn't even blink. She says congratulations, by the way, because you've snared an incredible woman."

"She's right, I have." If Beanpole had a problem with it, Leo would sort him out.

"Look, Zoya, you don't have to be here every Monday and Friday, or every weekend. I know you'll be traveling a bit and some weeks you'll need to spend more time in Canberra.

And that's okay. We can make this work."

Silence...he checked his phone, but it still had strong signal.

"Zoya?"

"You always make me cry."

"I love you."

"I love you too. Gotta go. Ciao, beautiful man."

"Ciao, bella."

He put his phone down, bursting with relief and joy. If anything was going to roadblock their plan it would have been her job. Now that hurdle was history. He got out of the car and walked down the path through the park. The last bit of sunlight tickled the leaves on oak trees, pink sky behind them.

Melbourne is beautiful in winter when the wind stays away.

"It's going to work, it's going to work."

He thought he was speaking quietly to himself but a skateboarder coming the other way said, "Go, bro," and stuck up a hand for a high five as he rolled past.

Leo slapped his hand then yelled, "It's going to work!"

24

US

"They'll have to change the carpet in the main bedroom. If they do that, we could do the painting in the other bedrooms, lounge, and my office." Zoya walked from the main bedroom, across the hall and into what had just become her Templestowe office.

Leo breathed deeper into his chest. The last couple of minutes the air had barely cleared his throat on the way in. They were walking through the only house that she'd wanted to see a second time. He couldn't get a handle on why she hadn't liked a couple of the others. It created some tense discussions.

Beanpole hadn't helped Zoya's mood. His reaction to Zoya's engagement was "*Congratulations, when's Leo moving over?*" Zoya was so thrown, she never brought up Macy's commuting suggestion, deciding it would be easier in an email. Leo helped her draft the email to Beanpole, but it had been ten days now and still gathering digital dust on her home computer. He hated Beanpole more than any man he'd hardly known.

She said, "my office." Cut her some slack, schemo, she's here, in her office, in your village.

The rundown light brown brick house from the early seventies had an addition tacked on, maybe ten years later. The new wing housed the main bedroom with ensuite and walk-in closet, a small study, and this spare bedroom, which Zoya was claiming as the unofficial satellite office for Digital Media Australia. He'd gladly take the small study. Heck, he'd work in a wardrobe if Zoya was happy here.

She was at the floor-to-ceiling window gazing at the heated swimming pool, shimmering crystal blue under a sky with a few swirly clouds. The house surrounded the pool in a U-shape. The back of the pool was shaded by shrubs, green climbers and bunches of flowers. It was a beautiful surprise when they first checked the house.

Past the pool, sliding doors opened to the family room and kitchen. Three bedrooms for the boys across the front section of the house and lounge room meant they wouldn't drive Zoya crazy. Plus, the mini bungalow in the corner could be cleaned up as a private hangout for teenagers. The place was perfect for them and because of its age, the rent wasn't ridiculous for the up-market area. The boys would be close enough to buses for school, and their mum, but not too close.

He wrapped his arms around her waist.

"I feel like diving in. We should make an offer," she said.

He closed his eyes, sighed into her neck, kissed it.

Water's good for Zoya.

THE ZOYA MAGIC WATER EVAPORATED QUICKLY ON SUNDAY, LEAVING A toxic vapor.

When he had to leave for Tommy's soccer game, she'd been silent and grumpy, even though she'd known about his coaching commitment for months. When he got back from the game, he wished he brought the team's goalkeeper with him. Zoya was in attack mode, and her emotional grenades were flying in from all over the place.

"I'm risking my job for us, and you don't have to miss a beat in your cozy routine. What if your 8-Crocs game is a one-off? Who's going to cover the rent and overhead on two places? Me. I wanted to buy a house in Hobart, now I have to put that dream on hold. What are you sacrificing? I'll always be second to *your* boys."

"That isn't fair. I—"

She held up the palm of one hand. Made a show of checking her watch on the other.

"I brought my flight forward. You can take me if you promise not to speak. I want you to digest what I've said properly before we communicate again. Otherwise, I'm happy to call a cab."

Her bags were by the door. He was barely inside. Their relationship had left the building.

The Antarctic divide between them didn't melt on the way to the airport. Something compelled him to drive her, yet he didn't dare speak first. Shock, anger, a million responses all cluttered his brain into zombie mode. He didn't get out, she didn't say goodbye or thanks. Just grabbed her bags and stormed off, head high.

On the way to his place, he detoured to what was supposed to be their first home together. Sitting in his car, he wondered if their engagement was over after just two weeks. A cold spear hit his chest. He shook his head, short and vigorous, to shake the idea away. Rubbed his chest.

That night, after trying two hundred and fifty thousand positions under his duvet, he gave up on sleep.

Three-fifty a.m. his radio clock beamed. He threw on a sweater and beanie, flicked the central heating up and shuffled to his desk. A poem. His poems had always broken through with Zoya, set their communications back on track. He picked up his pen and adjusted the writing pad. By five-thirty a.m. he'd doodled through five or six pages, but no words stuck. Not one decent couplet. He headed back to bed and fell asleep just as the alarm blared.

BY THE NEXT NIGHT THERE STILL WEREN'T ANY WORDS FORMING. HE picked up his phone many times to text Zoya, but he didn't know how to broach the subject. Every romantic fiber in him was tuned to them being together forever. Every bunch of words he came up with reflected the fear of another ending.

Then a Zoya email hit his Blackberry.

Subject: Us

He scrolled through it quickly to check the length, careful not to read any of it. Another epic. He jumped over to his laptop, brought it over to the futon and fired it up. *Us.* That could go either way. It might be positive...

Hi, Leo.
I know yesterday I jumped off a cliff of negativity that triggered an
ugly avalanche for us. I realize now from the rubble I'd been feeling
lost and sad and alone while you were at Tommy's soccer. I know
I'm a better person than this.
By coincidence, this was the subject of part of today's leadership
workshop—emotional self-management. Turns out I am quite bad
at understanding my emotional impact on others. To be honest, that
was quite a shock. I didn't realize how self-focused and indulgent I
have been.
As you've pointed out, I can choose to wallow in self-pity, or I can
choose to be empowered and not feel like a victim, and to take
control of my life. I do, however, feel we can become better at
communicating with each other.
I have let my inner fear drive me and as a result, I have gotten
angry at you too often, as though I am somehow suffering for some
unknown thing, which I have kind of made you responsible for. I
can see now this is impacting our relationship terribly. I can't really
apologize enough because I haven't been fair to you at all.
You deserve to be loved fully and with the same passion and
commitment that you give. You are so loving. You really do give so
much in a relationship. It's amazing and precious and special. I
know I have resisted throwing myself completely into our relation-
ship. I know I have feared the commitment. I guess in some ways, I

have not been ready to be in a long-term adult relationship, and in a beautiful way it is your fault because no one has loved me this deeply before. Not even close. You must sense this? It must add some anxiety in you.

Lesser men than you would not have felt secure in our relationship at all and called it quits some time ago. But not you. You stay, you don't leave, you keep calling, you keep smiling, you keep kissing, you keep loving. And I keep being surprised that you stay.

I want to be alive to all that we are, and all that we can be together going forward. And I want to give to you as much as you give to me. I understand how strong you have had to be to carry us both. I haven't been there to support you emotionally in the way you deserve. I hope these words resonate with you because they are coming from deep within my heart.

I have chosen to be with you and to not have a child because I love you and want to be with you. I want to enjoy my life and have fun and share it with you. I also don't want to compromise your passions in life. I know you love your boys (I am actually very fond of them too), and that coaching Tommy (and maybe Jake in future years) is important to you. I really didn't mean to make you feel guilty about it yesterday. I didn't manage my feelings around that very well at all.

I know that when we are settled in Templestowe that I will relish having a Sunday afternoon to read, and relax and do yoga or what-ever, so it was probably partly that feeling of being in a transitional phase, and partly that old chestnut of knowing that we only have a few hours together for the rest of the day and just letting small silly emotions blow up into big negative feelings.

I also appreciate how much you have adjusted to accommodate me into your life. You have missed time with your boys to stay with me here. You also gave up tennis comp on Saturdays, and I really did appreciate that. It meant that we were able to maximize our time spent together even though I could only come for such a short period. I probably have never said thank you or appreciated you for this. I am doing it now.

Thank you, lovely man of mine. xxx
I am not perfect, Leo, but I am learning. I know you are frustrated.
I know that I have been hurtful and unsettling and probably fright-
ening and exhausting too. At least I know it.
And I have the power to change this.
I do love you and us together and want to spend the rest of my life
with you. Happily, and to wring out every moment of joy together
that we can. And this is a definite positive shift in my feeling. Macy
said to me today "Take every moment, because you don't know how
long you've got," and it struck a chord. We don't know how long
we've got on this earth, and we are so lucky to have each other. It is
a blessing and the greatest gift, so I'm going to just go with it and
feel the joy of it.
There'll be challenges ahead but you don't have to carry my feelings
anymore, Leo, and you don't have to be strong for us all the time,
okay? Emotionally I am with us, committed to us and to making us
work.
I adore you. I miss your twinkling eyes and your happy, happy
smile that lights up like a Christmas tree and guides me to your
loving arms.
Your girl always,
Zoya xxx

25

COMMUNICATION

LEO READ THE EMAIL THREE TIMES IN FULL AND THE FINAL THREE paragraphs another half a dozen times. He printed it and read the whole thing again while sitting on 'Zoya's couch', sunlight streaming over his shoulder. His inner carnival back, like she'd said *"Yes"* again and again and again.

He left the email on the couch, jumped up to the entertainment unit and flicked through the CDs on the top shelf until he found the greyish cover of Lionel Richie's greatest hits. He slipped in the CD, picked up a large blue pillow from the futon and waltzed to the caressing percussion and piano of track one, Penny Lover.

"THAT'S RIDICULOUS. WHO'S GOING TO PAY THAT MUCH RENT FOR THAT dump?" said Zoya.

Leo's eyes clenched, his grip testing the Blackberry's strength. *That dump* was supposed to be their new home, their first home together. The one with Zoya's unofficial satellite office. With her oasis in the backyard.

The Lionel Richie CD had been on high rotation for three days at both camps. Zoya had loved Leo's reaction to her email so much she danced with him on Sunday night in her bedroom, while he danced to the CD in his lounge room, both phones on loudspeaker.

By Wednesday night, the mobile airwaves were crashing the vibe, voices louder and louder. He opened his eyes and leaned forward on 'Zoya's couch', staring at the orangey-red haze from the square red lamp in the corner.

"It's only the lounge and boys' rooms. They're not even living with us full time. They don't care about the carpet."

"I care." Two-syllable full-stop. Conversation over. Subject closed.

He slumped back on the couch. The landlord had received two offers on Saturday for their Templestowe oasis, so she was in a strong position to demand more rent for the changes Leo and Zoya had requested. Accept the carpet as is and they'd have the edge because they offered to paint. Otherwise, the rent hike for new carpet or they lose out.

"We can do the carpet in six months," said Leo.

"We?"

"My mate Con knows how. James and I will help him."

Silence.

"I meant 'we' as in who's going to pay for it?"

"We both will. I'll have 8-Crocs up by then. My financial situation will be—"

"You already owe me three thousand dollars."

Zoya had slammed down a sledgehammer on a giant steel peg. A marker on her limits, her fear, and through the one fragile piece of his self-esteem.

He'd been so obsessed with getting the production funding he and Pirate Bunnies needed for their 8-Crocs iPhone game from Multi-Media Victoria, he'd let his freelance copywriting work slide. Economic reality crushed his creative delusion when he had his car repossessed back in April. Zoya didn't just lend him the eighteen hundred dollars he needed to cover the three monthly payments and fees, she insisted on paying off the balance of the loan so he'd own the car outright. She turned one of the most embarrassing moments in his life into a beautiful, loving gesture.

Three thousand dollars.

Zoya had trusted him unconditionally and never hinted about the loan again, even in her wildest anger. Not even when she'd ended the relationship in late June before resurrecting it again. He'd been able to bury it deep under his self-confidence, sheltered from his ego. Now she was throwing three thousand rocks and he couldn't avoid them nor justify any defense. It had been such a loving, generous gesture. He should say something kind, appreciative. Reassuring.

"I didn't know this was a bank of Zoya meeting. I would've worn my armor."

"Fuck you, Leo."

Just before midnight, his phone chirped. He was in bed but hadn't been able to sleep, and the message from Zoya may as well have been a caffeine injection.

"I'm sorry for hanging up and swearing. But you definitely need to add passive-aggressive to your list when you meet your therapist."

He jolted up, blood surging through his veins, assaulting his heart, pounding his head.

Passive-aggressive? That's twice now. She pulled the three-thousand-dollar loan out of the blue to bludgeon our plans of living together, then calls me passive-aggressive?

She insisted on lending him more than he needed. She knew how hard he worked. She feigned admiration for creative people with innovative ideas, the risks they took, sacrifices they made, then ridiculed him for taking those risks. As soon the funding was approved for 8-Crocs production, he'd pay her back every cent, plus interest. He didn't need a holiday or any other toy. He needed to clear that debt with Zoya ASAP. Remove another excuse she'd plucked for delaying and diluting her commitment.

No government funding was ever guaranteed for a creative

project. But the 8-Crocs prototype won an award in Cannes and from Multimedia Victoria. He'd been paraded around Australia by Multimedia Victoria, Australian Universities and even MIPCOM and MIPTV in Cannes as some kind of authority. No way could MMV not approve their application for 8-Crocs.

He started typing a response text. Stopped. A scathing, honest poem would be more powerful. He flung the bedding off, bound into his office, and fired up his computer. First, he'd use her own words to show her how unfair and hurtful she was. He searched 'passive aggressive'. Instinctively, words floated into his head. *Massive defensive. Therapy heresy. Alone for a loan.* He jotted them down on his big pad, then focused on the screen for definitions and other info on passive aggressive.

The more he read, the more he slunk back into the chair. He never fully understood the term before. Zoya's attack wasn't an attack. It was accurate. Without even knowing the term, he slipped into a brilliant exponent of passive-aggressive comments. Hurtful attacks wrapped in a bit of sugar.

He turned off the laptop, grateful he hadn't sent off a response. Embarrassed by the words jotted around his pad, he ripped off the page, scrunched it up, and dumped it in the little bin.

You, schemo. You were passive-aggressive. She lends you three thousand dollars with no day job or payment deadline, and YOU feel aggrieved that she mentions it? Ricoglionito.

He grabbed his phone and punched in a text: *Hey, Zoya, I'm sorry. Your loan is a beautiful gesture and I'll always be grateful. It is a loan, and I will pay you back. I'm sorry.*

He shuffled back to bed to bury his shame under the sheets. Hide his pride deep in the pillow, the weight in his heart testing the mattress.

LATE THURSDAY AFTERNOON HER RESPONSE HIT HIS PHONE.

*I accept your apology. Have to cancel trip this w'end. Don's called
special budget meeting for Sat. All departments need to cut 10%
more off new (recently approved) budget!!!
Talk later.*

At least he and Zoya weren't throwing rocks or other shit at each other. First time that he had felt a short communication with Zoya was a good communication. Usually, he tried to squeeze every drop of juice out of their schedules or exchanges.

By the end of the third week of their engagement, they were under attack on three fronts: logistics, financial and practical.

Five p.m. Friday, General Beanpole, who led the major logistics battle, had sent Zoya an email advising her suggestion of being based in Melbourne "*...was against the spirit of her contract. It would make it impossible for him to defend her position with the Minister. Also, I cannot approve your request for the organization to pay for commuting with taxpayers' money, especially since they'd already paid for your relocation costs to Canberra and twelve-months rent subsidy.*"

On Saturday, a digital grenade landed in Leo's email that could explode into major financial disaster. His partners in 8-Crocs, Nicholas and Jason, were getting cold feet and didn't want the pressure of creating the retail iPhone version, which was first going to be released in the USA then Japan.

Sunday morning, he got a confirmation text from the agent that they'd leased out the Templestowe oasis to the other family. Ground zero with their Melbourne home.

Underneath all of that, or on top of it, or permeating through it like acid, was another battle with Michele. He'd lost count of all the cluster bombs his ex-wife had dumped on him. None of them rational, all of them horrible timing, which often happened the weekend the boys were with him.

What a shitty weekend.

"Why do we have to find a place straight away? Why can't we just keep going the way we have and sort out the long-term stuff later?" said Zoya.

Leo was driving, connected to his phone with the cable and ear jacks. It was a wet and windy Thursday night, but he didn't have time to stop because he'd finally nailed the Pirate Bunnies to a meeting and no way could he let Nicholas and Jason off the hook after they'd avoided him all week. He'd have to post the funding application by six p.m. next day, less than twenty-four hours.

Week four of their engagement and Zoya's domestic suggestion tasted like she diluted the concept so much they were drinking a large bottle of water with the tiniest drop of romantic cordial.

"The whole thing was your idea," he said.

"Macy's idea. I just went with it."

"You loved it, embraced it and sold it to me."

"Well, circumstances change." She was trying to keep it conversational, no edge, but no love.

"You mean Beanpole changed your mind." Circumstances, baloney. The guy needed a circumcision, starting at his forehead.

"You really have a communication problem. I'm trying to talk through this. Suggest other solutions."

"Throw an ultrasound over the nine months we've been together, and you'll find a few lumpy bits when we've been apart too long." Leo winced, punched his thigh. Throwing 'nine months' and 'ultrasounds' was ripping open a deep scar in Zoya.

Silence.

He asked for that. "I'm sorry. That was dumb."

Wheesh wheesh, wheesh wheesh. His car windscreen wiper blades got louder, screechier.

"Zoya?"

"We need communications counseling."

"That's crazy. You've got your weekly therapy, and in eight days I'm starting with my therapist. We don't—"

"Together. We need communications counseling together."

Wheesh wheesh, wheesh wheesh.

Three counselors between them. Ridiculous.

He reached Bebida Café on Smith Street, and despite the rain and wind, this Bohemian piece of Melbourne was busy with the street parking taken. He found a spot about a hundred yards down.

Ding-ding-ding, ding-ding-ding. The loud tram bell startled him. He had his indicator on, obviously going to park. What was the moron's problem?

"I'm here now and need to focus on parking. I'll think about it. Ciao."

"Ciao."

By Friday evening, Leo had placated his partners on 8-Crocs, dropped their funding submission in an Express Post bin, then collected Zoya from the airport. For twenty minutes they talked about the three properties they'd be checking out in the morning.

"Did you think about communications counseling?"

"Yes. We're booked in for eleven a.m. Sunday."

"Really?" she shifted in her seat towards him.

He nodded, glancing at her.

Angled brow aimed at him, chin high. "And she specializes in couples?"

"Yep. Apparently, she's got a Masters in feisty Ukrainian Gypsies and a PhD in stubborn Calabrese."

At the red lights he stopped the car and looked at her. "I missed that smile."

She took his left hand. "I'm so proud of you."

"And I'm still scared of you." He winked.

She snarled like she was going to bite his hand but gently kissed it. Soft eyes. He missed those too.

A horn tooted behind them. They both turned forward, holding hands as he rolled the car through the green lights.

26

ULTIMATE SACRIFICE

"Your love is conditional on me not having a baby," said Zoya, like a casual conversation about a movie.

End of the session for Leo.

They'd barely gotten comfortable on the brown fabric couch. Frana had offered Zoya the chance to open the discussion, since she'd requested the counseling, and *bam*, that's what flew out of her mouth.

"I thought this was about us communicating better?"

"It is. I just thought Frana should have some background." No angst in her tone or eyes. Not even the angled, furrowed brow.

He searched the room for some balance. The small desk and office chair faced away, into the corner, like they were avoiding his eyes. The mint green walls offered no support.

He turned to Frana in her brown leather armchair. Possibly late-fifties, greyish hair with silver spectacles, and the way she held her hands in her lap gave her a librarian feel. But there was something behind those blue eyes. Leo was desperate for that something to be wise and experienced, and to come out through her mouth. Reboot the session. Reboot their engagement. Reboot their love.

"Well...Zoya...Can you see how Leo might take that statement as manipulative?" asked Frana.

End of session for Zoya.

Frana had unknowingly unleashed the nuclear word. He could sense Zoya tensing up, increasing her body mass by at least twenty-five percent.

"How do you feel about that, Leo?" Frana said, either oblivious to Zoya's reaction or trying to save the moment.

He turned to Zoya. All her concentration was lasered on her boots. Any more intensity and she would have branded the leather.

"I think we might have some stuff to cover before we can make the most of your guidance," he said.

Zoya got up, grabbed her handbag, walked out.

He turned back to Frana. "Sorry."

She patted his arm, sympathy in her eyes.

THERE MUST HAVE BEEN AT LEAST TWO YARDS BETWEEN LEO AND ZOYA as they trundled along the bitumen path. Fifteen minutes since the 'Communications Shutdown Counseling' and they hadn't spoken a word.

He stared at the river bend to the left. He loved Westerfolds Park and the way the track wound its way through natural bush, every now and then kissing the river. He'd chosen a section they hadn't walked before, a clean path, not affected by any of their history.

"Your love is conditional on me not having a baby" cannoned around his head. He thought they crossed that bridge, left it far behind, but Zoya couldn't burn it.

He turned onto a dirt track that hugged the river. Zoya swung around with him, forced to move a yard closer but staying at the extreme side of the path, her boots brushing long grass.

Despite being in one of his lush green comfort spaces, his stomach was heavy, chest tight. He could see only one outcome from her opening line in their ultra-short counseling session. He snuck a look at Zoya, who focused down, about two or three yards ahead, not taking in any of the scenery. Maybe being in a room with a counselor was one of her comfort spaces, so the whole baby thing filtered through subconsciously.

His soul was still booked on the happily ever after flight, wasn't ready to give up his seat next to Zoya. But she was already in the aisle walking towards the exit door, boarding pass on her empty seat.

"You know, Zoya, it works both ways."

She took a few steps before responding, without stopping or lifting her head.

"What?" Part word, part grunt.

"I could say your love is conditional on me willing to have a baby."

After two or three steps, she stopped, giant gum trees behind her, watching over them like referees, the gurgling river about ten yards behind him.

"It's not the same." She lifted her head, dark sadness in her eyes. "Having a child with someone is the deepest form of love you can show...the ultimate commitment."

"When people all died by the age of forty and only married once. The world is different now. Besides, it still works both ways. Not having a baby so you can be with someone is the ultimate sacrifice."

"You're impossible." She turned away, stood tall, arms by her side, fists clenched.

Threw him back to their suite in Freycinet, the last time he saw her standing for battle. His right leg shuffled back a little for a more defensive balance, or ready to pounce forward in attack. Every sinew tightened. A third-person experience, surreal and involuntary.

"Your idea of good communications is any communication when I agree with you," he said.

She swung around, a furrowed brow you could sharpen a knife on. "And you're an arsehole who doesn't respect everything I've done for you."

"So, your loan was just a baby mortgage." Externally he stared at her, chin high.

Internally, he cringed at the low blow that hurt them both at their most vulnerable point.

Zoya's eyes transformed from dark pit to a searing inferno. She stormed back down the path.

The temporary engagement ring on her finger reflected the sun like a prism of pure truth. Zoya's desperate desire to have a child was never going away. His heart struggled with the emotional punch. The knock-out punch. No words or tears trickled out. Unlike the flowing current of the river, he was drought dry.

27

DEAR LEO

LEO PULLED HIS CAR INTO THE CHURCH PARKING LOT NEAR HIS PLACE. Three cars sat close to the back entrance of the church, and he stopped at the opposite end. He had no intention of getting out or praying. He simply wasn't ready to face Zoya. Something died on the Yarra path earlier that day and he couldn't see a resurrection.

He had Tommy and his team to distract him for a few hours, although he must have taken some of his frustrations out on the innocent referee because his assistant coach, Jimmy, had to calm him down a couple of times. Post-game, Tommy devoured a large Big Mac meal, ten nuggets and a Coke. A double chocolate sundae soothed Leo's throat but nothing else.

Whatever else was said or done between them, the bottom line was Zoya's need to have her own child. Specifically, a girl, which was really about her own childhood. If she was going to end their engagement, she needed to come out and say it. He'd been clear from day one and consistent throughout their time together.

Zoya hadn't.

She had a responsibility to be clear one way or the other. He didn't have the emotional strength for more arguments with the woman he loved so deeply.

He ran his hand down the empty seat. The grey cloth had witnessed hours of laughter and silly singing from Zoya and him, passionate conversations, and other kinds of passion. The late afternoon Melbourne winter demanded he turn his car and heater back on or get out to put his jacket on. No signs or answers had fallen from the sky or through the stained-glass church windows. He started the car and eased into his street. The little sedan felt like a semi-trailer loaded to its maximum, as reluctant to chug up the short steep hill as his heart.

"I'VE EATEN," SAID ZOYA, WITHOUT LIFTING HER EYES FROM THE LAPTOP or packing up her paperwork on the dining table, making her Sunday night agenda clear.

Spaghetti Bolognese was a meal for many, two minimum. He shut the Tupperware lid on the leftover Bolognese sauce, put it back in the fridge, stared at the chilled options.

"I should get a taxi in the morning."

The back of his neck chilled. He'd always picked her up from the airport. Always dropped her off.

Always.

Sandwich and cup-a-soup. He juggled his go-to ingredients to the counter and flicked on the kettle switch.

Sensed her glancing at him.

He concentrated on scooping avocado with a spoon and squashed it over the chunky piece of sourdough. Sliced the tomato slowly, four thick pieces, slapped them on the bread, then stared at the salt and pepper shakers. Salt and pepper worked well together. They worked okay on their own yet had a core compatibility that brought out the best in each other.

By the time he looked up, Zoya was typing on her laptop again.

I should get a taxi in the morning.

"Yeah, good idea."

LEO WAS AWAKE AT FIVE A.M. WHILE ZOYA GOT READY FOR HER TAXI, BUT he kept his eyes closed and faced away from the door.

Not his proudest moment.

He doubted either one of them slept for more than an hour or two. The queen-sized bed somehow doubled in size that night, the distance between them noisy, annoying, and persistent.

Toot.

The taxi driver's don't-wake-the-neighbors-toot barely carried through the front door, let alone to the bedroom. Maybe he sensed the clear-and-present-silence from out there.

Zoya stalled at the bedroom door for a couple of seconds, then her footsteps creaked through the usual suspects of floorboards until the front door closed. Closed with a thud in his heart. Clamped his lungs. Clenched his body into a ball. Couldn't breathe as the taxi gently revved to make the tight, three-point turn and head back up the driveway past the three front townhouses. Dared not breathe as the taxi's engine faded down the street.

Air gushed back into his lungs. He rolled out of bed and checked the wardrobe for slippers and clothing she'd parked at his place over the last few months. All gone. The only thing she'd left behind was the scent of her favorite perfume in the air. It was only a couple of weeks ago she'd finally ended their running gag and told him it was vanilla.

All his hanging clothes looked heavy and five sizes too big, like the bed. He pulled the duvet, wrapped it around him and slumped to the floor, back to the wall.

LEO HAD SLUSHED THROUGH MONDAY AND TUESDAY IN A HAZE. HE neither remembered nor cared what filled the days. Lying on his back in bed Tuesday night, there was no way of avoiding the midnight mirror. Dark stillness reflected the fear and deep hollow in his heart. Vanilla oozed from her pillow.

Zoya hadn't ended it, but it felt ended. He knew she'd survive Monday and Tuesday by focusing on work as she was heading straight to an off-site strategy conference and wouldn't get home till ten p.m. on Tuesday at the earliest. So intense was his belief she wouldn't call, the content of her potential call consumed him.

The call didn't come.

EARLY WEDNESDAY MORNING, DETERMINED TO GET BACK INTO A functional work mode, Leo fired up his laptop with a coffee and marmalade toast at his desk. Didn't get past the first bite. One entry beamed from his inbox among the dozen or more new emails:

Eleven-fifty p.m....Zoya...Subject:

No subject. Blank. Empty.

Eleven-fifty p.m. Tuesday. She'd gone from their worst fight, to not talking for their longest time while in the same space, to a five a.m. taxi, flight to Hobart, straight to a two-day intense conference, to home, and then must've written this physically and emotionally exhausted. Couldn't have been a positive love note. He clicked on the email.

Dear Leo,

The two-word greeting dumped two tons of sand in his gut, quicksand his heart dropped into.

Dear Leo. The first email she had begun that way. Formal, distant. Dead. He slumped back into the chair and pulled the laptop closer, a couple of inches hanging over the desk.

Dear Leo,

I am really sorry and really sad that I had to leave the way I did Monday. I couldn't find any words that morning. My whole vocabulary seemed irrelevant.

I wanted so much to fit into what I thought we both wanted, and it just depressed me, which just made me angry at you.

So much of my journal lately explores how I will get used to not having a little girl. And I'm sorry, because I know these thoughts will cut through you, but I understand now, no matter how hard I try to ignore it, having my own little girl is a joy I need in my life. I have also struggled with your dogmatic need since our engagement, to 'be based in Melbourne' and your resistance to negotiating our living arrangements. If we had found a middle path, with more flexibility, where I could live here and in Melbourne and also you come and be here too when you can, so that we share our lives, rather than me simply be absorbed into yours, well, that would have made things easier for me.

Then there's our fighting. I can't explain why there is so much verbal abuse, but like any abuse, it takes its toll.

So, for all the times I have behaved badly toward you, I am sorry. I am sorry for the hurt I have caused and the suffering I may have inflicted.

I don't want to resent you in the future, and I don't want to continue negative and angry. As hard as it was, I had to make a decision the other night. One of the hardest of my life. I know it's not your job to look after me. It is my job to take responsibility for the choices I make.

If this seems selfish, then so be it. As you have made your choices about your future and have very clear goals going forward, so I have made a decision about my life and the direction I want it to go in.

I am going to have a child, and I am going to buy a house here in Canberra and I am going to give this job all I can. And through everything, there will be the raising of a precious little girl. Because if I don't, I will never ever forgive myself.

I can't imagine another relationship. Because I love you still, and I know it will take me some time to get over you, and I don't really even want to. I wish with all my heart that we could both have gotten what we wanted together.

So, I wish you all the love and happiness you deserve, with someone that is on the same path as you. I love you and will miss you with all my heart and mind and soul. I tried, I really tried, but I can't change what I want and what is in my heart and what I know I deserve to have.

I am too sad to write anymore.

Take care.

Zoya

P.S. I won't say sorry for saying yes to marrying you, because I meant it with all my heart, and wanted so much for it to work.

28

HONOR YOUR LOVE

LEO FINISHED SINGING ALONG TO *THIS OLD HEART OF MINE* WITH EVERY ounce of his soul. The live Rod Stewart/Ronald Isley up-tempo version was one of his go-to torture tracks post-any-relationship-ending. The lyric of the Holland-Dozier-Holland classic, a song they wrote with Sylvia Moy, could have been written for his madventure with Zoya.

No logic to his end of romance ritual. Before making sense of what had happened with Zoya, formulate any words in thoughts or on paper that could rise above the shock and agony, he had to bury himself in other people's heartache. Their suffering somehow soothed his heart. A communal bond bowing to the ancient truth, love often follows a path from torch songs to torture tracks.

What possible encore could follow six repeats of that song? He considered the other Rod Stewart romance stretcher-bearer, *I Don't Wanna Talk About It*. Danny Whitten must've etched those words on his skin with thorns, blood dripping onto his guitar. Enough Rod. He lifted the stylus arm and slipped the record into its cover. Gazed over the albums scattered across the coffee table.

Intimate friends.

Maybe the comfort hug of harmonies from The Eagles. Let Don Henley torment his soul with *The Best of My Love.*

A tear dripped onto Earth Wind and Fire's *I Am* album. A sign. He wiped his eyes and cheek with his sweater sleeve, pulled out the record, flipped it between his hands a couple of times, then set it onto the turntable, side one, and carefully lowered the stylus onto track three. The lyrics weren't exactly relevant, but the raw, tender, moody atmosphere was perfect. Together with the band, Foster, Graydon and Chamblin had created one of the greatest harmony key changes of all time. The melody swept you up and soared you through the brightest blue sky all the way to the shiny moon of your love...before dumping you back into a dark cesspool of desolation.

That's what happens *After the Love Has Gone.*

CAMPFIRE EYES.

Leo had never seen anything like them, not even in films or photoshopped magazine models. Golden honey and sparkly flames, huge ovals with almost no white. He just wanted to sit in front of Aysha's campfire eyes and warm his soul.

The soul Zoya had frozen with her silent walk out of his townhouse and shattered with her *"Dear Leo"* ice pick.

In the first session, he'd been in a myopic victim zone. The therapy was supposed to be about his relatively recent anger fueled by his ex-wife, however, coming just two days after the email, he'd spent fifty-five minutes dumping his pain and anger about his cold-blooded ex-fiancée.

By the second visit, he was keen to get his money's worth from Aysha.

She put her pen down and looked up from her large brown notebook. "What do you think love is?"

"It's a feeling...an emotion that you feel strongly about someone."

She nodded gently, sitting back in her chair of dark green fabric and curved wooden arms. Not an extremely high back but with her petite frame her head only just reached the top. Hands were clasped in the lap of her long, sandy dress, which somehow worked with a deep purple cardigan.

"But how would you describe that feeling on a practical level?"

"It's kind of indefinable. The whole beauty of love is its esoteric nature. Can you really define it?"

"Love is care and kindness. Love is built on virtues, but I feel those two are at its core."

He nodded. Hadn't been expecting an answer to his rhetorical question. *Care and kindness* didn't sound as grand as he'd imagined love. Too simple. Basic.

"Did you always act from care and kindness with Zoya?"

Her voice was gentle, eyes warm, yet something in the question tightened his stomach.

"I cared about her deeply." He looked through the window at the gum trees swaying wildly in the mountain wind, leaned on the chair arm and plonked his head on his hand. "Maybe not always in kindness." He snapped his eyes back at her. "But it was always provoked. You're not saying I pushed her away?" He didn't mean the defensive tone, but what did Aysha expect? He didn't walk away from his commitment, from his love, from their engagement. Zoya did. With a bloody email. He shoved his hands under his thighs.

"No, you're the expert on yourself. Only you can answer that."

Not even two full sessions and he was already tired of that line. *You're the expert on yourself.* He wasn't paying this much money for his own opinion, he wanted her wisdom and experience to give him answers. Really good answers. Clarify all the stuff clogging up his head and heart.

"If Zoya fully resolved the baby issue, would you take her back?"

"No." Leo spat the word out of a barbed-wire throat. He leaned forward, feet angled up, heels of his shoes up the base of the armchair, toes on the rug.

She let his answer float around the room for a few seconds. "Less than two weeks ago you were engaged. Did you love her then?"

I proposed to her. Wanted to spend the rest of my life with her...

"Yes."

"Zoya wasn't born in a bad peoples' factory, was she?"

He shook his head in agreement. "But how can we possibly find closure when she goes all emu?"

"Emu?"

"Sends that email, then sticks her head in the sand. Won't respond to any calls or texts or emails."

Aysha smiled, nodding, then leaned forward.

"You can't control her non-communication. But you do need to honor your love for her. You can't let go and move forward unless you first honor your love."

*H*ONOR *YOUR LOVE*.

Leo's inner eye had rolled when he heard the three simple words, and he resented Aysha for throwing them at him. Yet the longer the words rattled around his brain, the more they slowed down the anger train he'd been riding on the rusty tracks of hate and blame.

He shifted his weight on the rock to the left side of his bottom. Rubbed his right butt cheek and upper hamstring. Three brown ducks paddled their little webbed feet against the Yarra's current, bobbing up and over tiny ripples.

Honor your love.

Before his therapy, life had shoved some lessons down his throat and the toughest was that you can't avoid the grief. In his younger days, he'd tried pushing it up Mount Delay, lashing out with a hurricane of words, and self-marooning on Melancholy Island. Temporary delusional therapy. Grief has its own timeline.

He faced the Zoya grief head on. Maybe too much head, not enough on. Like care and kindness.

As his anger train slowed, Leo ticked off the stations he had to spend time in: appreciation, respect, fondness and forgiveness. Forgiveness. It would take a while to work his way through the many levels at that emotional hub. He found himself drifting back to it via different routes until he had to swallow a new life lesson. Forgiveness wasn't a destination; it was the platform that launched every other worthwhile journey. Every peaceful journey. Every kind journey. He wasn't quite there yet. Wasn't something he could schedule.

The ancient gum trees hovered above like caring elders as the sun snuck under their canopy. Friendly sunshine caressed the left side of his face. The three ducks had given into the current and floated back past, while he flirted with memories of Zoya and his new life lesson.

Honor my love.

Smiling Chalice
Some places have arsenic in their water
Some carry cancer in the sun
Death from life
Beauty of nature, demons below
I drank from a smiling chalice
Basked in her outer glow
Death from love
Blissful nature, demons below
I poured love from my deepest well
Shined my heart in her darkest shadows
Death of soul
Beware of nature, demons below

LEO CRINGED AT THE POEM. IT CERTAINLY DIDN'T HONOR HIS LOVE. Then he read the bottom line of the email:

Wow, Zoya, you continue to be an amazing inspiration.

Where was the care and kindness in that? He pulled out another printed email he'd sent in the week after Zoya's *Dear Leo* ice pick and read the poem:

Nine months was all we lasted
How ironic for this bastard.

He stopped reading, scrunched up both pages and threw them in the bin under his desk. He wasn't surprised his anger inspired creativity, and maybe there'd been some therapeutic value, but sending them to Zoya bordered on evil.

He picked up the little plastic bin, walked outside, dumped the scrunched-up papers in the green recycle bin, then slammed the big lid shut. Needed to have that negative energy out of the house. He shivered. Maybe it was his socks, soaked from the wet concrete after the spring shower, or the shame of his callous words to Zoya.

Every time Leo's car wound up Mountain Highway heading to Aysha's home office in Sassafras, a flutter tickled between his stomach and lungs, and it wasn't due to the altitude. Always a believer in personal development, the therapy was another dimension, simultaneously deeper and higher. Aysha didn't spend the whole time digging into his past. He liked learning something about himself and walking away with tools. Sometimes the new awareness was enough. Mindfulness, she called it.

With her encouragement, he started a journal for the first time in his life. A happy green cover with the words *'For Life'* printed across it randomly. The pages were filling fast. In between raw ramblings about Zoya, and Michele's behavior, were his life lessons from Aysha.

Reflect and respect, rather than react when angry. Not rocket science, but much easier to write than do. It would take a while before this became part of his natural psyche. At least he had a hook to hang his anger on in difficult moments.

Love is care and kindness.

Fascinating how powerful this was, the more he analyzed and observed. He also had a page listing his *Irreplaceable Worth* right next to *Collect your Gifts*.

Aysha had explained during session four, *"Life is full of gifts for us. We can't see them when we're buried in anger or fear. Collect your gifts, Leo. Cherish every little one of them."* Her velvet voice made as much impact as her words. Within the first month of working with Aysha, he was able to reminisce about the many special moments with Zoya without simmering anger, appreciating how lucky he was to have experienced those gifts.

AT THE END OF THE FIFTH SESSION, LEO HELD OUT A SMALL BLUE envelope for Aysha.

"Last week you inspired a poem."

She stared at the envelope. For an awkward moment he didn't think she'd take it, couldn't read her eyes. Then she took the envelope, pulled out the folded blue page and adjusted her body so that the light from the desk lamp came over her shoulder.

He'd memorized the words:

What gift to give to a gift?
A beautiful flower will not do,
Nature's no match for her sweet eyes.
A book of knowledge isn't enough.
She already is so worldly wise.
A grand story will not help,
She can see through any lies.
A moment of passion is all wrong
Until this relationship dies
What gift to give a gift?

He tried to sit casually, leaning back, hands flat on the chair arms. Searched for a curl at the end of her lips, or an extra sparkle in her eye as she read.

Nothing. Steady hands, still face, eyes scrolling across the words. He couldn't discern her cultural background, but it wasn't Anglo.

With her long, black hair and olive skin, she could've been Spanish or Greek. No, the cute little nose wasn't Greek, maybe Argentinean. Put a bindi on her forehead and Indian wasn't out of the question. Her surname, Le Ferre, must have been from an ex-husband, or maybe her mother had re-married.

Aysha folded the poem, put it back in the envelope and placed it on her desk. She turned back with the slightest furrow on her brow and sat rod-straight on the edge of her chair, not like her usual open disposition.

"Leo, our relationship is purely professional. You're my client, I'm your therapist." She pointed at his shoes; toes on the rug, heels raised and resting up the base of the chair,

"Your feet aren't even on the ground yet. There is a lot more work to do before you're back on your path." She rose and brushed down her long skirt.

He scrambled his journal into his knapsack and stood.

She put out her hand to shake, which is how she always greeted him and sent him off. A simple, professional handshake. "I'm happy to continue as your therapist but if that doesn't work for you, we can make this the final session."

29

BOOKMARK

Schemo. So bloody stupid. And so fucking predictable, flirting with your therapist. Call yourself romantic and you hug a cliché. Ricoglionito.

Leo got out of the car, locked it and ambled down the bush path, hands stuffed tight into his jean pockets. Aysha didn't throw him out, so that was a positive. Of course, he wanted to continue working with her. He'd heard from other people how difficult it was to find the right therapist. He'd been lucky and wasn't going to walk away now. She was one of his gifts.

Had they met under other circumstances he had no doubt they'd connect socially but reality had cast them in different, more important roles. He was still struggling to begin closure with Zoya, let alone get over her. Certainly not the time to throw himself at someone else, especially his therapist.

Whoosh, whoosh, whoosh.

He stopped, spooked by three birds swooping across his path. The three little birds perched on a branch, probably searching for their last scraps of dinner as the sun disappeared over the hill. The crimson and orange sky stilled him.

Beautiful.

The spring mountain breeze cut through his shirt and t-shirt, always five to ten degrees cooler up the mountain. He trudged back to the car, opened the door and stopped.

She didn't give it back. Aysha liked the poem. My gift to my gift.

She reminded him of the professional boundaries, gave him no feedback on the poem at all. But she'd kept it. A fire flickered in his tummy, sweeping a warm flutter though his heart. A smile braved his cold face.

She kept my poem.

ELEVENTH OF SEPTEMBER WAS A GOOD DAY FOR LEO. STICK A SUNNY flag in the calendar for an annual private holiday kind of day. Amelia, the head of Multi-Media Victoria, called personally with the good news that the full production funding for 8-Crocs had been approved.

Bless her socks.

He used to joke that too many creative people in Australia didn't get out of bed without a government grant and now he was joining them. He didn't realize how much his financial pressure had weighed on him until it wasn't an issue, at least for the next six months or so. Much longer, if the game got any traction in the market.

He had fun celebrating with Nicholas and Jason. Coke, donuts and chocolate, watching their faces roll from excitement to terror along with their sugar rollercoaster as they realized there was no hiding now. They would have to actually convert 8-Crocs from a prototype to a fully functional iPhone game for the masses.

Most satisfying for him was the ability to pay back Zoya her seven-thousand-dollar loan out of his allocated fees in the funding. He fired off an email to her:

Subject: 8-Croc$ is a go!
Hey, Gorgeous,
Yes, the funding was approved today. The only sad note was not being able to celebrate with you. Thank you for believing in me and your insights with the funding application.

This also means I will be able to pay your loan back in full when
the funds come through. I will always appreciate the generosity
and faith you showed at my difficult financial time.
I look forward to talking soon, preferably in person. We will never
be able to begin a
path to closure by ignoring the ending of our relationship.
I hope you're well and happy. I really do.
Ciao,
Leo

Aysha would be proud of him, he was honoring his love. He was more than hopeful of a response this time, and to Zoya agreeing on catching up. But it wasn't a night to waste time projecting or pining.

He shut his laptop, grabbed his wallet and keys and headed off to catch a Tuesday night bonus movie with his boys. Outside his door, he stopped, turned around and opened it. Took out his mobile and threw it onto the futon, stepped back outside and closed the door. He didn't want to be checking for a Zoya response every few minutes. Jason Bourne and his boys were getting his full attention, along with a big tub of popcorn and a giant box of Maltesers.

Hi, Leo,
Thank you for acknowledging the loan. It would be good if you
could pay it all by first week in November as I am settling the
purchase of my house on 9 November.
Regards,
Zoya
P.S. Congratulations and good luck with the game.

C OULD HAVE BEEN WRITTEN BY HER BANK MANAGER. L EO'S EYES DRIFTED back to *purchase of my house on 9 November. 9 November...*After all the dreams of them setting up a home together, reading the cold reality of Zoya buying a house in Canberra on her own dumped him under the positive wave he'd been surfing since the funding approval.

He flicked his laptop to 'calendar' and studied the dates working back from 9 November. If it was a sixty-day settlement, she must have bought the house within a week of breaking up. Even a thirty-day settlement meant she'd acted bloody fast.

He chewed slowly on his marmalade toast. Zoya's speed in domestically moving on left a bad taste. He pushed the plate with the second piece of toast away and gulped down the rest of his black tea. Saved her email in the bulky *'Zoya'* file and picked up his to-do list, which was borderline overwhelming: liaising with Apple marketing, which he'd found unexpectedly clunky, organizing the contracts and payment schedule with Multi-Media Victoria, booking flights and accommodation for MIPCOM in Cannes, and setting up as many meetings as possible with potential mobile phone companies and games distributors attending.

Oh, and preparing his notes as a speaker on a panel for mobile games at MIPCOM, which was just three weeks away. Traditionally a market focused on TV content, MIPCOM had in recent years added mobile and internet content as a growing part of the conference. The iPhone had been released in the USA in July. The UK, German and French launch was a few weeks after MIPCOM, just when they were releasing 8-Crocs. Perfect timing and crazy times.

THE SMALL BLUE ENVELOPE HE'D GIVEN AYSHA A FEW WEEKS EARLIER containing her poem sat beside the notebook. A fountain of warmth flowed out his heart, reaching down to his toes and bubbling back up again through every vein.

"Why are you smiling?" she asked.

Because you like me more than you've told me and it's a beautiful feeling.

"You kept my poem." He pointed at it.

She looked at the envelope and color filled her cheeks, again noticeable. As far as Leo could tell, she never wore makeup except a pastel mauve lipstick.

Nine sessions, ten weeks it took. Six weeks since she pushed me back into the Dumb Poet Corner.

"Ah, yes, handy bookmark. I keep separate notebooks for all my clients." By the end of the sentence her voice was back in serene-neutral mode, therapist to client.

He wasn't buying it and his heart was never going back to that professional contract.

Maybe the tumultuous time with Zoya was all about leading him to this unique therapist. Fate, destiny. If it wasn't for Zoya pointing out his anger and pushing him to do counseling, he would never have found Aysha's campfire eyes or velvet voice that gently caressed his soul with every word. Aysha liked him as more than a client. He felt it in his bones.

Patience.

He normally didn't have time for it, taking after his dad regarding that elusive virtue. Passion: tick; persistence: tick; patience: tick-tock, tick-tock, tick-tock...But just because Aysha opened the door didn't mean it was a good time to barge in and make himself at home. That was old Leo.

Aysha had helped him understand the power of patience. Of letting feelings sit before they became clear. Now she would benefit from his new patience.

30

REUNION

Aysha scribbled them down in her 'Leo' notebook. Through the window behind her, giant gum and pine trees high-fived in the strong breeze. The community choir of birds chirped and sang in the distance as the late afternoon October sun created secret nooks and angles through the branches.

She looked up, smiling. "That's very good, Leo. I've never had a client give nicknames to their patterns before."

Turned out Aysha was right, he was the expert on himself. She helped him understand how everyone tended to follow behavioral patterns. Recognizing his patterns would help make him more mindful and less likely to react negatively. Ego Man, Mister Defensive and Super Prover were tags that helped him identify his negative behavior quicker, react slower.

"Did you have time to reflect on our discussion regarding your lapse into passive-aggressive behavior?"

He nodded. "My dad's a stirrer. Never gave compliments that could build my ego or reassure me. He felt more comfortable making fun of me...'stirring.'" Leo raised his pointing fingers to emphasize the italics.

'Stirring' or 'taking the piss', was a national sport in Australia, and Calabrese fathers weren't too shabby at it either.

"Stirring can be fun but it can also be vicious. I went to a private boy's school. You cop a lot, and I gave a lot. I wasn't a fighter, but I was good at attacking with words." He stared out the window then turned back to Aysha. "I'm creative with words, so now as an adult I can be spikier when I get defensive or extremely angry. What I thought were clever or funny little hooks were actually hurtful spikes."

Aysha nodded.

His heart bobbed up and down with her eyes. In her bungalow office, he was a deep sea diver. Aysha had guided him through the oceans in his heart and soul he needed to explore. Leo thought he knew the waters well, but all he'd done before her was splash the surface. She held the safety cable, and he dove down deep until his heart and mind adjusted to the darkness. Some of it was tiring, sometimes scary, but he trusted her.

"How do you feel about it now?" she asked.

"It's amazing once you see them, how some of the patterns are linked. Dad and the school stirring were the foundations of the defensive and super prover stuff too."

"Mindfulness is powerful and something that becomes stronger with practice. Patterns are like habits—you can change the bad ones."

He nodded. "I know my parental stuff is minor. I'm not blaming my dad at all, I'm forty-seven now. The passive-aggressive stuff only came out of an extreme situation with Michele. That's her stuff, not something I can control."

Aysha studied his relaxed hands resting on his lap, his red sneakers with soles flat on the rug. She looked up, smile beaming brighter than he'd ever seen.

"Your feet are on the ground. Leo, you've come a long way in..."

"Ten. This is session ten." He'd only missed one Friday session when he was in Cannes.

She nodded, rose and opened the door as he picked up his knapsack. Late afternoon sunlight streamed into the room. Photographers call it magic hour, nature's spotlight focused on Aysha. Angelic

Aysha. The magic light shining on her yet warming his heart. When he moved closer, she put her right hand out to shake. This time there was a comfortable looseness, and her soft skin sparked an energy through his body. He was sure she felt it too.

Must have.

She let go. "See you next Friday."

He didn't step outside. "You should never stand still at an art gallery because people will stop and stare at your amazing eyes. No one will want to look at another painting again."

Somehow her eyes spread wider, her cheeks pinkish.

"Next Friday," he said as he walked through the door. Before he turned the corner of her house, he glanced back at her office bungalow.

Aysha watched him from the door. He saw her hand come up like she was going to wave, then she quickly spun around and closed the door.

A grin or smile lifted his face as he floated around the corner and down the driveway to his car. His traitor muscles were welcome.

Zoya country.

Flying into Canberra Airport created more inner turbulence for Leo than he'd imagined.

Zoya country.

Assume crash positions, screamed his soul, fastening the seatbelt tightly around his tummy. *Give me a parachute,* his heart pleaded, desperate to float directly into Zoya's office and hug her.

He sat in the back of the taxi on the way to the Hyatt, laptop and overnight bag beside him. Melancholy dominated his mixed emotions as they rolled across the bridge, staring out towards the town center.

Sounds like a fruity dog, melon-collie.

He smiled at the memory of Zoya's heavy but witty observation.

Bits and pieces of their time together had randomly popped into his head over the previous three months. In

Canberra, she was on high rotation.

The one-on-one sessions with digital project teams from the A.C.T. were scheduled before the *Dear Leo* email. Five, back-to-back, seventy-five-minute sessions in one of the hotel's meeting rooms. Planning the sessions forced Zoya to communicate with him but she kept it to email and focused on the work stuff.

In one email he mentioned he couldn't imagine them being in the same space for the first time after their break-up, in a purely business situation.

She ignored it.

In a later email, he re-stressed that it was impossible for either of them to truly move on until they could meet again and talk.

Zoya ignored that too.

Two days before the trip, she sent an email suggesting dinner at Lotus Bay Restaurant. Neutral territory as they'd never eaten there in their time together, although they had bought fish and chips from the café downstairs. Plus, it was part of the Canberra Yacht Club precinct, where Zoya had first driven him before they consummated their relationship at her place. So many moons ago, it was like yesterday. All of Canberra felt like yesterday. Like he was still in a relationship with Zoya. She'd swung from silence and avoidance to dinner. Swung him into emotional chaos.

Facilitating the five creative sessions left him on a high and had forced his head away from the shadows of Canberra memories. He'd planned a swim and spa before getting ready for Zoya, but he slumped onto the edge of his bed in his board shorts, towel around his shoulders. How could he possibly prepare for a reunion with Zoya? No real communication for three months after her Dear Leo email, after committing to spending the rest of their lives together.

How much 're' and how much 'union'?

31

HARBOUR

Leo stopped mid step, took a deep breath.

Zoya stood in front of her car, watching the moored boats, not ten yards from where she'd parked on their first ever super-short tour of Canberra. She must have sensed him and turned, dark hair fluttering in the breeze. High, black leather boots, black skirt, tight black blouse with orange and red swirls and her favorite red jacket. She smiled and stepped towards him.

His last few steps quickened but still couldn't keep up with his racing heart. He dropped his leather jacket, she dropped her bag and he hugged her. She hugged right back.

Like they'd never been apart.

He moved his head back, arms still around each other's waist, back in his favorite swing as her eyes swayed between his left and right eye.

"You're beautiful," he said.

She lifted a hand, wiped a tear. "You always make me cry."

"I could say the same lately." No edge.

Zoya's eyes dulled, and she looked down, dropped her hand from his waist. Then her smile bloomed again. "You wore my shoes."

He smiled, nodded. Zoya had bought them for him. He never

imagined wearing any kind of red shoes in his life, not even sneakers. But she'd insisted he could carry them off and she was right. He caught her Dorothy-Wizard-of-Oz bug, and the red sneakers with three black stripes became his favorite.

"THAT'S WONDERFUL ABOUT JAMES. YOU MUST BE SO PROUD," ZOYA said. "Please congratulate him for me." She lined up her knife and fork on the empty plate, next to some salmon skin.

"I am and I will. His adult independent life takes off next January." James' dream since he was fifteen was to join the Air Force and he survived all the RAAF hurdles to land the gig he was aiming for as an Air Electronics Analyst, based on the edge of Adelaide.

"How do you feel about that?"

"Relief. He got through our parenting without ending up in jail or a junkie. Bruce reckons that's all we can aim for as parents these days. If they picked up some decent values along the way, that's the parenting trifecta."

They already talked about their respective families, yet Zoya had circled around again to James, avoiding the mammoth in the room. Sitting on opposite sides of the table rather than their natural adjacent corner. Bobbing yachts and lights twinkled below the window on his right, the colorful lights from Black Mountain Tower over Zoya's shoulder, across the lake. Under normal circumstances, it would have been a perfect romantic setting.

He tried hard not to project or second-guess Zoya, but it was hopeless. His inner world—a new term he'd learned from Aysha— was all over the place. The progress he thought he'd made in the last three months dived into the Lake Burley Griffin as soon as he saw Zoya. As a soccer player and on junior coaching courses, he found the concept of muscle memory fascinating. His heart and sexual muscles were gym kings with their own agendas.

It wasn't just the setting and company that confused him, Zoya was drinking water. Maybe she wanted to be in absolute control that night. Maybe it was a way of showing him she'd taken on board the courageous concerns he'd shared back in Freycinet.

She shifted in her seat, straightened up, took another sip of water. Red lipstick stuck to the lip of the glass.

"You were right, this was a good idea."

He nodded, bit his inner lip. He wanted, no, he needed Zoya to say whatever had to be said. He'd shown his commitment. He didn't walk out on their engagement. He didn't bury his head in sand for the last three months. And right there and then, he wasn't sure what he'd say or whether he'd just get up and steal her red lipstick with his lips.

"I'm sorry." No buts or ifs. No excuses, reasons or explanations, just tears sneaking into her eyes.

A lead ball in his stomach melted away. Every sinew in his body relaxed. He had no idea he was wound up that tight until he heard her three syllables. He felt the million words and emotions behind her apology. Didn't need more.

"One thing I didn't say in that...letter." Her eyes made another silent apology for referring back to the email. "I loved the expression of our feelings through our sexual intimacy. The places you have taken me to...you celebrated my sexual and spiritual energy and—" She wiped her tears with the back of her hand, leaving them brighter. "—you never shied away from my feminine intensity. It was a beautiful and loving part of our relationship for me. Very precious and special and I will always cherish this aspect of how we were together."

He reached out and squeezed her hand gently. She didn't withdraw.

"What a beautiful thing to say. Can I have *that* in an email?" He smiled and raised his eyebrows to make it clear it was a joke.

Zoya laughed. The soul-mama laugh that first hooked him in Batemans Bay stopped most conversations in the restaurant as patrons turned to see who was singing the joyous hymn.

"Oh, God, I'm making a scene." Zoya wiped her laughter tears with the napkin.

"You have a duty to create a scene with your magical laugh in every corner of the planet."

She put her napkin down. "Why are you so good to me?"

Because I loved you so much I wanted to marry you, to share the rest of my life with you. Because love that deep doesn't disappear into thin air... and because I'm honoring my love.

He sensed the guilt in her question. If he hadn't worked on himself with Aysha's guidance in the last three months, he was sure this moment would have had more sour than sweet, hope and desperation from him, spiced with tension and anger.

"I forgive you, Zoya. I know you didn't plan on hurting me, or us." Hadn't prepared those words, they simply spilled out in the moment.

Zoya lifted his hand and kissed the back of it. He noticed the missing ring. Somberness flooded him. That wasn't what he'd imagined when he called it a temporary engagement ring. He turned her hand, brought it to his lips and kissed the finger where their ring had lived for just over a month, slow, gentle. When he came up, Zoya's eyes were streaming tears.

"Back in a sec." It was a barely audible hoarse whisper as she took her handbag and disappeared.

Earlier in the evening he was surprised to hear a little voice from his heart, or maybe his loins, cheering for a full reunion. But now it was clear that in their reunion, there would be no ugly rehashing painful memories, reacting in anger. They were in 'union' as kind, affectionate friends. There would be no sexual union, despite Zoya's glowing review of their lovemaking.

No, they definitely couldn't go there tonight. No, that would be pazzo.

ZOYA RETURNED WITH FRESH LIPSTICK AND DRY EYES. SHE POURED THEM both more water. "You're probably wondering why I'm on water?"

No way was he going anywhere near the hyper-sensitive, hyper-dangerous topic of

Alcohol flirting.

"I start on the IVF program next week. I'm going to try and have a baby on my own."

She slowly spun her glass around on the white tablecloth then raised her eyes. "I'm giving it one year, till next November."

He turned towards the yachts with sails packed tightly away, masts tilting with the waves. Felt the intensity of her eyes. Two emotions seeped through, relief and happiness. He was relieved that this was the final unquestionable proof there was nothing he could have done to save their relationship. Plus, he was truly happy for her.

"That's terrific, Zoya. Good for you."

"Thanks." An edge, like she expected or hoped for a different reaction. She leaned forward, one arm on top of the other on the table, cleavage glittering in the candlelight. "Aren't you even a little jealous that you won't be the father of my child?"

A tornado swirled inside him.

Reflect and respect. Reflect and respect.

Zoya's loaded question would have triggered an angry response from him just months ago. Would have ended the moment.

Respect and reflect. Respect and reflect.

He might not respect Zoya's wording and tone, but he respected her desire for him to father her child, the most precious of compliments. But they'd covered that muddy territory and there was no point getting bogged down again. He turned away from her hopeful glare, filled his water glass, then hers.

"Is Kiara looking forward to being a godmother?" he asked.

"She is soooo excited. Maybe more than me. I mean, we have a long way to go, but she's introduced me to this wonderful naturopath who's helping me tune my body, giving me the best chance." She raised her water glass as a nod to her naturopath.

Seamlessly accepting his diversion and releasing his tension.

"You are looking well, Zoya."

"Had to do something. I put on fifteen pounds in the nine months with you."

It wasn't him, it was the first nine months in that job. Mindfulness is amazing. No point saying it, raising the tension again. They'd started the closure process and he was determined to not slip back into their old patterns.

"You know, Leo, I've done some research."

"Research?"

"You don't need to reverse the vasectomy, they can stick a needle in and—"

He raised both hands as stop signs. Pushed back in his chair.

Stick a needle in? In my... Seriously?

He rose. "I'm going to the bathroom. While I'm there, think about what you just said." Despite his twister-stomach, his tone was soft, steady.

Zoya's mouth opened, but he dropped his napkin on the seat and spun away.

32

A PLAY

MANIPULATIVE.

Leaning back against a wall in the stall, the word glared out at Leo as if it was scrawled in a thick black felt pen on the door. He'd defended her when Beanpole called her manipulative at work. It passed over him when the communications counselor had suggested it in front of him a few months ago. This time Zoya may as well have tattooed it on her forehead. He wasn't angry. No negative reactions were bursting to lash out. He was simply disappointed to see Zoya in that light.

More importantly, there wasn't one piece of his heart or soul jealous about Zoya creating a baby via IVF. He leaned on Aysha's wisdom, repeating the little mantra as he returned to the table.

Zoya wasn't made in a bad peoples' factory. Zoya wasn't made in a bad peoples' factory. Zoya wasn't made in a bad peoples' factory...

As Leo approached the table, Zoya signed the bill and the waiter left with the little black folder. He sat down.

"That was a dumb thing to throw at you. I'm sorry."

"It's okay. The whole thing is tough...messy. It's okay." Leo took his wallet out of his pocket and removed some cash.

"Tonight should be fifty-fifty."

"No. Please. Take it as my apology. Plus, I really appreciate you paying the loan in full so quickly. You got big brownie points from my sister."

Fat lot of good those brownie points were now, but he was grateful for an opening to steer the conversation away from apologies and babies.

"Congratulations on your house. You didn't muck around."

"I bought it two days after...well, let's just say you caused my biggest case of retail therapy ever." Smile warm, eyes caring.

His ego liked that, his heart, not so much. Before they planned on a Melbourne home base, he'd enjoyed exploring her Canberra real estate options during their time together. He would have bet on Manuka, where her original apartment was because of Manuka Pool, which she loved. But he didn't ask, and she didn't say. The memory of her apartment would fade with the moments of their time together.

Their closure 'date' that night had needed to happen, and now it needed to end.

THE GOODBYE HUG WAS WARM BUT NOTHING LIKE THEIR GREETING. Some kind of barrier had slipped between them in the restaurant, probably the beginning of true closure. He kissed Zoya on the cheek, watched her climb into her SUV and drive off. She waved before she left the parking lot. He raised his hand in acknowledgement.

He zipped up his jacket, walked to a bench seat facing out to the lake behind a building near the restaurant. Same spot he ended up after their Ides of March spat. Like it was yesterday. An eternity.

For a while, he just sat there with the crisp air a sorbet for his heart. A mediative rhythm from the water lapping against the wharf, boats bumping against the protective rubber tires. Eventually his thoughts and feelings found their own sails.

Zoya had once said if they had a baby, she'd move anywhere to live with him, but he doubted that. Baby or no baby, she was committed to her job and nesting in Canberra. It didn't matter how soulful her need was or how logical or irrational, that's the choice she'd committed to before they'd met, and she was never able to let go. Along their short and intense journey, she tried to guide his heart to the Australian capitol, while she knew it was anchored by his boys in Melbourne.

With the connection they had, he couldn't imagine them not remaining fond of each other and friendly when their paths crossed through work. But they couldn't be friends. True friends talk and share and support. With the best of intentions, he wasn't sure if he wanted to hear about Zoya dating other guys, and he was sure she didn't want to hear about his future romantic life.

He also didn't want to wait around a year to see if she'd been successful down the IVF path. But a piece of his heart was humming a different tune: *it's only a year... everything will be easy when the baby thing is off the table. Based on the past crazy year, it will be November 2008 in a blink.*

"It's beautiful," said Aysha, looking up from the small blue note.

Leo breathed out, removing his hands from under his legs.

She turned back to the page, reading his poem again:

Campfire Eyes...
Camping in our inner world
Walking without a compass
Wisdom drifts among the stillness
Shadows clearing with every breath
A river of rhythmic veins
Magic in your campfire eyes
A jungle sauna of emotions

Million stars guide a hungry student
And reflect feelings you cannot teach

The words had come to him that morning, nine days after the Zoya IVF dinner.

Following a couple of bike rides, a session with Aysha, long chats with Bruce and Maria, and a couple of quiet moments sitting beside the Yarra, Leo's heart guided his thoughts more and more to Aysha.

She'd opened up about her personal life near the end of the last session. She had a son with her first husband, and a daughter with husband two, who she divorced four years ago. In between the marriages, she thought she'd met her soulmate, a psychologist. Like many therapists, he had a tortured soul and ended his own life a year into their relationship.

He felt no jealousy or insecurity as she reeled off the names of the men in her love life. Yet something had changed during her confession session, confirming the inkling tickling in his heart that Aysha liked him more than just as a client. Her exotic looks came from a Swiss mum and French–Algerian dad, but that's all she shared about them. He sensed a story there, but she wasn't ready to tell it.

Aysha put the poem back in the sky-blue envelope, placed it on the brown notebook on her desk and faced him. It was the end of session twelve, yet she didn't get up. Her coy smile took twenty years off her actual age of forty-eight. She wore sandy-brown ankle boots and purple pantyhose below a white frilly skirt with a couple of layers that covered her knees as she sat, legs crossed. Purple blouse and sandy-brown vest. Part gypsy, part cowgirl, all cute.

"I'm going to a play this Sunday night. An independent thing at a small theater. I thought you might be interested." His pulse pumped so quickly he was sure she could see his veins throbbing.

"Oh, what's it called?"

Didn't say no. Half a yes, good sign.

"Letters from Animals. Set in the near future, it explores psychological and philosophical themes."

"Sounds interesting."

Interesting and teasing but she hasn't kicked me out.

Bellbirds, nature's think music, oozed in from the nearby bush.

"Starts at eight. I could pick you up seven."

"Don't be silly." She got up and opened the door.

Don't be silly, I can't go to a play with you or don't be silly, we'll meet there?

Her breezy tone suggested the latter, but he moved like a ninety-year-old to the door, tight and slow and tender.

"I'll pick you up at quarter past seven," she said, holding her hand out to shake.

His Judas muscles partied. He just hoped he didn't look like a fool. She lived forty-five minutes in the opposite direction of the theater, it made sense for her to pick him up.

"Cool." It didn't sound remotely cool coming out of his mouth. Think of the un-coolest way to say *cool*, multiply it a million times, then polish it with a thousand coats of dork varnish. He skipped down the timber steps.

As he turned the corner of her house, he looked back and Aysha waved. He saluted and spun around. Maybe saluting and spinning was un-cool too, but who cared? He was going on a date Sunday night.

With his super-smart, wiser than wisdom, exotic therapist.

Aysha.

33

OCCUPATIONAL HAZARD

"I don't think I'm the right therapist for you," said Aysha.

He'd blown it.

It was obvious to Leo from the beginning.

Aysha had picked him up late and texted him from the top of the driveway, didn't come near his front door. She steered the conversation towards their children during the thirty-minute drive to the venue in North Melbourne. They had to rush into the small theater above the pub, making it just before the play started. You could have squeezed a child into the space between them on the terraced bench seats, the no-touching zone.

Post-show, he just sat back at a table in a corner of the pub with their gin and tonics when she blurted it out. Not even a few minutes of analyzing the play.

He'd blown it by asking her out, and now he was going to lose her as a therapist. He didn't want that. The last three months had been invaluable. She helped him not just re-align, but also shift to a better version of himself.

"I shouldn't have invited you, put you in this position. I—"

"You haven't done anything wrong Leo, I..." She leaned forward, elbows on the table, palms up towards him. "I have feelings for you."

190

The words bounced between his heart and brain for a couple of seconds until his brain handed the baton to his heart. *This one's yours, go for it.*

I have feelings for you.

The velvet honey words flushed through his heart, opening doors and pulling up windows that Zoya had slammed shut two months ago.

"Wow. Aysha...I can't tell you how good it feels to hear you say those words but..." He waved a hand between them. "We have this situation, and I didn't know how to..."

She nodded and smiled, campfire eyes building to a bonfire. She'd been sitting on this romantic nugget all night. What he'd pictured as aloofness was probably nerves and fear, maybe a touch of shyness.

"Has this ever happened before?"

"Male clients falling for me is an occupational hazard. Me falling for a client...this...you...it's a first."

His heart wrestled his ego down. It was a battle. "I'm honored. I really am." He wanted to hold her hand, hug her, kiss her, pick her up and spin her around in the air.

No rush.

He'd felt comfortable with Aysha from the first second he walked into her quaint bungalow office. This was a massive step she'd made, and he wouldn't scare her by rushing anything.

"I'm not sure what to do next," he said.

"Me neither." She laughed.

He joined her, their laughter a joyous release, shaking up the established comfort zone of client and therapist. Unlike a snow globe that eventually settled exactly the same way every time, they had no idea where and how they'd end up, just knew it was something worth shaking together.

LEO GOT CRAMP IN HIS LEFT CALF JUST AFTER MAKING A JOKE ABOUT how he hadn't sat cross legged to eat since primary school. Rubbing his calf helped but not as much as Aysha's laughter, so sweet and soothing. If it could be bottled as medicine, it would cure half of the world's sick people.

"We can go to a table with chairs," she said after her laughter settled. "With the other older gents."

He imagined a playful side, and her grin shining across the low table flew way past playful to his favorite playground—cheeky.

"It's okay now, thank you, Miss Flexible." He gingerly crossed his left leg again and settled on his cushion. "It's good to see the real you." He angled his head a little and squinted at her. "I think."

They'd chosen Patee Thai on Brunswick Street to continue their breakthrough after the play. It wasn't really a date, more like their 'coming out' socially. The plates of delights they'd shared were mostly empty, tummies full, but he could've devoured another hundred courses of Aysha's words, face, and hands.

"You are so beautiful, Aysha. Your eyes, hands, and mouth group dance when you laugh."

"I hope they're all dancing to the same tune." She broke out in laughter, launching the choreography again.

He laughed with her. Wasn't natural, mutual laughter the ulti- mate happy space?

She dropped her head a little, in a humble kind of way.

"Thank you, but I don't understand the fuss about my eyes." She lifted her head again. "You have beautiful brown eyes, Leo. I trust your eyes. I feel safe with you."

"And I've never felt more comfortable with anyone."

She smiled then her mood darkened. She uncrossed her legs, then crossed them with opposite leg in front.

"I'm messy," she said.

"Ha! You should see my kitchen."

She shook her head. "When I was thirteen, my mother told me she loved my older sister but didn't like me."

His heart pushed through his chest, desperate to comfort hers.

"When my sister finished high school, my parents took her to Europe for a holiday. They never came back. Didn't tell me until they'd settled into their new place in Switzerland. I was sixteen."

"That's horrible, Aysha. I can't comprehend any parent being so evil."

She shrugged her shoulders. "I told you, I'm messy."

"They're the messy ones. Is that what led you to becoming a therapist?"

"Kind of. I dropped out of school and went to Bali with an older guy..." She dropped her head on an angle again but kept eye contact. "On a drug binge." She took a sip of her water then gently swirled the water in the glass. "It was stupid and dangerous." She put the glass down. "And then I met Shupta" Her face lit up, body straightened. "I was stumbling around a little village market, dazed, tired, thirsty. He just came up and stared at me with these amazing black eyes like deep tunnels, and said, 'Come with me.' I followed him up the hill to his hut. He taught me meditation and how to live on local fruits and vegetables. Then I followed Shupta to an ashram in Thailand and studied Buddhism. Three years later, I returned to Melbourne committed to becoming the best therapist I could be."

"What an amazing story. I bow to Shupta and your courage." He brought his hands together and bowed.

Aysha returned the bow. "Khaawp khoon khrap Shupta."

"Is that Indian?"

"Thai. Thank you, Shupta. It's confusing. Shupta is Indian but he's based mostly in Thailand.

"Have you reconciled with your parents?"

"No, but I've forgiven them. In their own bizarre way, they helped me find my life path."

What a special woman. He struggled to believe she had fallen for him, yet it had all flowed so naturally, like every movement of her body.

"Did you know in eighty-five percent of divorces it's the woman who leaves or ends it?" asked Aysha. The contrast in her tone with the rest of their frolicking conversation contrasted as much as the cold ice cream with the warm chocolate cake they shared.

Mario's in Brunswick Street was always busy, but the acoustics allowed easy conversation. They'd sauntered there for dessert after their Thai feast, neither of them keen on ending the landmark night.

"No." He put his fork down. He could understand why so many men hung in with a troubled marriage when kids were involved. Moving away from the boys was torture. Ninety percent of his agonizing was about how it would affect them and his relationship with them.

"Most men who leave, walk out with another woman already on the scene. Your situation is rare. You're rare."

He leaned forward, squeezed her hand. He'd been called many things in his life but never rare, especially not with the awe and kindness oozing from Aysha. "I'm just me."

He carved out a chunk of cake and ice cream.

"Do you believe we have a soulmate?" A lightness to her words, a touch of curiosity, not a therapist tone.

He finished chewing. "No."

Her eyebrows raised.

"I believe we have more than one, but you can only connect with a soulmate when your paths are aligned. You might have a moment, a mutual recognition of something special, but if the timing isn't right, no matter the reason, you can't truly connect."

She smiled, nodded. "I agree."

I think you're my soulmate but there's no way I'm going to tell you tonight...maybe not for a few weeks or months. Everything I went through with Zoya was to make me the best man I can be for you. Your parents led you to Shupta, my ex-wife and Zoya-land led me to you.

"Two years?" Leo slipped down the edge of the couch to the floor, hunched over his knees. He closed his eyes, cordless phone to his ear.

"I'm sorry, Leo. I should have known this before."

"It's okay, Aysha, you probably weren't sure how you felt till we went out last night."

Aysha's words echoed down an ethical black hole: *"A therapist and a client aren't allowed to have any kind of relationship until two years after therapy has ended."*

"Not even as friends?"

"No." Defeat dripped off the solo syllable.

Chest caved in, he had to focus on a couple of deep breaths. More than a couple. Oxygen trickled into his brain.

"Is it a law or regulation?"

"Does it matter?"

"If it's just an industry guideline we can be careful. We can—"

"My integrity is everything." Firm, no huskiness. Decision made.

What about your heart? Your soul? "Doesn't seem fair considering we're both in our late forties. It's not like I'm suffering from some psychotic thing."

"No, it isn't fair." Back to husky sadness.

Despite clearly crossing a dotted line in their relationship last night, they hadn't crossed any boundaries. Not even holding hands or a kiss on the cheek. He'd spent most of the day imagining the feel of her lips.

"I don't think I can go back to being just your client."

"Mmmm..." A long, saccharine sigh.

"So, it just ends? Now, after we hang up?" It took all his energy to push the words out. "That's the shortest romance ever." Not even sixteen hours.

"I don't want to end like this. Maybe...maybe we should speak to Counselors Australia. But..." Her voice was barely a whisper.

His back straightened, chest puffed out like a lion. Whether she'd thrown them a final straw or strong rope didn't matter, it was proactive, positive. "I could make the call anonymously. Tell them about our situation, not mention names or locations," he said. This was delicate territory for Aysha, and it wouldn't have been right to push her decision. He took in a long breath of hope and clung to it.

"Yes. Let's do that. Maybe we can get an exemption," she said, with the first splash of sun in her tone that night.

He breathed out and kissed the phone. "Did you feel that?"

"Mmmm..."

34

AND YOU ME

DURING THE FIRST THIRTY MINUTES OF THE PHONE CALL, THE President of Counselors Australia shoved Leo deeper and deeper into the black hole of ethics minus romance. Every little safety rope he tried to throw, Greg Carr kicked off with cold, professional logic.

"Can't we have independent analysis to confirm we're both reasonably intelligent, stable adults? Prove the therapist hasn't seduced me with her professional witchcraft... and I haven't fallen for her because of her power in the relationship?"

Leo stopped by the open sliding door, checking the cordless phone was still on. This was the first hesitation, a sliver of silence from Greg. He'd been pacing his unit in circles, from the meals area, through the lounge, the entrance foyer and around again. Despite working from home that day, he'd dressed up a little for this call in his best jeans and a new light brown shirt with blue flashes.

"I'll tell you what I'm prepared to do. We'll call an ethics committee, and they can make a decision on your specific case."

A lawnmower fired up in the distance.

He closed his eyes with relief, imagining Aysha's smile when he told her the good news. Until fear snaked down his spine.

"Greg, how many cases have been successful with the ethics committee?"

"None."

He slumped on a chair at the dining table, energy and hope draining out of his body like workers escaping factories on a Friday afternoon.

"Not one?"

"We've never done this before."

"Never?"

"Never."

Hope whirred in his heart. A back-up generator, not full power, not enough energy to get his whole love-factory working, but hope whirred.

"Most people in your situation usually end up having a clandestine affair. Inevitably, it breaks down and usually the client sues the therapist."

"Really? What happens then?"

"The therapist loses their insurance and destroys their career. That's why I'm willing to call an ethics committee. I appreciate the integrity both of you have shown."

He had to mention the last bit to Aysha. She'd be happy to have her high standards of integrity validated. Then he slumped back again. The enormity of this step on her career was colossal. Potentially dangerous. But what choice did they have?

"If we do this, what do you need from us?"

"Separate letters from you, your therapist and one from her supervising therapist."

He jolted up, toppling the chair behind him onto the carpet. How did he know her supervising therapist? Had he given away Aysha's name?

"Her supervising therapist?"

"Every therapist has a supervising therapist, so we don't dump our own stuff on clients."

His shoulders and neck relaxed. He didn't know that. Then again, there was a lot he didn't know on this Aysha journey. He prided himself on constantly stepping out of comfort zones but his feelings for Aysha were shooting him out in a spaceship.

LEO COULDN'T REMEMBER HAVING TO WORK THROUGH THREE consecutive phone calls that had such major significance in any other relationship. Not even with Zoya and she lived interstate.

He struggled to focus on work in the afternoon after the anonymous call with Greg, so he pushed through a punishing twenty-eight-mile bike ride. On a couple of the hills, and one crazy forty-seven-mile-per-hour descent, he'd managed to forget about the ethics committee.

He wasn't surprised by Aysha's reserved happiness on the phone that night.

"Aysha, whatever you choose, I'll accept and respect your decision."

"Thank you, Leo. Thank you."

She faced a massive dilemma. Once she went public with her peers, who knew what long-term impact it might have on her career or professional reputation?

So much pressure just to START a relationship. Crazy.

"I only ask one thing. You let me know in person, not by phone or email."

"Of course. Let's meet Thursday night in Templestowe. What's the name of that place on the corner at the roundabout? Opposite that old orange brick gift store."

"Carlucci's."

"Yes, see you at Carlucci's at seven. Please give me till then to sit with my thoughts and feelings."

If it wasn't for the work he'd done with Aysha, he would never have had the strength to leave her alone the forty-eight hours she'd requested. Luckily, he'd also been thrown a couple of marketing opportunities for 8-Crocs in Japan, which took up most of his time with phone calls, emails, and documents he needed to create.

But there was always the midnight mirror in bed.

He liked Aysha and had no doubt something special could develop between them. Universe in the shape of a heart special. Yet he had absolutely no control over her decision. He couldn't add to her pressure with any creative wooing. Put him in front of the ethics committee and he'd plead their case with all the Calabrese passion, humor and romantic reasoning in his bones.

Make them an offer they had to infuse.

If, *if* Aysha felt as strongly about him as he did about her. If she was willing to face the first-ever ethics committee in her profession just to get to a first date. They had a shot at something amazing. Unquestionably the biggest relationship 'if' in the history of his romantic life.

LEO ARRIVED FIFTEEN MINUTES EARLY AT CARLUCCI'S, WHICH WAS bubbling with locals eating and drinking outside in the warm spring evening. Aysha had already claimed a table at his favorite end, with the northeast view over the hills and parklands in the distance.

He stopped a few yards from her. His breath rushed out of his lungs and wrapped tightly around his stomach, gushing blood through his heart. Not because of nerves regarding the momentous decision she was about to share with him, she was simply stunning.

The first time he spotted her in this way. A normal way. As a woman, not therapist. A woman sitting at a café, waiting for him.

This is how it would have felt if I met her at a party or restaurant rather than her office as a client.

She sipped on her Chinotto as he approached. Looked like she'd ordered one for him too.

Aysha saw him and her face lit up. She rose, closed the distance between them in two steps, grabbed his upper arms and kissed him on the cheek. Not a peck. A warm, lingering melding of her lips on his skin. The sweetest, most romantic kiss on his cheek of all time.

He knew her decision before she pulled away. Adrenaline fizzed through his body. Her face floated back, campfire eyes smoldering.

"You have no idea how happy you've made me," he said.

"And you, me."

And you, me.

He'd never heard those three basic words in that order sound so adorable. Three syllables that would give grammar Nazis a migraine. Three syllables to launch a library of romantic stories. Their romantic stories.

They sipped their Chinottos, talking a little, but mainly smiling and grinning at each other. Then they walked for almost an hour around the village and nearby outdoor basketball courts, the whole time talking, laughing smiling and grinning.

His ego couldn't help crashing the party. To have his therapist fall for him after discovering his ugliest edges was one hell of a compliment. Ultimate validation.

I can't be that bad...

On a more practical level, he didn't have to change or prove himself to Aysha. He could just be. Any way he explored it, joy and contentment flowed through him. Not an overwhelming, head-over-heels freefall, a sweet, peaceful joy and contentment.

He was proud of Aysha too. She'd already set her appointment with supervising therapist, Darius, and was determined to not let '*a bunch of stuffy men tell me who I should fall for and when.*' For the latter part of the walk, she slipped her hand into his like they'd been walking side by side for years, her skin softer and warmer than all their handshakes.

He doubted they would have stopped walking that night if Aysha didn't need to race off to collect her daughter from her dad. At her car, she rested her hands on his arms again, his hands on her waist.

His delirious hands on her cute waist.

"I'm meeting Darius at two on Saturday. See you at Carlucci's again around three-thirty?"

He nodded, "Same table."

"Same table."

"You keep smiling like that, and I'll still be holding you right here through Saturday and into the next century."

She let go of his arms, turned to her car, and unlocked the doors with the remote.

"Get in," she said, pointing to the other door.

She wants a real kiss in private.

He zipped around the car, opened the door, and dove into the passenger seat before she changed her mind. Another test of inner strength as he stayed on his side of the car, letting her control the tempo of whatever was about to happen.

"I'd like you to listen to something." She clicked the keys over till the CD player and other dash lights glowed, then pressed play.

He recognized Anastacia's powerful, raspy vocal but not the song. The lyric lobbed straight into his heart. It was Aysha's way of saying, *you'll never be alone because from now on I'll always be there for you.*

Aysha stopped the CD after the chorus and stared at the steering wheel.

He kissed her cheek, closing eyes as his lips savored her sweet skin.

When he pulled back, it seemed like she was watching him through a new lens. He'd never felt the power, the desire, and the safe harbor in anyone's eyes all blended into one longing stare. It took all his willpower not to kiss her—deeply kiss her—then wrap her up and take her home.

"Good night, Leo."

"Ciao, Aysha. Ciao."

He slipped out of her car, watched her back out then drive off. She was gone for the night, but they were on their way for life.

"IT'S A BEAUTIFUL DAY..."

Leo sang along to the U2 song on the radio with the throat and lungs of Superman. He loved the track but those were the only words he made out. Singing was good for his soul and his lousy, no-key, tuneless voice was a painful paradox for friends. He packed his breakfast stuff into the dishwasher and danced around the tiled floor.

"We'll find our way," said Aysha on the phone earlier while he was chewing on his toast with avocado and tomato.

What a sensitive, beautiful thing she is, calling to reassure me.

"I'm looking forward to the ethics committee," she said.

"It's not an ethics committee, it's a love committee."

Aysha's laughter was still bouncing through his core as he danced.

"It's a beautiful day…"

He and Aysha would find their own way through the Love Committee and any other potholes. Their lovemaking would be amazing but that wasn't driving him. He also knew this wasn't a rebound relationship. Aysha fascinated him, excited him, stilled him. Before her, he'd never understood the notion of *stills me.*

Earlier, he'd sent Zoya a 'happy birthday' text, then got the call from Aysha. Every emotion in its place and a place for every emotion.

"It's a beautiful day…"

35

PARTY

Leo jumped up from 'their' table at Carlucci's when he saw Aysha approach.

She didn't kiss him on the cheek.

Didn't say anything, not even a handshake. Aysha sat down and stared at the distant hills, clasping her bag to her stomach.

He was rooted to the brick paving, the noisy Saturday afternoon crowd silenced by headphones of shock. A surreal, third person moment, looking down at both of them, like he was watching the wrong screen at a drive-in theater. The pictures didn't make sense with the story laid out in his head.

When Aysha looked up at him, he didn't recognize her eyes filled with anger and pain. He sat down in slow motion.

"No way," she spat out the venom.

"Did you get to explain—"

"Non-maleficence, power imbalance, transference, vulnerable with an engagement that just ended three months ago. He..." She leaned back, arms crossed. "He said 'no way.'"

Without Darius's support, they couldn't get to step one. *Fucking Darius. I should have known with a name like Darius, we were doomed.*

"How can he make that analysis without talking to me? Or seeing us together?"

Aysha gave an imperceptible shrug of her slender shoulders.

"So, to explore our...our feelings, we can't talk or see each other for two years."

Aysha nodded slowly as an elephant on Valium. She poked at the piece of lemon in her Chinotto with a straw.

"That's fucked. Two years."

She perked up a little. "Actually, he said one year. Due to our ages, our transparency, and the fact we haven't crossed any line yet, he was willing to look at it again in one year."

"One year..."

His head slowed from spinning to super slow motion. One year was late November 2008, the same November 2008 that Zoya was ending her IVF experiment.

Aysha put her glass down without drinking. "I need to process this, Leo." She got up.

He stood, dropped some money on the tray of a waitress walking past.

"I can't work through this with you," she said. Hadn't heard that tone since his early therapy sessions.

He stared at her tight eyes. "You can't just dump this on me and run."

Her eyes softened, his anger melted. This wasn't just about him. Darius had dumped an immovable boulder in front of their sunny plans, and it spooked her. She obviously hadn't been expecting it and had no idea what lay behind the shadows. Maybe she'd been projecting their future a little, like he had. But it wasn't just about her, either.

"Can I at least walk you to your car?"

She nodded.

They didn't hold hands. Didn't talk. Goodbye hug was one-way. She couldn't seem to relax, rigid under his embrace, keeping her cheek and lips as far from him as she could.

Her car rolled out of the car park slowly, yet it was the most abrupt ending he'd ever suffered. Hands deep in the pockets of his leather jacket, shoulders drooping to his waist, watching her rear lights fade down and around the sweeping bend, his heart rolling down the hill behind her.

"I HAVE A DUTY OF CARE," SHE SAID.

He was grateful for Aysha agreeing to see him a couple of days post Darius-Anti-Love-Committee shock, but Leo hated Aysha's therapist-to-client tone. They weren't client-therapist anymore, couldn't go back to that even if he wanted to. "Shouldn't you have thought that through before coming to the play? Before sharing your feelings for me?"

She stared at the mini rapids gushing below them, her cheek flushed. In any other circumstances she'd have looked cute and teenagerish with her legs dangling over the rock they sat on, hands tucked under her jeaned thighs.

He liked this secret spot on the Yarra, on the edge of Templestowe. If you jumped the rail of the viewing platform and snaked down a short dirt track through bushes, you ended on a secluded large rock, right on the river's edge.

"Seriously, Aysha, if Darius is willing to say okay in a year, why not just keep going now?"

She spun her gaze on him, flames searing his core.

"I can't believe you want me to abandon my integrity."

"That's work integrity. I get the principles, the need to protect vulnerable clients. But those rules don't make sense in our situation." He pointed to her heart. "What about your personal integrity...the integrity to your heart, your feelings?"

"I didn't know it was going to be this complicated."

"Maybe not, but you led us to the mountain of the love committee then stopped at the first incline."

"Darius is one of the most esteemed psychologists in the world, not just Australia. I respect his judgment."

I'm not dating your psychologist! I haven't fallen for Darius, I've fallen for you.

A déjà vu moment. He was sure he had the same inner conversation with Zoya about her psychologist.

Aysha was giving up so easily without a fight, she couldn't really have felt anything for him. Maybe it was a fleeting crush or curiosity he'd blown up into a long-term dream.

"I wish we'd met at a party," she said.

Her words lapped around him like warm bath water, unwinding every knotted sinew.

She did care.

Their frustrating romantic cul-de-sac hurt her as much as it hurt him.

Aysha scrunched up her legs, wrapped her arms around her shins and leaned on him, resting her head on his shoulder.

He kissed the top of her head, a couple of long black hairs clinging to his lips as he turned towards the rapids. He brushed them off gently. This was the last time he would see Aysha for a year, he didn't want it to end in rocks of anger, ripples of blame.

He didn't want it to end.

Their relationship had flowed from professional to personal smoothly, like the river to their far right, then their potential romance hit the quick-fire rapids, battering them from rock to rock, to a hint of sun, before dragging them back under and spinning them blindly until his heart ended up battered across a rotten log on the bank to their left, and hers drifted downriver, drenched in shock. Alone.

Leo emotionally limped to the end of the year.

Exhausted from launching 8-Crocs, including two trips to Sydney, one to Canberra and a seven-day dash to Cannes within five weeks. Worn out by his hyper-stressed young partners, who had already declared they wouldn't be involved in another commercial game, effectively killing off a potentially lucrative income stream.

Which all combined into a speck in the extraordinary emotional universe he'd traversed with Zoya and Aysha.

He'd just dropped off his boys and there wasn't enough Sunday evening light for a bike ride, so he trudged up the nearby hill to sit on the grass in front of Mia Mia Gallery. Over the trees and down the hill, the reddish sunset dulled to a deep purple. A bit to the south-west, lights from the tallest city buildings flickered for attention.

You learn more about yourself in a relationship. Zoya's insight made sense. *Between Zoya and Aysha, I learned more about myself in the last year than the previous ten. Ten lifetimes.*

Didn't dilute the confusion and deep melancholy. He'd been consistent, brave. Open with his feelings. Yet he was alone.

Would he have rather not met them?

No, despite the jarring suddenness of both endings. He couldn't have ignored the intense, rare attraction to Zoya or Aysha.

I was blessed to meet and connect with two amazing women. I wasn't afraid to follow my heart despite the obvious complexities.

He didn't resort to his usual end-of-romance ritual, listening to torture tracks over Aysha, as their romance had never really begun. With Aysha, he'd lost a teacher and friend, no scope for contact at all, for at least a year. But it wasn't a bridge-burning ending to their relationship.

And what did that November thing mean?

Was it a sign or just a fluke? What if Aysha and Zoya were both available next year at the same time?

He didn't have the energy to process it, the first time in more than a decade he'd scheduled four straight weeks of holidays, and Friday, December twenty-first couldn't swallow him and 2007 up quickly enough.

Two more work weeks of admin and marketing stuff for 8-Crocs then nothing except a few weeks with the boys, which was always fun around that time of year. They wouldn't let him mope around.

No going out and meeting women.

No dates.

Nothing remotely romance-related.

36

MEXICAN CASPER

Leo was dragged out of shutdown lagoon, dripping with melancholy and exhaustion.

Her long blond curls were a snow-covered Christmas tree, lit with sparkling blue eyes, and an every-gem-in-the-store, Tiffany-diamond smile. One glimpse and he shook off the murky waters like an excited puppy, heart's tail whipping.

He'd been going through the motions at the industry Christmas White Party. Despite some friendly faces and well wishes for 8-Crocs, he didn't want to be there. His reward was to fall into his extended holiday two days early, right after the party at Docklands. He was making his way to the exit around eleven when she stopped in front of him in a tight space.

"Looks like a Mexican Ghost stand-off," she said, making fun of the white dress theme, which created a feeling of hundreds of ghosts drifting around the giant old shed.

"How do you say Casper in Mexican?" he asked.

"Casper in Mexican," she said in a mock-Spanish accent.

He laughed. It had been a few weeks since those facial muscles had gotten any exercise.

"Casper el fantasma amistoso," she said.

"Wow, do you speak Spanish or are you the solitary member of the Spanish Casper fan club?"

"Spanish dad."

"You don't look—"

"Polish Jewish mum."

"I like what they cooked up with those ingredients."

She did her Tiffany smile thing.

He took in her white vest with blue trim, matching belt, and loose, white linen pants.

Couldn't have been much over five feet and no stick figure. Petite, curvaceous. The cheekbones on her round face were beacons. He had an urge to kiss both of them.

"Jade," she said, offering her hand.

"Leo."

She had a firm grip, warm skin. Jade was doing a PhD with a thesis about *creativity in digital design*. After a few safe career questions, they exchanged business cards.

She slipped in that she'd been separated for nine months. In another time he had no doubt he'd hang around to speak with her longer, maybe head somewhere quieter for a chat. Maybe more than a chat. But nine months was barely scratching the surface. In his experience, it took a minimum of two years for someone to begin moving on from a marriage that ended unexpectedly.

"See you at some other industry event, Calabrian Casper."

"That would give me much allegria." Leo threw in his favorite Spanish word, among the few he knew.

They shook hands and he squeezed past her. Best he get away before she expected more. Despite the way she sparked him out of his zombie state, he didn't have the energy to explain his recent relationship status, let alone launch a new one. He didn't even have energy for sex.

Never afraid to miss. His core mantra nudged him to at least open a door for future fun. After just one step, he turned back.

She hadn't moved, smile still beaming, card still in her hand.

"Jade, that other card was for business purposes." He took

another, identical card from his pocket. "If late next year you feel like catching up for personal reasons, use this one."

He wouldn't forget her in a year. He'd need twelve months to recover from the last three. Twelve months was good.

JADE CALLED IN JANUARY, LESS THAN A MONTH AFTER MEETING. "I'M BIT of a foodie and have been keen to try the Press Club. My girlfriends are all away with their families. Boys are with their dad down the coast. Thought you might want to join me."

Leo's sister had told him about the restaurant run by TV Master Chef host, George Calombaris, and he'd been keen to try it. But it had only been ten months since her separation. He really should pass.

"Sure."

"WE MUST'VE SEEN YOU PERFORM AT LEAST A DOZEN TIMES," SAID LEO. "Three or four gigs just at the Grainstore. I didn't recognize you as J.A."

"I was skinnier then. Had my hair straight and short."

"You were the one with the crazy colors. Were they wigs?"

"Nuh. Bright blues, pink, green. My mood, my hair." She patted her wavy honey blonde locks. "Sticking with natural these days".

J.A.—aka Jade—one of three singers in Leo's favorite cover band back in the early eighties. Later she was a back-up vocalist on TV's biggest, Tonight Show. He'd grown up with J.A. as part of his backing track in the eighties and early nineties. Probably same age but she looked so young.

"I'm fifty."

Must've read his mind. Three years older. "Fifty going on twenty-one."

"Flattery will get you everywhere," she said, exaggeratedly fluttering her eyebrows and twirling her hair.

"You've gone from one of my favorite things, live music, to least favorite, academia."

She shrugged. "It was a fun ride, but I don't miss it. I love what I'm doing now."

She looked gorgeous in a blue cotton blouse that matched her eyes. With the linen white pants, she fitted right into the modern Greek cuisine.

"'J' must be Jade, so what's the 'A'?"

"Amante. Plain Jade Amante."

"Anything but plain."

She dropped her eyes to the empty dessert plate, cheeks blushing.

"Does Amante mean anything?"

"Lover." She twisted the corner of her napkin. "Guess I was misnamed."

A million things he could have said to brighten her but didn't want to mislead either of them. He liked Jade, no doubt about that. Loved the way she could jump from worldly to girly, from rock star to intellectual in a heartbeat. Like a whacky Barbara Streisand character.

She saved the moment, indicating to a waiter with her hands for the bill.

"We'll split this," she said, full smile back, her credit card out before he could answer.

He nodded, soaking up the course they wouldn't be charged for, Jade Amante cake, syrupy sweet with secret spices.

Brendan's an imbecile. How could he possibly walk out on such a beautiful, funny, and smart woman like you?

"I LOVE THIS ASPECT OF MELBOURNE," SAID JADE AS SHE LEANED against the thick concrete rail of Princes Bridge on her tiptoes, looking towards the tennis center. "Hate the commercial stuff on the other side," she said, flipping her thumb over her shoulder at the glitzier commercial end of Southbank.

Leo nodded beside her, enjoying the sun shimmering off the Yarra. A small cruise boat floated underneath, a couple of solo kayakers paddling towards the boatsheds on the right.

He pointed east, upriver. "I like the view from Swan Street bridge too, looking back this way."

She nodded. "Yeah, especially with the sunset."

He enjoyed her profile as Jade smiled at the river.

"Lunch was fun. We should do it again," she said without facing him.

"It was fun." *But we're not doing this again for at least six months, probably more.*

The food was good, but he struggled with the background noise bouncing off the concrete and marble in the vast space. However, his internal antenna had no problem picking up the signals his favorite foodie was unknowingly sending. Newly single women from long-term relationships had no idea how frequently they referred to their ex-partner or husband, often with an edge. In Jade's case, her eyes dulled every time she'd mentioned Brendan. And she mentioned him a lot.

He walked Jade to her car, which was parked close to the fountain alongside Alexandra Gardens. After she threw her handbag onto the passenger seat, she turned to Leo. "Maybe in a couple of weeks?"

"Jade, I'm not sure you've moved on from your separation yet. Even when breaking up is the right decision, it takes a while. You need time to grieve, to find bits of yourself again that got chipped away while you sculpted a life around kids and your husband."

She leaned back against her car, searching the grass.

It was the right thing to say, to do. He liked her too much to pursue her just for sex.

Jade eyed him with a diluted smile, head on an angle.

"You're an unusual guy, Leo Devecchio. Perceptive and..." She bounced to him, kissed his cheek. "And kind."

You can probably thank Zoya and Aysha for that, you sweet thing. Walking away from your zaniness isn't easy.

37

INFINITY

LEO CHECKED THE TEXT AGAIN WHEN HE'D GOT BACK FROM HIS Saturday ride with Paul. His bike buddy had patiently listened as he processed the layers and hidden dangers among the little letters sitting on his phone. Two hours of sweating through a scorching February morning and a long, cool shower didn't sprinkle any clarity.

Hello, Leo, why don't you join my next beginners' yoga term? First class next Tuesday seven p.m., school hall near my place. Look forward to seeing you. Aysha.

Just over two months of no contact. Of trying to forget about her. Of wondering how he'd manage any of that until November.

How could attending Aysha's yoga class help? Sure, they'd be able to see each other for a precious hour or so each week. Was that worth risking her career? Or ruin the chance of being together properly post November? Plus, it would be as student-teacher again. Her domain, her control. Any angle he looked at reflected negativity. The suggestion seemed out of character. The only clear positive was confirmation she was thinking about him, missing him.

Normally, the pining scampering around his chest would be

sweet. But his ribs were like bars, chest a cage. His heart couldn't follow its romantic instincts. He and Aysha should be together. Exploring, discovering, laughing, and learning as a couple. As equals. He'd have already registered for her class, probably two. But they had this ethics issue with a love committee snooping over their shoulders in November that year.

Bloody Darius.

He closed the screen on his phone, shoved it as deep as it would go into a pocket in his shorts and headed out to do the shopping. When he opened the front door, the thick January heat hit him simultaneously with an opposing thought.

Maybe she's given up on November and the whole idea of the two of us being together?

He shut the door, leaning his head on the wood.

Can't be.

He straightened up and headed out again.

LEO DIDN'T RESPOND UNTIL SUNDAY EVENING, ALMOST THIRTY-SIX hours after Aysha's text. It took him a while to craft words that answered her suggestion, and his nagging question about their future without raising unnecessary negatives.

Hey, Aysha, what a lovely thought. I miss you. But I can't see how joining your class would help our case in November. If you don't agree, please call me. Ciao, Leo.

If she had reached out because she missed him, he was certain patience was their best course, as much as he struggled with the notion. If...if she'd given up on them, he opened the door for her to clarify her feelings. He didn't expect a quick response.

Chirp, chirp.

Leo stirred awake and turned to his phone on the bedside table.

Thud.

He jolted wide awake, a touch of fear tingling his nerves until he realized the book he'd been reading had dropped to the floor. Radio clock beamed eleven-oh-nine p.m. He scrambled for the phone without turning the light on. When he saw it was a text from Aysha, an inner warmth flooded his inner-world.

As he read the message, his lips tightened, and the only warmth came from the stuffy air in the non-air-conditioned bedroom.

I was expecting you at tonight's class. Now I feel manipulated.
Reading your text again, your response was pushy, expecting a
commitment to something I'm not in a position to give.

He stumbled out of bed, flicked the hallway light, and placed the phone on the kitchen counter, pulled out a jug from the fridge and poured cold water into his favorite thick glass with a handle. He stared at the phone in between long gulps. The icy water didn't cool down his anger.

How on earth did she read 'pushy' or 'manipulated'?

Aysha's attack threw him right back into his Mr. Defensive, Super Prover zones. Zones that she'd helped him recognize. He scrolled through his text. Even if there was the slightest chance of her misreading it—and there wasn't—he'd ended it with *If you don't agree, please call me.*

So, she chooses to lash out in a text? How could she get it so wrong?

He called her number. It was the only way to sort this out. Clarify each other's words and feelings.

Brrr-brrr, brrr-brr...

No answer. She was awake five minutes ago.

He hung up before her voicemail message and rang again.

Brrr-brrr, brrr-brr...

Still no answer. He didn't leave a message. Wednesday morning was her quiet time with no client appointments. He'd call her then.

Probably best we don't speak tonight if we're both angry.

Wednesday, he called twice. She didn't answer or respond. A text wouldn't do, neither would an email. So, he typed a letter:

Sweet Aysha,

I have absolute faith in our ability to talk anything through. I have absolute faith in us… if the spirits allow that opportunity sometime after 15 November.

I'm not planning on it. I'm not living my life around it. But if that opportunity is still there for us in November… I'm not afraid to explore it. I want to explore it.

Aysha, we are in an unusual situation. An extraordinary situation. Not many people would be mindful enough and internally strong enough to keep our friendship alive, let alone potentially more than that.

Last year you warned me that you're 'messy', that I shouldn't put you on a pedestal. If this is the messiest you can get with me, relax. You don't scare me! If things don't work out between us, that's life… but to finish like this based on misunderstandings, via SMS… that would be sad. We are better than that.

From the first moment that we confirmed our feelings, I've trusted you unconditionally. Whenever you talked about your ex-husband and other relationships like David, I never felt even a twinge of jealousy, not even when you accidentally called me David. I knew you could spend time with any of them again and I had nothing to fear. That's a reflection of my realignment under your guidance and of our soul connection.

As a teacher, what you have done for me will stay forever. That's why I hope you accept this gift. It represents infinity. If I never get to see you again as a friend, I will accept and respect your decision. But if, as I hope, we do work our way past this little 'blip', then I look forward to seeing it on you later this year. Tomorrow it's three months down, nine to go… but who's counting!

With care and kindness,

Leo

He folded the letter into an envelope, along with the infinity pendant he'd bought after her commitment to face the love committee. He never got the chance to give it to her when Darius had dumped the giant roadblock across that path.

He dropped the envelope off in her letterbox. He'd looked forward to visiting her home as her boyfriend or partner, rather than rear bungalow office as a client. Instead, he felt more like an intruder even though he was doing a good deed. Maybe everything would sort itself out later that year.

TWO DAYS LATER, LEO WAS KICKING HIMSELF THAT HE'D WRITTEN SUCH an overcomplicated letter, his old super prover routine.

Probably took her two days just to read the bloody thing.

He assumed by then she must be sending a letter back to him. Until he got her six-word text on Friday evening.

38

REVERSALS

Thanks for your letter and gift.

Aysha's text. All of it.

Underwhelmed. Let down. Leo wasn't sure what he'd expected. Despite his best intentions, he obviously invested hopes on more. No explanation behind her yoga class suggestion. No affirmation about their connection. No positivity at all about November.

Not even a friendly sign-off.

He stepped out into his small courtyard and plonked onto the picnic chair. The pavers were warm under his bare feet but by that time of the day the sun was hiding behind his garage and neighbor's huge gum tree. He wasn't sure how long he'd sat there, must've been a thousand cockatoos, galahs, parrots, and other birds flitting across the nearby trees searching for dinner. The setting sun created a crimson-orange umbrella over his thoughts.

Aysha's a listener, not a talker. She's never sent long messages or any emails at all. Romance isn't her comfort zone. She didn't question anything I wrote, and most importantly, she didn't slam the gate shut on November.

With each thought, his inner world melted away a layer of stress.

There wasn't anything to gripe about. He couldn't rush November. His tummy grumbled and the only feeding taking place was by the mosquitoes feasting on his legs. He slapped one away and headed back inside.

39

ONION SONGS

"Hey, Yo-Yo." Janey waved Leo over to a window table with Giga.

He sat down at the chair she'd pulled out. "Two bloody interstate VIPs have just canceled."

"Who do you know in Melbourne that might be available for tomorrow?" asked Giga.

It was already late Thursday morning and they needed someone who could make the two-hour drive to Cape Schanck by two p.m. the next day, preferably earlier.

"There'll be a fee and we'll put them up for the night."

He looked out over the golf course and trees to the blue ocean. There were worse places on the planet to stay a night. The late March autumn sun wasn't too shabby either.

"Try Andy or Simon from Portable Studios and... Jade Amante."

"One of the Portable guys is a great idea. Who's Jade?" said Giga.

Good question.

"She's doing a PhD about interactive design. Used to be a singer and worked on TV, so she's kind of a walking cross-media story."

"Sounds perfect."

"Sounds like a cross-bedroom story," said Janey with an exaggerated wink.

"You want their details or not?" he asked Janey with a bite, but his damn Judas muscles framed a grin.

As he walked back to the presentation room to help Matt give each team the final feedback on their pitch, he wondered why the grin and the warm buzz high in his stomach.

Jade knows I'm a mentor here. It's a safe way of reaching out. If Jade comes, it means she's moved on from her husband. It's about twelve months since they separated, might be enough. If she doesn't accept, no one loses face.

It's like a movie moment.

Late in the wind-up dinner, the instant he looked towards Jade, she turned across from her conversation, and her Tiffany diamonds thing shimmered across the empty glasses and cutlery on the tables between them.

Air slumbered out of his lungs, warm and dreamy.

Apart from a quick greeting and introduction to Giga and Janey when she'd arrived that afternoon, he hadn't had time to talk to Jade. Friday madness of the Digi-Tent workshops.

Fellow mentor, Matt—the real deal as a published novelist and creator of major brand games—followed his gaze, then gave him a wink and a gentle nudge. Leo liked his New York mate.

He tilted his head towards the foyer. Jade nodded, turned to her fellow VIP, Martin, shook hands with him and headed across to meet Leo.

"The article was in the *Age* so it must be true," said Jade, in a fake posh accent.

"The Australian Psychics Awards... that's hilarious."

She straightened up on the couch and put on her announcer voice. "And winner of Australian Psychic of the Year…but the winner is already walking on the stage, grabs her award and says: *Thank you. My talented peers already know my speech, the pretenders can check it out on my website where I posted yesterday.*" Uninhibited laughter with nasally harmonies and golden mane waving all over the place.

"Maybe there's a Psychic's Club. Can you imagine the short conversations? *'Hey*

Jessie, your sister gets breast can—' 'Yeah, I know,'" said Jade.

"Bob, your son's going to win—" said Leo.

"Yeah, I know."

Their laughter bounced around the small space they'd claimed, away from the post-midnight party animals raging down the foyer. A tiny private lounge, just them, their wines on a small coffee table, and silly conversation with all sorts of zany tangents.

Jade settled back into the couch but kept her eyes on him.

"Did you leave your wife for another woman?"

If he got a dollar for every time he'd been asked that…

"Yes."

Tiffany diamond face closed shop, lights out.

"I just don't know who she is yet."

Her face brightened. But it was fleeting as she focused on her glass, swirling the red wine.

"How did your separation happen?" he asked, sensing that was what she really wanted to talk about.

She slumped deeper into the couch, like the question was a physical weight plonked on her shoulders. "Last year we organized a huge shindig for our twenty-fifth anniversary. Two nights before the party, Brendan went out and didn't come home. Sent me a text that he would still be celebrating with me at our party but no other explanation. Wouldn't say where he was." She downed her wine, put the glass on the table gently, stayed on the edge of the couch, staring at the empty glass. "He turned up with his twenty-eight-year-old assistant on his arm."

Wow. I've heard some terrible-men-in-relationship stories and this one was top-shelf, or gutter-level. The young assistant thing is a pathetic cliché, but the timing and public humiliation, criminal.

The party noises down the foyer jumped in decibels.

"I don't know what to say, Jade. What a horrible thing to put you through."

"My friends rallied around me. His mates partied on the other side of the hall. It was like each side had to prove what a great time we were having anyway. Insane. The whole thing didn't really hit me till a few days later."

Brendan just added to Leo's theory that there was nothing special about him, it was the dumb and awful men out there who helped him look good. His heart laid itself out like a blanket, wanting to cover her, protect her from that idiot ex-husband and all the other stupid men out there. Her hand scratched at the couch beside him. He placed his hand on top.

She studied their hands then looked up, tears, lips slightly apart. Jade removed her hand, picked up her handbag. "Sorry, Leo. Been a big week and long day. Time for this old shrub to hit the old garden bed." Like a chirpy pop song despite her sadness.

A friend once told Leo she believed women fell in love with their ears. Jade must've brought out his feminine side because her sweet tones tinkled up his spine, amplified in his brain, and reverberated in his heart.

"I'm no green thumb but I can make sure you make it to your garden." He'd almost said BED instead of garden. Leo consciously fought his rogue face muscles from going cheeky or grinning, or anything remotely cocky. It was a valiant effort.

She stood and inched around the coffee table. He joined her and she looked up a touch, eyes barely visible under her curly fringe bag clenched to her side.

IT WASN'T UNTIL THEY STEPPED INTO AN EMPTY CORRIDOR, A LONG WAY from the party rebels, that Jade interlocked her arm with Leo's, old school.

"Sorry I killed the party," she said.

"Our party hasn't even begun."

"You're not coming into my room."

"I'm honored you've been thinking about it."

She looked up at him for a couple of steps. "You might be the first guy I've met who's cocky *and* nice."

"Thank you. And that's very clever, because now I have to live up to the nice bit."

She stopped, let go of his arm and pointed to a door. "This is me."

"You're a special woman, Jade."

She kept her eyes down as she shuffled in her bag. "Thank you, but you're still not coming in."

"I'm just glad you're here."

She looked up at him, room keycard in her hand, head on an angle.

"Want to hang out with me tomorrow? We can go for a walk, maybe a winery lunch and then I can drive you home," he said.

"Hang out? It's like high school again." She patted him on the chest, acting coy. "Shucks, Leo."

"Or you can take the minibus with Martin."

"Let's have breakfast together in the restaurant, see what happens." She kissed him on the cheek, swiped her key and opened the door. "Don't go alpha male diva on me. I don't really think I like you that much, I just want to see you again to make sure."

His Judas muscles surrendered, never stood a chance.

She blew him a kiss and closed the door.

His heart rippled like his tummy rumbled when he was starving, as uncontrollable and unpredictable as a West African percussion troupe.

"You to me are everything…" Leo sang along to the Real Thing CD with every ounce of feeling in his soul. Something about the seventies track hooked him into a zone from the launch of keyboard, percussion, and funky guitar, forcing him to blast it out of his lungs. And it needed all the lung work his hopeless, toneless voice could muster, because it wasn't an easy chorus to master. Kept his eyes on the highway as he dug deep for the climax, "…come on and take the rest of me, oh, baby."

He stopped singing when he saw Jade's tears trickle around her smile. He turned down the volume, eyes back on the highway.

"Can't believe you're singing to me," she said, wiping tears with the back of her hand.

"You're a former rock chick. You must've had a million guys sing to you."

"Doesn't count with pros. Takes guts when—"

"When you've got a shitty voice?"

She nodded, tears still flowing.

"I've created a whole new genre—Onion Songs. My voice uncovers layers in a song that no one's heard before, brings everyone to tears."

She laughed. "I love your onion songs. Keep singing." She turned up the volume.

Any woman who asked for more of his voice was the woman for him. He hit repeat, and sold the song like his life depended on it.

Earlier that morning, they had waved everyone off at the resort, raising a couple of eyebrows, a grin from Matt and a wink from Janey. They soaked in the spectacular scenery with a long coastal walk, the conversation ranging from deeply philosophical to plain silly. On the drive back to Melbourne, Jade knew exactly which winery was right for lunch on the Mornington Peninsula. Two wines and four or five sumptuous pounds on their waists later, they'd hit the road.

He felt comfortable singing his signature onion song to Jade despite her once being a pro herself. Everything about the previous night and the day's road trip was cruisy and fun. No kiss, not even holding hands, yet it was one of his favorite ever first non-date dates.

"STOP HERE," SAID JADE.

Leo wasn't totally surprised. Their silence had a heaviness to it as they approached the city down Beach Road. He'd taken the scenic route along the bay. The longer route.

I guess she doesn't want the day to end either...continue on with dinner, maybe.

"There." She pointed to an empty parking spot.

He slowed, let a car pass then reverse parked. Turned off the engine. It wasn't the busier, trendy end of Fitzroy Street but he wouldn't question the taste of his favorite foodie.

"I can get a cab here."

A sledgehammer may as well have smashed through the windshield. Fragments of fear and doubt cut through him.

"That's crazy. We're so close and I'm virtually going past South Yarra anyway."

She stopped shuffling in her handbag. "Brendan moved back in. Three weeks ago."

40

SNEAKY U-TURNS

Two trains crashed Leo's soul from opposite directions.

The Brendan Monster locomotive. How on earth could she let him back into her life?

The other steam engine funneled all the warmth out of his heart while fueling a burning rage in his head and stomach.

"Interesting timing, Jade. You don't think you maybe should've mentioned that little fact last night?"

"I was going to, I really was." Eyes on her bag, as if it carried all the answers, then back at Leo. "I like you...a lot. I wanted to see you again but that just made it harder. I'm sorry, Leo."

"That's why you were crying earlier. Nothing to do with my onion songs?"

"Both."

"So where does that leave—"

She shrugged, a frown making her almost unrecognizable.

"That's not very adult, Jade, or fair. I've been open with you all along." An edge in his voice but he wasn't angry. Maybe it was just a jarring contrast to the rest of their playful banter.

"I need some time. He just...it was out of the blue. The kids were excited and I...I haven't processed it yet. Please don't hate me."

Brendan Monster, the spin king of Melbourne, with the larger-than-universe personality, had spun a web of pain and confusion around Jade, and now he was being dragged into it.

"Better get your bag." He flicked the trunk open, rolled out of the car, pulled out the bag and brought it to her on the pavement.

"I'll call you," she said.

"I'll answer." Hollow banter on autopilot.

No kiss or hug. She turned away and jumped into a taxi.

The taxi made a sneaky U-turn, inciting angry toots from two cars. Jade waved to him. He raised his palm to waist level. The lyric of his favorite onion song haunted him, the bit about just being a clown. Jade peeled off yet another layer of the song and left him raw.

Leo checked the radio clock, the red digits glaring three-twenty a.m. A bunch of words kept shining a lamp inside his head, mucking up his circadian rhythms.

All you share in your bed is the linen that covers your loneliness.

He gave in to his mini insomnia and headed to his office.

By four a.m. he'd clicked send on his laptop. Maybe he should've slept on it before sending the email to Jade. He read the poem again.

All you share in your bed
Is the linen that covers your loneliness.
Listen to his endless autobiography
While you float in my onion songs.
Touch him by distant memory,
Yearn for my lips and loving caress.
Watch him breathe in his secret sleep,
Dream of my open smiling eyes.
He gets to share your bed.
Which one of us is the fool?

He shuffled back to bed. Sleep or no sleep, he was in no rush that day.

THE TEXT LEO GOT TWO WEEKS LATER IN EARLY APRIL WASN'T FROM THE woman he was expecting.

Hello, Leo. The two books I recommend are Shantaram by Gregory Roberts and A Path with Heart by Jack Kornfield. I look forward to your thoughts. Take care, Aysha.

The message felt like part of a conversation they hadn't had, although he did mention during his therapy he was interested in eastern spirituality, especially curious about Buddhism. That was about six months ago.

She's still thinking about me.

A campfire in his inner world. Of the three women he'd opened his heart to in the last nineteen months, Aysha was the only one who was off limits purely because of third-party rules, not her own desires or decisions. Whether she'd gone through her notes or remembered his interest didn't matter. She was thinking about him and looking forward to his thoughts.

The timing was interesting, the universe telling him to forget Jade. Good advice.

I see on your timeline you're in Sydney tomorrow night. Me too! Time for a drink? Summit Bar Six p.m. xxx JA

LEO SHOOK HIS HEAD. WITH HER PHD STUDIES AND COMFORT IN THE social media space, it made sense Jade reached out to him via Facebook. At least it was a private message.

But she doesn't get it. Nothing can work while she's still living with her Brendan Monster. Didn't she even read my poem?

Just as he was about to rattle off a reply, another message popped up from Jade:

PS: Loved the poem. Just like your onion songs, so many layers...
and tears.

He leaned back on his black leather office chair, hands running up and down the curved plastic arms. Was Ego Man pushing him to say yes to the rendezvous, or was Jade hinting at changes? Changes that meant they were cleared for take-off as a couple.

He was tired of holding patterns. Between Air Zoya, Aysha Airlines and Jade Jets, his heart had been circling above Soulmate Airport forever. Sooner or later, it was going to run out of romantic fuel and crash.

One thing he'd already learned from reading A Path with Heart is that projecting was an extension of longing, and longing for anything was not a good state. He'd been a world-class projector, screening major love scenes in his heart way before life had finished writing the introductions. A walking case study on the pitfalls of longing. He decided he needed more time, typed his reply.

Sounds good but won't know if I can make it till tomorrow. I'll
text you.

41

REVOLVING HEARTS

Jade's eyes and energy sitting on the two-seater black leather couch outshone the glittering skyscrapers behind her. And the Sydney Harbor Bridge. And Opera House.

"I would've picked you for a grungy pub in Balmain, maybe Newtown. This is more classical than rock 'n roll," said Leo.

"If life didn't change…" Jade turned back from the view, mischief all over her face. "You wouldn't be here."

"Touché."

As the forty-seventh-floor bar-restaurant slowly revolved, her words swirled in his forty-seven-year-old heart.

Change… was that a hint?

He was surprised he never heard of the Summit Bar during the three years he'd lived in Sydney for his last day job. The high-networking sports marketing gig had drawn him into many opulent corners of the town, but not the Circuit Bar. Took a zany ex-rocker, born again digital media guru from Melbourne.

"So, you're a chocaholic too." She clinked her German chocolate martini with his.

He nodded. "You can trust me with your money and children but neeeever leave me alone with your chocolate."

"Don't get why they bother wrapping chocolate, just gets in the way." She put her glass down, pretending to shovel chocolate into her mouth with both hands.

He smiled. "And what's the point of use by dates on chocolate? Waste of ink."

She laughed then shifted her legs closer to him. "Use by dates on lovers would be handy, stamped right here." She slapped her forehead. "Good in bed but emotionally immature. Spit him out after three weeks."

They chuckled.

He slapped his forehead. "Sexy body but high maintenance, one night only."

Jade laughed, her nasally sounds adding harmony. "Starts interesting, good provider." Slapped her forehead. "Set up life then run before he dumps you." The tone spiraled down as she spilled out the second sentence. She gulped down her martini and swirled the glass between her hands like she was rubbing a genie bottle.

She's opened another door. That was no accident.

"Has Brendan Monster moved out again?"

He asked the question with Sydney Tower over her right shoulder. The clockwise revolving view passed the Bridge, and he could see the Opera House in the corner of his eye before she lifted her head and met his stare, eyes smoldering and vulnerable, lips parted and doubled in size.

So, so beauti—

Jade kissed him on the mouth. Sweet, chocolate lips and fiery tongue stirred a cocktail of chocolate, vodka, pheromones and endorphins. His fingers explored her neck, around her ear, skin smooth, hot. Her hands slipped around his shirt, fingernails digging through the cotton into his back.

Her tongue did a lap of his lips before Jade pulled back. Showtime cheeks, carnival eyes, rollercoaster lips.

He wasn't sure if it was the two martinis, the spinning restaurant in the sky, or pent-up desire to kiss her, but his heart was doing Cirque du Soleil somersaults.

"That was the longest, most amazing first kiss."

Tiffany diamonds smile with a hint of pride, maybe some relief. He was probably the first new guy she'd kissed in over twenty-five years.

"I think we did a few laps," she said, swinging her finger around in circles towards the ceiling to floor window. She landed her finger on his lips, traced around them then came in for another kiss. Squeezed her body closer, wedged a leg between his, her foot tangled under his calf.

Kissed him harder, longer, hotter. By the time they came up for air, three young women nearby were leaving and an older couple who'd been sitting behind were talking to the Maître D' while pointing at them.

"I think we're about to be thrown out," said Leo.

Jade pumped a rock salute. "That's rock 'n roll, baby."

He laughed.

Jade checked her phone. "Jiminy jeepers, I'm late."

"Really? You have to go?"

"Supposed to be at my brother's in fifteen and it's at least a thirty-minute cab ride."

She picked up her handbag and they headed for the exit.

"What about later tonight?"

Shook her head. "I'm staying at his place."

Jade collected her overnight bag from the Maître D', whose badge said 'Julie', and face said, '*we don't do passionate romance here*'.

In the elevator, he wrapped his hand around Jade's waist and brought her in tight. They kissed all the way down the forty-seven floors.

When they stepped out of the lift Jade grabbed his arm.

"Forgot my umbrella."

They kissed all the way up in the elevator, got her umbrella from Julie non-romance, then kissed all the way down.

He followed her to the taxi stand. "What time are you finished tomorrow? Maybe we can get the same flight?"

"Nuh. Can't do." Jade jumped into the back of a taxi.

Turbulence from an all too familiar holding pattern tensed his body.

Jade yelled out, "Sunday. Dinner in Melbourne!" She blew him a kiss and shut the door.

Sunday's only three days. He could work with three days.

"FOLLOW ME!" YELLED JADE OVER HER SHOULDER. IN A FLASH, SHE snaked through the stationary cars, jogged around the back of the tram, then jumped in.

Leo was stuck at the curb, mesmerized by her effervescence. Like his favorite drink as a child, creaming soda, she bubbled and fizzed, super sweet.

"Come on!" she yelled, hanging from the tram door, one foot in, half her body out. "Before the lights turn green."

He darted across, jumped on and plonked himself on the seat opposite just as the tram took off.

Jade beamed her eyes through the window, taking in every little detail. "They say coffee is Melbourne's international icon, but I reckon it's the trams. Always be the trams."

Rock chick energy, gentle sentimentalist. Elegant dresser, raw sexiness. Digital guru, nostalgic purist.

"See, you look so happy," she said.

"That's because I'm looking at you."

Her cheeks zoomed past crimson to bright red, smile and eyes so bright they almost blinded him. She turned back to the window. He liked that pocket of Chapel Street, away from the commercial shop-ping end, closer to Dandenong Road. Jade had chosen a dark and grungy café for dinner, which was perfect. After dinner she'd wanted a walk, then jumped on the tram.

"I like facing forward. Always feels strange moving backwards," he said.

"I love facing backwards. Everything's a surprise." She jumped up. "Come on, we have to get a tram back again."

They barely traveled more than two or three stops, could've walked back to her car.

Waiting for the return tram, she pulled him in tight and kissed him, her hands around his neck, his under her long, unbuttoned blue coat, teasing every muscle in her back. When they peeled their faces back a little, it struck him how big a deal it was for her to be so free with him in the open. In Melbourne, not far from her home.

"Your lips under-promise but boy, do they over deliver." She closed her eyes and her whole body shuddered as she sung the final two words.

"That's my mantra," he whispered into her ear.

"Under-promise and over-deliver?"

"Make every kiss like it's the last one you'll ever have."

She swooned, pretended she was fainting.

He held her tight.

"I have an early start tomorrow." She didn't try to untangle herself, resting her head on his chest.

"Jade…"

"Leo."

"I…I can't keep doing this." He felt her arms stiffen a little, but she didn't move.

"It's okay," she said.

He stretched back so he could see her face. "It's not okay, I'm falling for you but you're living with—"

She put her finger on his lips. "It's okay because I'm telling him to move out. You've gotten under my skin, Leo Devecchio, and it feels kind of cozy with you there."

He kissed her. Relief, passion, and euphoria tasted sweeter than an endless vat of creaming soda.

Talk about déjà vu.

Hanging around, waiting for another woman to confirm she could be with him. Zoya and her work. Aysha and her supervising therapist. Jade and her Brendan Monster.

Despite beginning meditating recently and the wisdom he read in 'A Path with Heart', anxiety kept sneaking up on him. Jade was planning to conduct 'Operation Fuck Off' Monday night. Remembering how evil Brendan Monster had been to her made it easier to believe she would go through with it.

He told Jade to not rush calling him. It was going to be emotional doing OFO with BM, no matter how much he deserved it. A day or two gap before calling was probably a good thing. By ten p.m. Wednesday he wasn't so sure. Sunday night's euphoria seemed eons ago. It was impossible not to think about Jade and her mission. Up to two days seemed reasonable, longer signaled disaster. He was trying to watch a new TV show but the lack of drama on screen didn't help distract him from the drama clogging up his head.

The new guitar melody ringtone on his phone startled him. He knocked his phone off his lap. He grabbed it off the futon, knowing it was unlikely to be anyone else at that hour.

"Hey, J.A."

"Hey, L.D. Sorry about the time."

"No problem. You okay?"

She inhaled and released a long breath. "Brendan agreed to move out."

Euphoria burst through him, pumping his free fist high. It was a delicate time for Jade, so he didn't want to go crazy blabbering on the phone. He rolled off the futon, did a silent jig.

"But he made a good case."

His jig stalled in slow motion, finished as a statue in his lounge room. Something in her tone turned his body hairs into antennas.

"A good case for...?"

"We agreed that it's best if he leaves after our youngest finishes high school in November. He's worked so hard in his final year we don't want to fuck it up for him."

His ears heard the second sentence, but his brain stopped working after 'November'.

"It's only six months," she said.

November...

He sat on the floor, his back to the futon, left elbow leaning on his bent knee.

"I'm sorry, Leo, but I have to put Pablo first."

"I understand, kids first."

Understanding was one thing.

His heart bled out, creating a heavy pool of blood in his stomach. Blood that turned acid, but this acid didn't burn through anything, just kept burning where it was, wave after wave after wave. Didn't want to hang up, didn't know what to say.

"Maybe I'll see you on a tram before then," she said, trying to perk up.

November...

"Yeah, maybe."

"Ciao, L.D."

"Ciao, J.A."

He pressed end with his thumb and skimmed his phone across the carpet, hitting the timber trim at the bottom of the wall.

Unbelievable.

He had a date with destiny and three women in November.

42

ONE TWO THREE

Just to meet three women in a row who Leo connected with so deeply was a miracle. He'd lost count of the detour women he dated in the two years between his marriage ending and meeting Elly, the first true relationship which only ended because Elly's biological clock suddenly began ticking. His dating slowed down a little in the two and a half years from that break-up to Zoya, but it must have been close to twenty. He heard countless complaints about how many frogs most women had to go through to find a prince.

Same swamp stats for guys.

Not counting the first year frenzy post-marriage, he dove into every date and relationship with long-term hope, his heart always half full. Unlike most men and many modern women, the big 'C' word—Commitment—wasn't a problem for him. Its cousins, Chemistry and Compatibility were more elusive. It took two to C and C.

Then he stumbled into Zoya, Aysha and Jade. Three smart, dynamic women in a row who'd captured his heart, and he somehow swelled theirs.

Crazy. Crazy-lucky maybe, but still crazy.

Now all three of them, with their own unique reasons and

personal circumstances, had to push his heart away, put their feelings on hold until November.

The very same November.

November, 2008.

Insane.

Normally he would have been drowning in melancholy deep into his torture songs over the frustrating situation with Jade, but the serendipity of the November thing dictated his thoughts, dominated his heart. At first, he couldn't help blurting out the situation with his sister, close friends and anyone else who would listen.

"It's a great story, you have to write it," said Bruce, echoing everyone else.

"It's not a story, it's my life. I want to end up with one of these women." He shifted the phone to his other ear.

"I don't know what to say, mate. It really is incredible. You need heaps of chocolate for this one."

"Yeah. The really good stuff."

Haigh's... Haigh's frogs and dark-mint buttons and...

"And if you meet another woman this week, don't be so bloody greedy. Give her MY number." Bruce unleashed his baritone laugh.

That infectious laugh. Took them a while to settle. He'd needed the release and Bruce's humor never let him down.

"See ya, Bruce."

"Bye, mate."

He relaxed back into the pillows on the futon. Bruce had shaken some perspective onto his myopic mess. Whatever happened in November, he'd been lucky to connect with three amazing women. None of the break-ups were clinical break-ups. Neither he nor the women had done anything stupid or hurtful. All three relationships were on hold. This wasn't something to get down about. Thousands, maybe millions of lonely souls would've given their right hand to have had one-third of his recent romantic luck.

But his heart clock wasn't built on the precision of logic and perspective.

Tick-fucking-tock, tick-fucking-tock, tick-fucking-tock. How do you possibly count down to this triple date in November? What do you even count?

ONE TWO THREE, FIVE SIX SEVEN. ONE TWO THREE, FIVE SIX SEVEN.

"And that's it for tonight," said Liz as she turned off the salsa music. "Great first lesson, everyone, this is going to be a fun term. See you all next week."

One two three, five six seven. Leo repeated the unusual beat as a mantra while he walked down Swan Street in Richmond, keen to mentally lock it in. He zipped up his coat as his body cooled in the frisky May night.

It was fun.

As soon as the music had started in the studio, he wondered why he'd been talking about salsa dancing all these years and never done anything about it. He'd been infatuated with the music since he was first mesmerized by couples sizzling around the dance floor at the Night Cat, his favorite club post-divorce. Liz was a brilliant dancer and gentle teacher.

Before he jumped into the car, he practiced the basic steps and unfamiliar timing on the pavement.

One two three, five six seven. One two three, five six seven.

Driving home, he was convinced he found the three-pronged strategy that would lead him to November with his sanity intact: salsa dancing, meditation, celibacy.

His meditation guide was the book Aysha had recommended, *A Path with Heart*. Giving up on 'longing' was a big message in the early chapters. He decided he'd need to give up on something important to him, like chocolate or sex. So, he committed to six months of celibacy. He wasn't aiming for Monk level. Six months of no sex by choice would prove a point to him and wind up conveniently in November.

Salsa lessons were a perfect avenue for social interaction with women for one hour a week without messy strings attached. Meditating five or more mornings a week tied it all up. Helped him resist contacting any of his November women.

He had no idea which one he'd end up with, or if he'd end up alone. The key was to live his life and avoid projecting or longing. Let everything play out in November and whatever rolled out in front of his heart, be in the moment.

Salsa. Meditation. Celibacy.

No contact with any of the three women.

"Hey, Zoya."

"Hi, Leo, is this a bad time?"

The busiest diversion plan, built on massive bricks of logic, crumbled from a swirl in his soul as soon he heard her voice. "Never a bad time."

"I've got some potential work for you."

Work. Of course.

"Okay, what have you got in mind?"

"We've got a couple of funding applications with mobile game elements. We need someone to assess the projects and write a short report. We can pay you five hundred per assessment, probably three to four hours work for each one. Do you have time?"

Probably seven or eight hours each, based on the same work he'd been doing for the state government funding agencies, but that's okay. "Sure. Thanks for thinking of me."

Silence for a beat.

"I'll get Bec to send you the docs. Thanks for helping out."

"It's good to hear your voice, Zoya." He bumped the conversation out of her work zone. Couldn't help it. A deep yearning to know if she missed him, if she was pregnant.

Longer silence.

"Got to go. Ciao, Leo."

"Ciao, Zoya."

Fascinating how the world works...how souls work. Zoya's call was all about work. But she called today, of all days.

The anniversary of their engagement. Friday night in July, exactly one year ago, he'd proposed naked to Zoya at her favorite little beach spot.

She wanted to, needed to connect with me today. But had to limit the conversation to work. Why?

He didn't try to analyze it any deeper. It was a nice moment and another easy gig. He'd leave it at that.

MEDITATING THE NEXT MORNING, ZOYA KEPT FLOATING INTO HIS MIND. Memories of her tapped away at his conscience post-meditation. Kept him company during a two-hour bike ride. So after showering, he picked up his phone and called.

"Hi, Liz, is there still a spot open for the beginners showcase?"

Liz was running a showcase for her salsa school in late October. It meant an extra two-hour class every Saturday morning, probably another practice session with his partner one night a week as well. Something else to focus on.

"Yes, Leo, I need a partner for Jill. You'd be perfect."

It meant a five-minute public performance on stage in front of a few hundred people. Choreography wasn't his forte, but Jill was good. Worst case scenario, he'd let her back-lead, as if he'd have a choice.

"Okay, count me in."

Potential public humiliation was more acceptable torture than scouring through every angle in his triangle-heart again and again and again.

Jade's photo had been teasing him on Facebook. Snippets of her life popping up that should've—could have—been shared moments. He thought about unfriending her. Never felt right. The strong thing to do was leave her in and not click on her posts, but Facebook's algorithms had kept calculating against him, testing him, teasing him.

Seemed like every time Jade posted something, Facebook sent a direct notification to his heart.

He'd gotten into a routine of meditating most mornings, at least ten to twenty minutes. Then he read a chunk from *A Path with Heart* with breakfast. Just looking at the book sent his heart to Aysha. Whenever he contemplated some of the wisdom from the pages, her velvet voice joined the discussion in his head. It was a natural conversation to have with her, real or imagined.

By July, he had managed to not mention or think of Zoya when he worked with Canberra-based Bridget on her project. Fortunately, or nobly, Bridget came to Melbourne for a creative workshop.

Bless her socks.

Avoiding Canberra physically was crucial for Leo, Canberra Airport a gateway into too many feelings he couldn't strap down with a plane's seatbelt. Somehow, he'd managed to lose his banged-up luggage with Zoya.

Until she called today...on our engagement anniversary.

He looked around his bathroom, unable to remember why he'd walked in there. Went back to his bedroom. Saw his sweaty Lycra and stuff from his bike ride on the floor, picked them up and drifted back to the bathroom.

Schemo.

Spun around and headed into the laundry then dumped the gear into the washing machine, but the lid was closed.

Schemo.

He needed to use the broom to scrape up a sock wedged in the small gap between the machine and wall. "Aww, fuck." He'd banged his head on the dryer above the washing machine. He rubbed his head then carefully bent over to work the sock up with the broomstick. Waved the sock over the sink to shake the dust and fluff off, opened the lid and dropped the smelly gear in.

Found himself leaning back on the kitchen bench, waiting for the kettle to boil. Looked at the kettle and shook his head. He'd come in to get a Gatorade out of the fridge. Flicked off the kettle, opened the fridge and grabbed the drink. Guzzled half the bottle in one go.

He wasn't sure if he was being nudged around by three elephants or one elephant with three women riding.

The fresh air and workout from the twenty-eight-mile bike ride hadn't been enough to escape that romantic jungle. He needed something else to clear his head. He shuffled over to his sound system in the lounge and hit play on the CD.

The vivacious beats of the tune Liz had selected for the beginners' performance simmered through his bones. He skittled over to the slippery kitchen floor tiles. Bent his knees a touch, white-socked heels automatically rising to the beat. Lifted his arms, imagining Jill's pretty but focused Chinese face in front of him, and let the rhythm dance his soul around the kitchen.

One two three, five six seven. One two three, spin, five six seven. One two three, side-turn, five six seven. One two three...

43

NOVEMBER 2008

A BSENCE MAKES THE HEART GROW FONDER IS A POPULAR TRUISM.

Leo had read an article with scientific confirmation. He'd proven it himself a couple of times. But neither his experience nor the research data could have predicted how his heart would deal with three absences that all drifted back into his life in the one month. Always been a 'one-woman in his heart kinda guy'.

Loyal.

Committed.

Obsessed. Therapy, reading and reflection had led him to this self-confession. Obsession was at the extreme spectrum of longing and fed unhealthy projecting, something he'd have to be more mindful of.

On his forty-eighth birthday in September, he'd lapsed into the *what if?* triangle of melancholy over his November women. Apart from those few days, the closer the calendar edged towards November, the calmer his inner world. Wasn't forced or based on any artificial mantras. He just felt stronger.

Absence makes the heart grow.

That was his new revelation—sometimes absence just makes the heart grow.

"You must have an inkling. There must be something about one of them that stands out by now?" asked Bruce.

Leo closed his eyes, laying back on the sun lounge in his courtyard, mobile to ear. With other people in recent months, he avoided the subject, not wanting to project or muddy the November waters. Mostly he regretted sharing the story because they all wanted to offer suggestions. Bruce was different, their talks having saved him thousands of dollars in therapy over the years, despite being based in Sydney.

"Aysha. Deep, deep down, if I had to make a prediction, I'd say Aysha."

"Why?"

"Because of the therapy she knows more about me than any of them. Yet she still likes me."

"She needs to call me. I'll sort her out of that foolishness."

They laughed.

"I trust her too. Unconditionally."

"Do you think you might've dodged a bullet with Zoya?"

He knew what Bruce meant. She obviously had a few more demons that her therapy hadn't exorcised yet, including her obsession with having a girl.

"I really don't know, Bruce. If the baby thing was off the table, it might take the whole edge off her stuff."

"Does that mean I can have Jade's number?"

Despite being nine years older, Bruce's romantic appetite and energy hadn't diminished.

"Kind of the same thing with her. If her husband's out of the picture—"

"But?" said Bruce.

"They say the best predictor of future behavior is past behavior and...her choices with her husband haven't made sense."

"So, I can have her number?"

"No. Speaking of past behavior, Aysha's relationship track record is quite messy too."

"You haven't got a bloody clue."

"No idea."

THE FIRST CONFERENCE LEO AND ZOYA BOTH ATTENDED SINCE SHE declared her baby-IVF mission fell in early November, almost exactly one year later. His Zoya sense hadn't lost any power during the event's opening cocktail party earlier, constantly aware of where she was. They'd both drifted to this couch at the same time, their hug and kiss, soft, warm, and friendly. A homecoming, when he hadn't realized he'd been homesick. He and Zoya had been marooned on their two-seater cane settee for about thirty minutes, oblivious to the cocktail-infused conference crowd around the pool.

"I laughed with the moon tonight. A private joke without a punchline, like so much of my lifetime. Waiting for wisdom to wash over me, shine a star on this mystery. I laughed with the moon tonight."

"That's beautiful, Leo. I can imagine you sitting in your courtyard at night, staring at the sky," said Zoya, pointing up at the glorious night sky.

"You triggered something in my creative bones last time we were up here. Before that, I hadn't written any poems since my twenties."

Her smile stayed but she stared down at her low-heeled black shoe, leg crossed over his way. "Two years ago." She faced him, "Ready but not prepared."

His inner world glowed that she'd remembered that first poem.

Splashes of color on her dark chocolate dress, which had scrunched up above her knees, skin on her thighs collaborating with her cleavage.

"Feels like yesterday," he said, then moved a wavy strand of hair that had fallen across her eyes. *Also feels like we're going to bed.*

He'd already forgotten what they'd joked about for the first twenty minutes or more. The content didn't matter. She laughed a lot, unconsciously stroking his calf with her foot.

He remembered that.

And the swing-thing with her eyes. His heart dizzy, navel assembling the machinery, in itself a relief, he'd been curious, maybe a touch concerned as to how his mechanics would work after six months of celibacy.

"It does feel like yesterday." Husky, sultry.

"Did I ever tell you your eyes are like marshmallow stars? Sweet and mushy and sparkly all at once."

Even under the low light he couldn't miss her cheeks flush red.

"Charming as ever."

"I miss waking up under them."

The tip of her tongue worked slowly around her lips. "Me, too. I'm staying here this time." She waved her hand towards the accommodation wing.

In Zoyaland, that's a yes.

It really was like they had never parted.

"Hello, Leo, Zoya." A deep Manchester accent.

He unstuck his eyes from Zoya's face to see Mount Giga.

"Hey, Giga," he said, standing and shaking his huge hand.

"Hi, Giga." Zoya waved from the couch.

"Sorry to interrupt," Giga said to Zoya, then leaned in close to Leo. "You haven't seen Lauren by any chance?"

The sheepish look and shy tone were unusual for the big man. Giga was hooked. It had looked like a perfect match for the two mega geeks back at the Cape Schanck workshop where Lauren was a first-time mentor, but shy time works slower than normal time.

"Saw her in a little alcove. Here, I'll show you." Leo turned back to Zoya. "Two seconds."

He guided Giga through the doors and pointed Lauren out in a corner, sitting with her trusty chaperone, her laptop.

"Don't know what to say," whispered Giga, as he subconsciously swung his laptop-appendage in his right hand.

Another example of love making the smartest people feel and act dumb. He tried to come up with something Giga could relate to. "When it comes to romance, content is not king."

Giga looked down at him.

"The key is to be in the same media platform at the same time, really be there. Love writes its own software, it's not something you can program."

Giga nodded once, then loped over to Lauren without a 'thanks' or 'good night', but Leo was happy for him, for both of them. Romance was definitely in the air.

Wild sex, too.

He rushed back out, but Zoya had disappeared. He scanned the area, no sign of her. Stepped back inside, not there either. He sat on the couch.

She's probably gone to the ladies' room to 'freshen up'.

Fifteen minutes later, still no Zoya. Phone screen said ten-thirty-seven. He sat back and called her number.

*Brrr, brrr. Brrr, brrr...*Rang into her voicemail.

Shit. Surely, she couldn't be angry that I took a minute to help Giga?

He thumbed off a text:

Hey, gorgeous, are you close? Or do you want me to come to your room?

Sat there as most of the delegates emptied the space, a familiar tightening in his stomach.

Don't be silly, Leo. It's been a while. It was a sweet reunion. Maybe she just had second thoughts about sex so quickly. That's fair enough.

His mission wasn't sex, it was much bigger than that.

She could've at least dropped me a text saying 'goodnight, see you tomorrow' or something...

But there was tomorrow, and the third day. She knew he'd be there. No rush.

"I KNOW THOSE SNEAKERS," SAID ZOYA AS SHE DESCENDED THE FINAL few steps with her one-woman entourage, Bec.

Late afternoon and Leo was checking his phone after a conference session, while Zoya headed for the room he'd just left.

Is that why I wore these today? My subconscious one step ahead again.

She pointed to his red Adidas sneakers. "But orange is the new red." A teasing tone, like Bec was in with the fashion joke and he wasn't. Zoya in an orange blouse, Bec with an orange-brown, V-neck dress.

"Orange works on you."

"Ha! What a charmer."

Last night I was charming, today a charmer.

"Got a sec?"

"Not really, next session's about to start." Her stare was laced with icicles of indifference.

The hairs on his back stood to attention. Even by Zoya standards, the polar shift from their intimate moment on the couch the previous night spun his inner world off balance.

But he stood his ground.

Zoya stood hers, broken by a quick glance to Bec.

"I'll save us a seat," Bec said as she headed in.

He led Zoya away from the throng to a private space under the stairwell.

"You disappeared last night," she said.

"I disappeared? You..."

He took a breath. Back in the familiar Zoya spectrum, complete avoidance or mortal combat. All Scorpio.

Took another long breath. "I said I'd be a minute."

"I didn't hear that. One second, we're all cozy, then you're running off with Giga."

He studied his recently out-of-fashion red sneakers. He could've pointed out his unanswered phone call and text. Unanswered since last night. "Zoya, we're not a couple of teenagers, stumbling to a first date. We were cozy because..."

Because we're still in love? Because we were once engaged and still can't help ourselves whenever we're together. Because we're confused? How many times were these questions going to bog him down? Slap them down?

"Session beginning in thirty seconds." The volunteer closed one door and stood with her hand on the other.

Zoya looked across to the door, back at him. "I know our history, Leo, I was there." It was served with a bucket of ice over his head. She shuffled towards the door.

"Dinner tonight?" It came out desperate and in a way he was. Desperate for clarity. Desperate to avoid more avoidance.

She shook her head.

He remembered the big conference dinner. He wasn't going because he couldn't imagine himself at a long party in the same room as Zoya unless they'd tied up their loose end with a forever-after knot, or forever-never noose.

"Let's do lunch by the pool. Twelve-thirty. We can pretend we're in Cannes." Full smile, sweet tone, squeeze of his arm.

Just when he thought he'd worked out Zoya's extreme spectrum, she slapped another one over the top like a cross.

If she wasn't a Scorpio Superstar, she'd be the poster-girl for Geminis.

44

RIGHT

 and two glasses with the other hand.

That's got to be a good sign. She wasn't drinking on IVF. That means the baby thing is definitely off the table.

Leo was glad he'd gotten out there early and scored the furthest table from the hotel and pool, the closest to the beach. The more distance between her and the work environment, the better.

He got up to help with the bucket, but she plonked it on the table with the help of her hip. He kissed one cheek then went for the other one, Italian style, but she turned away and slumped into the chair.

Zoya took off her sunglasses and rubbed her temples. Heavy makeup couldn't hide dark, baggy eyes almost as furrowed as her brow.

"Big night?"

"Yeah."

She slipped her sunglasses back on, filled one glass, picked up the other.

"No thanks, I'm good." He emptied his little Chinnoto bottle over the remaining ice in his glass. "I'll get some food from the buffet for us."

"Don't feel like food, help yourself." She skolled more than half her glass.

Drowned his appetite.

"I take it you're not on the IVF thing anymore?"

"You have no right to ask me that question." Forty-four caliber finger shooting at him

A black pot of disbelief and disappointment simmered in his gut, steamed his chest, burnt his heart.

She picked up the bottle, filled her glass, had a gulp.

"I have more right to ask that question than anyone on the planet."

She stared at her beloved Pinot Gris.

"I just thought..." He didn't know what he thought. His tightening body was screaming, *shut up...go get some food...jump in the pool.*" "I just thought with you drinking again it meant you'd given up on—"

The heat from her glare burned through her sunglasses.

"How convenient for you. And don't start with the alcoholic thing again."

He didn't start anything again. His soul drifted away from the hotel, stopped under the shady trees near the beach, recognizing the ending with Zoya, waving him to catch up, a few steps ahead of his mindfulness.

Slap. Slap. Slap. When a woman keeps slapping you with your own heart, eventually you had to see past the shock, the numbness. The delusion.

Enough endings with Zoya.

He peeled himself off the cushioned chair and stood before her. She looked up but didn't rise or remove her sunglasses. He put his hand on her cheek and kissed her forehead. As he turned to leave, she held his hand with both of hers for a few seconds, then kissed his palm. When she let go, her head dropped down and he shuffled away.

"Bruce was right, I did dodge a bullet."

Leo knew the brown ducks with white flecks weren't listening, they were just keen to get their dark beaks to the bread he was throwing into the river. He'd tried to not over-think it for a couple of days following their private pool anti-party. Same as cream, your deepest feelings rose to the top as long as you didn't keep stirring around and around with spoons of logic and doubt or mix in fear and projection or sprinkle anger and blame. Life, especially Western activity-is-everything life, had a way of diverting you from feeling the cream.

By the time he sat on 'his rock' on the Yarra, so close to home, so far from the world, he knew he wasn't misleading the ducks. His heart was clear. He did love Zoya, and she once loved him. But her heart was muddied like the flowing waters in front of him. She blamed him for not having a baby yet deep down, he was sure her career and Canberra nest meant more to her than maybe she even understood.

He hadn't run, always believing they'd work their way around the logistics and other potholes.

"There's something special about a mountain meeting the ocean," she'd *said at Batemans Bay. I was the relentless waves crashing against her beautiful stubborn mountain.*

He laughed, scaring the ducks away.

She probably thinks exactly the same thing about me.

There were a bit of waves and rocky mountains in both of them. Their tides simply didn't align, some of their jagged edges too sharp. Yet the good with Zoya was special, fun, amazing.

"No fruity dog," he said to the returning ducks.

He smiled at Zoya's little play on words. There, indeed, was no melancholy.

In her own way she had taught him that the stages of moving on after a romantic relationship are a little different from the classic stages of grief: respect, appreciation, fondness, forgiveness. He respected her choices even though he didn't fully understand them. Appreciated the chance to meet her, love her, and their mutual courage to fully explore unmapped caves together. He would always be fond of Zoya. And he forgave her, even for the physical attack. Even the 'Dear Leo' email.

Zoya would forever have a special place in the museum in his heart. Bones of memories he'd flesh out now and then. Might make him smile or laugh, but not pine.

"Probably the last time he'll let me kiss him goodbye."

Leo stared at the post on his Facebook newsfeed. Jade and her 'baby', Pablo, in a series of selfies: kissing him on his grimacing cheek, hugging side by side, and another of him waving goodbye as he left for his end of school mayhem with his mates. Threw him back to the same time with James. On one hand, there's a collective family sigh as the stress and tension of the final high school year is pushed out the door. On the other, it's a seminal moment when your boy edges a little closer to being his own man.

No Brendan Monster in sight. Has he already been pushed out the door too?

Powerful.

Urge.

To call her.

He wasn't sure what the right procedure would be late in November and Jade wasn't an old-fashioned *the guy must make all the moves* kind of woman.

Looking closer at the photos, he sensed this might not be the right moment. She needed time to work through the emotions of her son 'suddenly' being a grown-up and closer to flying the nest.

He clicked 'like'.

That would remind her of him, if she needed reminding. Appropriate too, as this post was the line in the sand that had kept their beaches apart. Her son had completed his VCE. No other hurdles or reasons for Brendan Monster to hang around, or for Jade to stay away from Leo.

Orange café. Not a good sign.

Shook Leo back to Zoya's '*Orange is the new red*' barb. Jade's suggestion for dinner was near the restaurant where they had dinner six months earlier. Dinner and tram jumping and kissing and hugging. At least that was a good sign, like her quick text suggesting dinner following his Facebook 'like'.

She looked good, no question there, wrapped in bohemian layers and colors that blended in with the tinges of orange on the walls and dark brown timber around the café. She bounced up from the little couch in the corner when she saw him, her smile adding to the glittering bottles and wall mirror behind the bar.

"You look like a seventies rock goddess."

Her smile found another impossible level of sugary warmth that permeated through his skin and ribs until it gurgled in his heart.

"Stevie Nicks meets Carole King, but prettier."

She whirled around, then checked out his burgundy paisley shirt, blue jeans, and steel-blue boots. "Like, hey, man, I'm digging your groove too," she said in husky Californian. Pretended to take a puff of an imaginary joint in her hand, inhaled deep then blew imaginary smoke to the ceiling before flicking the 'joint' over her shoulder. "Come here, you dummy."

He walked into her open arms. Another homecoming. No smoke or mirrors, real and as loving as a hug could be. They sat down close, angled towards each other. Talked about their favorite seventys singers and bands until his Campari and soda arrived. Jade was already into a vodka and soda.

He lifted his glass. "Here's to revolving bars and silly white parties."

"To revolting bars and Barry White parties."

They clinked glasses.

"Those photos with your son are cute."

Her eyes brightened while her tight lips upturned a touch.

How does she do that? Joy and sadness in one look?

"My baby's all grown up. If he gets in, says he wants to live at the Uni hall."

"If they grow up any faster, they'll be older than us soon."

She laughed, held his chin with her fingers "You're doing okay. I still don't believe you're forty-seven."

"Forty-eight now."

"Oh, dear, that old? I thought you were my toy boy."

"Toy boy? I thought you loved me for my mind?" Throwing 'loved me' in was his machete trying to carve a path back to their romantic camp.

She studied him for a couple of seconds, head on angle, then turned to her vodka. "How old were you when you first kissed a girl?"

"Ten or eleven, grade five. But my first crush was in grade two, just seven years old."

"Seven?" she said, incredulous.

He nodded. "I still remember walking through the school at lunchtime holding Leanne's hand, some of the older kids stirring us and wolf-whistling. In hindsight, I guess that's proof that romantics are born, not made."

Now Jade's eyes had dulled but her mouth was smiling. She turned away, picked up her glass and finished it.

"Another vodka?" he said.

"Brendan isn't moving out."

45

FACING FORWARD

BRENDAN ISN'T MOVING OUT.

She'd made her confession to the squished lime at the bottom, hands gripping the drained glass like it was Brendan's neck.

Or Leo's heart.

His soul must've done some quiet work in the background, preparing him for the worst, because he wasn't shocked or angry.

"Are you happy about that?" Some fight still left in him. Was it a survival reflex? A competitive male thing? Or the last dribbles from his drying well of a hopeful heart.

She rolled the glass between her hands. Shrugged her shoulders a touch. "What's happy." Not a question, each syllable weighed down with defeat.

"You were happy last time we met up the road...and on the tram, and when we kissed at the Circuit Bar. And—"

"I was on happy pills." She looked up. "I've been on anti-depressants since he first left. You haven't met the real me. Who even knows what the real me is anymore?"

Clobbered by his own rule, his only rule: don't go out with a woman separated or divorced until at least two years after her separation. It always took at least that long for the person who'd been left behind. The person instigating the leaving did a lot of their grieving leading up to the end. For Jade, it was still lingering eighteen months later.

She poked at her lime with a straw, every stab spiking straight through his heart.

"How do you throw away twenty-five years?" she asked.

You didn't throw it away, he threw it in your face. All the grains of the sands of your time together... without any care for you at all. A public humiliation.

"The boys are much happier this way."

The messy complications of a destructive marriage when children were involved. Whatever tension gurgled through his veins diluted.

He couldn't argue with her. She knew the dysfunctional situation with his ex-wife, how it messed with the kids. He felt sorry for Jade, for what the monster had dragged her through, but he'd learned the hard way from Michele, feeling sorry for a woman comes from the same recipe as love—care and kindness—but sprinkling 'feeling sorry' as the main ingredient was no recipe for a long-term relationship.

"Anyway, you should be with someone younger and—"

He put his finger on her mouth. "Now who's being a dummy? Come here." He leaned back into the couch and pulled her in tight. She rested her head on his chest. He enjoyed her warmth and perfume, a hint of...his damn nose could never pick a fragrance.

They stayed like that for ages, at least ages in their short and intense romantic timescale.

"I'm another wife," she said, muffled in his shirt.

"You're another wife? You mean the jerk has—"

She pulled up smiling through glistening eyes, "In another life, you dummy."

They laughed, releasing tension, sadness, and frustration.

When they settled down, he took her hands, rubbing his thumbs over her warm skin. "In another life."

He leaned in and kissed her cheek, closing eyes as his lips lingered.

She let go a long sigh before opening her eyes, wiping tears with the back of her hand.

So many '*could've*' with Jade had they met younger, but no '*should've*' when they did meet. That little glimmer of pride was something worth hanging onto. Nobody knew for sure if we'd get a peek at another life. All he and Jade could have done was to give their romance every chance in the circumstances they'd been dealt. He had.

He leaned back into the couch and Jade snuggled into his chest for the last time. Smelling like goodbye.

JADE'S LOOKING BACKWARDS ON THE TRAM OF HER LIFE. I SIT ON THE OTHER side looking forward. Maybe a genius would have worked it out, maybe someone half smart, maybe someone awake. Our romantic tram ride was always going to be short.

Even if Brendan had been cut from Jade's life, his roots cast such a large shadow in her heart, there wasn't room for her to tangle up with anyone else. No trust left to sustain the faith needed for love. Leo had seen similar twisted shadows in the hearts of other women. Some men too, but mostly women. Some only had the strength, the courage, for one big love.

He pushed his sunglasses up to rest on his head as the sun dipped beneath the trees. There wasn't enough light for a ride after the Café Orange goodbye, so he'd taken a walk, ending up at the suspended footbridge across the Yarra, near Finns Reserve. The river snaked relentlessly through most of Templestowe, but a straight stretch of water, about seven hundred yards, ran from the east, under the bridge to the west. Orange light bounced off clouds.

Bloody orange.

His legs wobbled and he grabbed onto the wooden rail so deep in thought, for a moment he was afraid the hot spring evening and his heavy heart were overwhelming him.

"Rosana, stop running, you'll hurt the man," said a female voice.

He snapped out of his thoughts to see a girl walking past, dangling a kite over her shoulder at the end of a couple of feet of string, her parents behind, the bridge swaying a fraction to their collective steps. As soon as Rosana passed him, she sprinted to the other bank with her arm raised and the kite flying behind her.

"Sorry," said the mother.

"Don't know where she gets her energy," said the dad, winking at Leo and pointing at his wife.

"It's okay. I have three boys," said Leo.

He watched the girl run with her kite until she ran behind trees. When he turned back to the river it was darker, the light under the few clouds changing from orange to crimson-purple.

Amazing how slow it goes down and then the last few minutes whiz by. Just like his November sunset. Staring at a romantic oasis with three women for an eternity... then whoosh, two were just a mirage.

A flock of pink galahs soared overhead and disappeared into the trees. A shimmer of light on the water triggered a smile. For a few weeks in spring and autumn you could watch the sunset from this bridge as the moon rose in the east.

He blew a kiss to the sunset.

To Zoya.

To Jade.

Turned to the other side of the bridge and smiled at the new moon.

Is that Aysha grinning at me from the sky? Did she sense she was the last woman standing in November? Was she patiently orbiting my heart... waiting for a clear landing zone?

"HELLO, AYSHA," HE SAID AS HE WAS DRIVING. DESPITE THE EAR PLUGS with cable dangling to his phone with the tiny microphone in the 'V' half-way, saying hello to Aysha sounded as natural as breathing.

"Who's that?" said Aysha.

Not so natural.

"Leo, your November man."

Silence. He pressed his right earpiece in tighter.

"Aysha? You called me. Are you okay?"

"Ha! I was calling my lawyer, Len. Must've hit your name by mistake."

If I had a dollar for every time a woman hid behind the called-you-by-accident excuse...

"Lucky for you I don't charge like a lawyer."

"How's your inner world?"

Her voice oozed through the ear plugs and into his heart and belly like warm soup after a cold rainy day at the boys' soccer game.

"Good, thanks. I've got more maps now and I spend time frolicking in there...getting to know the place."

"That's a nice image."

He pulled into the parking lot outside the village shops. "You know it's over a year now. Maybe your inner world dialed my number?"

"Maybe it did. But I do have to call Len before lunch."

"Lunch sounds like a great idea."

More silence. Really? She had to think about it? He let out a long breath, relaxing his neck back onto the head rest. They were still in an extraordinary situation. A challenge on her career. *Give her a break.*

"Yes, that would be nice."

Nice. When Aysha said the word, it meant exactly what it was supposed to mean. Nice. Nice, nice, nice.

"Sunday?" He knew he was pushing it. Sunday was just three days away, the last day of November.

"Mmm..."

Sounded like a no was coming. He closed his eyes and silently repeated a mantra he'd learned from the book Aysha had recommended and spun it for her: *May she be filled with loving kindness. May she be peaceful and at ease. May she be happy and well. May she be filled with loving kindness. May she—*

"If it's Sunday, let's do brunch. If you have the time, of course?"

Was she kidding? Did she really have no idea I'd cancel my whole year for her?

"Perfect."

"Do you mind if we go somewhere in Fitzroy? There's a little market there I haven't been to for ages."

"You know I love the color and movement in Fitzroy and Collingwood."

"Okay, you can choose the café. I'll pick you up at ten," she said.

"And I'll pick you up at ten-oh-one and swirl you around like a teddy bear."

She laughed. "Ciao, Leo. Ciao."

"Ciao, bella."

LEO HAD BEEN TO THE ROSE STREET ARTIST'S MARKET YEARS AGO, BUT Aysha lifted it to a different dimension. Every stall-keeper wanted to chat with her. She had the unique gift to connect instantly with all of them. They proudly shared stories about the ethos of their crafts or their children's adventures. Many were generating donations or running projects for third-world communities.

It was hot in the tight outdoor section and stuffy inside the larger shed area, yet Aysha soaked up every product and story. He lifted his straw hat to wipe sweat off his forehead. He couldn't see a speck of perspiration on Aysha or her floral sundress, which was white with splashes of golden yellow and blue flowers that ended just above her knees.

He could've watched her hands dance through the air, her little nose twitch with curiosity, and the flames flicker in her eyes all day. At brunch earlier, Aysha didn't just eat, she infused every aroma, each delicate flavor like it might be her last taste on earth.

"I want to buy you something you can have as a memento for today and everything we've had to go through just to get here." He pointed at the African-themed paintings with vivid colors and striking human shapes.

She stared at him, deep, serious. Threw him back to her therapy office. Had he pushed it with the gift idea? Was she recoiling from his pedestal building?

"Okay. Over here." She grabbed his hand and led him to the leather craft stall. After perusing the many options, she pointed at what looked like a thin, plain, leather necklace, "That would be wonderful."

"Really? That's all?"

She nodded.

He paid and gave it to her. She opened her colorful little canvas shoulder bag, rummaged around for a while then pulled out something wrapped in purple tissue paper. She smiled. Was it a gift she'd been carrying for him? Had he underestimated her inner romantic? Super shy, hidden inner romantic?

She didn't hand the gift to him, instead unwrapping the paper to reveal the infinity pendant he'd given her earlier that year.

His heart filled with love helium so fast, he grabbed the side of the stall, afraid he'd float away. All the doubts anchored deep in his heart and soul drifted away.

Forever.

"How long have you been carrying that around?"

"Is that Ego man asking?"

"No, it's lover boy."

Her sweet smile and eyes must've seared the temperature above total-fire-ban levels.

She attached the pendant to the leather chain, put it on over her head and pulled her long hair through.

"Beautiful. Perfect," he said.

She stepped up on her toes and kissed his cheek.

His lips were getting extremely jealous of those lucky cheeks.

"Can we sit somewhere, have a drink?" Her voice was soft, almost a whisper.

He couldn't tell if it was emotion or tiredness. "Of course. You okay?"

"I...it's been a crazy few months."

Mega understatement.

You know it's been a special first date when brunch starts at ten-thirty and you're still enjoying each other's company five hours later. After topping up their sugar levels post-market, they walked to her car holding hands. At her car, she wrapped her hands around his back and kissed him on the lips. Passion poured out of her petite frame with ferocious heat and power, all the New Year's Eve fireworks from every city in the world for a private crowd of two.

Her body melded into him like seasoned dancers to the music orchestrated by their lips, conducted by their tongues. Time floated away. Their ridiculously complex fifteen-month history floated away, three as therapist-client, twelve in romance limbo. That one dreamy, fiery kiss could've been a teaching video for delayed gratification.

It would have gone viral.

46

PATTERNS

"Wow, I kissed Leo Devecchio."

Shapes passed behind her on the sidewalk, his eyes mesmerized by her campfire eyes.

"We started that kiss on the last day of November and I think it's Christmas now," he said.

"Christmas..." Aysha snuggled in tight. "My early present."

He liked romantic Aysha. "Can't wait till we unwrap it." So many ideas flying through his head and other parts of his body, but he kept his hands on her lower back.

"Mmmm... that's a nice image."

As soon as Aysha pulled up in front of his place, he unclipped his seat belt and leaned over to kiss her, making a wild man face.

Aysha laughed and laughed.

When she settled down, she unclipped her seatbelt and eased over, leading with her lips. Time looked the other way again.

Aysha eventually pulled back, rubbing her ribs. "Sorry, this console isn't very romantic."

He leaned across the stubborn console and nuzzled her neck. "We should go inside."

"I'm really tired and I still have a long drive."

He would have been delighted with the date ending after brunch. Delirious at the pendant magic moment at the market. Drunk with the first kiss fireworks on the pavement.

"Okay, time is on our side now."

Her eyes dulled like a city blackout.

"I...I'm..."

He sensed the love in her hesitant and husky syllables. He kissed her.

"Today..."

"Let's not label today. It doesn't need words. Let it ripple over the next few days, trickle through the months, flow into years."

Her face, the angle of her eyes, he'd never seen her so vulnerable. Made bits of his heart melt and ooze down to his belly. He caressed her cheek with the back of his fingers.

"I'll call you tomorrow," she said.

"Ciao, beautiful Aysha."

"Ciao, Leo."

The short goodbye kiss felt like a tiny commercial bar after gorging on boxes of Belgium chocolate delicacies. But he wasn't complaining. He got out, walked around to her door and opened it.

"I need to hold you properly one more time before you go."

"You're crazy."

She slid out. He picked her up and whirled her around, just like she made his heart swirl every time he saw her.

Aysha shrieked.

He put her down then backed away, smile beaming. "You like my crazy." Blew her a kiss.

Aysha caught it and blew it straight back at him, slipped into the car and drove off.

AYSHA DIDN'T CALL HIM THE NEXT DAY AND HE WAS COMFORTABLE WITH that. Nothing she could have said would have made the date more memorable or captured its essence. He knew Monday was her longest day, weekends being dark times for many of her clients. He enjoyed letting their special moment breathe.

*Breathe...breathe...*Leo hit pause on the EPL highlights show—his Monday evening ritual during the English football season—and skipped to his desk. Pulled out his thick profile Paper Mate pen and wrote like he was possessed, struggling to keep up with the words pouring through his mind and out the thick blue ink. What he ended up with didn't have any real structure. As he read the printed words, he wasn't sure if it was a letter, a poem, or poetic letter.

Last Breath
You asked me once
If my last wakeful breath at night
Was going in or out?
I could not answer.
You told me about a man,
So mindful, he knew each night
Which was his last breath before sleep.
If we twist the words
And you ask me which breath I would prefer,
My answer is clear and simple.
The last breath I want to be aware of
Before sleep carries me away,
The last breath I want to feel
At the end of each day... is yours.
Your breath on the valley of my neck,
Your breath on my shoulder,
Your breath on my floating chest,
Your breath on my protective arm.
We don't know how many breaths we have
During this miracle of life.
Patience is a virtue

Procrastination a disease.
Sometimes, slowly, our hearts forget to breathe.
I've met a million women and loved a few,
Was loved by one or two.
Didn't always choose the best direction
But was never afraid to choose.
All my path was an education,
Preparation.
For the day I met you.
Let your last breath be with me,
Let me resuscitate your heart,
Blow trust back into your soul.
Let's dance till we're breathless
And breathe in the stillness of meditation.
Not look back on this time
With the heavy sigh of regret.
Ripples from my soul
The honest words I would write.
If this were my last breath.

He folded it into an envelope, wrote her address, licked a stamp, and stuck it on. He almost floated down the street to the corner letter box, then posted it.

Such a romantic paradox: the longer the gap from their Sunday magic brunch, the sweeter the memory, the more Leo craved to be with her again. The subconscious outpouring in the epic poetic letter wasn't from desperation or anything to do with the November madness. The words reflected his raw feelings for Aysha, and he was convinced to his core that she felt the same.

He resisted till Thursday night, calling her mobile but it rang out and led him to her voicemail.

"Hey, beautiful, looking forward to hearing your smile again. Maybe dinner and flamenco show this Saturday night? Ciao."

No response by Saturday morning, so he sent her a text. Over the next couple of weeks, he sent four or five texts and left three messages, the last couple checking she was okay health-wise.

No response.

Sent two emails.

Nothing.

Not even a "Sorry, Leo, something's come up, call you soon."

How could she go through a year of waiting for their magical first date, then shut shop for over two weeks? That wasn't good for the heart business. Highly unfair to your sole customer.

Was she overwhelmed by '*Last Breath*'? Of all the people on the planet who should respect his honesty, clarity, surely it was Aysha.

Let down? Betrayed? He couldn't define the dark river bubbling inside him. Nothing was clear, the undercurrent scary.

The year wound down workwise, which just gave him more time to get frustrated. Long chats with Bruce didn't help. Neither did long bike rides, or grueling, three sets of tennis with Paul. Meditation must've helped but it wasn't something he could measure.

He refused to stalk her in Sassafras. They deserved better. He deserved better. He gave into calling her office number, scrunched up on the edge of a picnic chair in his courtyard.

Brrr-brr, brrr-brr...

It was a workday, so she should be around. If something major had happened, her message would have changed.

Brrr-brr, brrr-brr...

"Hello, you have called the office of Aysha Le Ferre. Please leave a message and I'll get back to you as—"

He hung up on her professional voice. He'd sensed his anger bubbling and didn't want to spill it onto her voicemail. He shoved the phone into the pocket of his shorts and slumped back. Felt the sun burning his arms, legs, and face. Fuck it. His heart was already scorched.

Sorry, Leo, do you have time for coffee this afternoon? Carluccis?
Dropping off Anna-Marie in Eltham about four.

Leo flicked from her text to his phone's home page to confirm the date: Friday 19
December.
Nineteen days. She really did want their first kiss to last till Christmas.
Tension flowed out of his back and neck, made him three feet taller. A mixture of excitement and trepidation swirled between his heart and gut. The text gave no clues, no explanation.
Did she need nineteen days to work out how she really felt? Surely, I wasn't imagining the magic that day? I didn't push any of it. She kissed me.

"Hey, beautiful, you look cute."
Heat sizzled off the brick paving, yet Aysha wore her little denim vest buttoned over a long-sleeved blouse and long white skirt and cute ankle boots. One of his favorite combos during his therapy sessions.
She smiled and pecked him on the lips before sitting.
He was expecting more than a peck.
At least she's here at Carlucci's, at our table. And she does look good.
Until she removed her chunky sunglasses and revealed a hollow face with eyes too heavy for the skin below.
His heart skipped a beat. She'd made the effort even though she was obviously under the weather. Maybe she'd been sick the last few weeks? He leaned on the table. After the torturous absence, he needed to be as close as possible.
They talked about his children while waiting for their order. She was evasive about her own kids. He hoped nothing major had happened.
Her chai latte and his Chinotto arrived, breaking the small talk.

He'd given Aysha every opportunity to start the real conversation. He jabbed the slice of lemon with the straw, extracting as much juice as possible, then poured the small bottle over the ice. Took a sip while sneaking a look.

Aysha focused on her chai latte, hands wrapped around the hot glass.

"You had me worried."

She looked up, face apologetic and caring. Flames barely flickering in her eyes. Sitting at a right angle, she faced forward again.

"Maybe I'm losing my judgment, but our first date seemed special."

She nodded, eyes on the distant hills.

"You froze me out for nearly three weeks and all I get is a nod."

His old passive-aggressive train built up steam. He didn't want it to leave the depot, consciously pushed it back, but she did owe him an explanation. He'd resisted the possibility of her not wanting to see him again, but the more Chinotto he sipped, the more it seemed a reality. The aftertaste of his favorite drink seemed more bitter than usual. He poured the rest of the bottle into his glass, as if that would help.

Aysha turned to him, leaned closer, put her hand on top of his. Despite the warm weather, and her unusually heavy clothes, her skin was cold.

"It was very special. The best first date I've ever had." She stroked the hairs from his wrist to knuckles.

Something in her tone and elusive eyes triggered his back hairs into emotional radar mode, pinging a *but* to his brain. A scary *but I can't do this* or something-like-that-but.

She stopped stroking, held his hand tight.

"I'm sick, Leo. A blood immune disease. Every month the results have been worse. Last month's test was...Doctors give me three months, six if I'm...lucky."

Her eyes wide, studied his reaction.

Tornados of grief, love, and despair crashed through his heart, spun his stomach tight and blacked out his brain. His spare hand closed over hers. A fragile, soft hand sandwiched between his, their romance sandwiched between a magical first date and her crushing illness.

In a third-person experience, he took out some money, placed it on the table, got up and led her to his car, holding hands. She followed without hesitation.

"IS THIS WHAT YOU WERE TRYING TO TELL ME... AT THE END OF THE date?" he said.

Aysha nodded.

The bench seat away from the gravel track, shaded by towering ghost gums was secluded, apart from the occasional fly. The river current below headed towards them then broke left in a wide sweeping bend. A mini rip dragged branches and leaves under the surface a few yards from the right bank.

"How are your kids?"

Her face lost all life, even her eyes.

Even HER eyes.

"Sorry, stupid question."

He raised his arm, she slid closer, nuzzling into his shoulder.

"It's fucked-up and anti-fair," she said. "That's what my Anna-Marie keeps saying. Poor baby." He'd never heard Aysha swear, not even close.

"Totally fucked up."

"Whatever energy and time I have left...I need it for them."

"Of course." He never felt more devastated agreeing to anything, like he'd cut his own heart out and thrown it into the rip.

He squeezed her tighter. Aysha was facing true devastation. She was dying, yet for both hearts, there was no cure.

47

LOVE AND DEATH

Aysha wanted six weeks to get through Christmas and the school holidays with her kids without any communication from him. He'd honored her request, except for her Christmas gift.

Strange walking up to her front door. For all their connection, he'd only ever walked down the side driveway to her bungalow office out the back twelve times, and once to her letter box, never inside her home. He placed the package on the retro wooden chair that was keeping guard on the front porch, chimes tinkling above.

Back in his car, out of sight of the house, he imagined her face when she discovered it. A cold clamp gripped his stomach, squashing the air out of him, eyes clenched in reflex.

How could death take away those campfire eyes? They are a gift to the world.

He thumped the steering wheel. Thumped it again. It jolted one of his favorite quotes from E. James Rohn into his head: *Sometimes things just happen. Sometimes things happen, just.*

She had an amazing spirit, healthy lifestyle. Still alive. While she was fighting, there was always hope. A cure or tiny miracle of nature could bounce her DNA into the air and rearrange the perfect puzzle of Aysha, with that blood immune piece in the bin.

He started the car, hit the 'back to start' button on his CD player. Anastacia wrapped an arm around him with her voice. He eased down the winding road, listening to the track that Aysha had chosen as 'their song'. By the time the last line poured out, *'You'll never be alone,'* his eyes were flooded. He had to pull over into a parking lot and release the blubbering mess of his soul.

THE SHADOW OF DEATH SHINED LIGHT WHERE IT MATTERED MOST. LEO made sure he squeezed out every experience and laugh he could with his boys during the holidays.

Three busy weeks with Tommy and Jake from Christmas day, including a ten-day break in Sydney staying at Bondi beach. The day after he dropped them back at their mum's, James moved in for a week. Leo was proud of the man his eldest son had become after just one year in the Air Force. They played pool at the pub, caught a Thirsty Merc gig, watched sports, and talked for hours about his RAAF adventures and goals.

Despite the engrossing fun with all his boys, every single night in bed, Aysha waltzed into his head and tormented him with two dilemmas. The first was the lack of contact. He should be there to support her, to make her laugh more than she might have, to hold her. Was it love and kindness or guilt? He was honoring her wish, but should he be?

The other Aysha snag he was struggling to untangle shamed him. Once the school holidays were over, was he strong enough to begin a relationship with a dying woman? What was the right thing for both of their hearts, their souls? Did he even have a choice? Was his heart already sitting on the chair on her front porch, waiting for her to open the door?

Death answered for him.

Leo had watched many film and TV scenes where a character was advised of a death of someone close to them, how they buckled at the knees and dropped to the floor from the shock of the news. He'd wondered if that was started by one creative actor and all after him mimicked the performance.

Until he got that phone call.

"Natalie died...my baby...she's dead, Leo," said his sister, Maria, in between deep, raw sobs.

His thirteen-year-old niece, the only princess in a family of boys, died on the Murray River near Echuca, Friday night of the Australia Day weekend.

It wasn't the weight of shock that made his knees buckle, his own life force sucked out of him. Every bone and muscle crumpled. He was just useless clothes draped over lifeless skin on the floor.

"Oh, Maria..."

James tip-toed into the kitchen, concern on his face, as Leo listened to Maria's request. Even though Maria had called an hour earlier to tell him Natalie had crashed into a tree stump while she was hanging onto a biscuit—a large inflatable donut towed behind a jet-ski—his soul couldn't possibly brace him for the worst case.

He was strong until Maria had hung up. Then he dropped the phone and wailed in between earthquake tremors of pain ripping through every molecule.

James drove Leo to his parents' home. Lucky James was there. Leo cried through the whole fifteen-minute journey until they turned into the street when he fought to compose himself. Without question, telling his parents their only granddaughter had died was the most difficult thing he had ever done. Previously, it was when Michele and he told their boys they were getting a divorce and he was moving out. Trivial in comparison.

THE NEXT EIGHT MONTHS WERE A HAZE BETWEEN CHERISHING HIS OWN kids and the hopeless helplessness of not being able to do anything worthwhile for his baby sister. Leo could manage work, just. In hindsight, it was a strange, zombie-like existence.

He'd sent Aysha a short text about Natalie soon after the funeral in early February. She never responded. He was okay with that. Now that death had slammed him into a depressing wall of grief, he'd also become clear on his Aysha dilemma. He couldn't start a relationship with her knowing she was dying. He was struggling to spend the time he wanted with his sister and boys, let alone a new relationship.

Even clearer, there was no way he could drag his boys and family through another death so soon. He never contacted her, and nothing came from Aysha's world.

NINE MONTHS LATER, LEO GOT A CALL IN THE LAST WEEK OF September, 2009.

"Hey, Leo, did you see the article about Aysha in the Australian?" asked Bruce.

Leo placed *A Most Wanted Man* next to him, pages splayed open, facing down.

Aysha's obituary?

If you have an emotional limit for facing the tragic death of someone close—the red-raw grief, the acid tears, the horrible injustice—he had been drifting at ninety-five to one hundred percent since Natalie's fatal Friday night in January. He didn't know if he had anything left for Aysha. He slumped back and closed his eyes, head resting on the high back of the futon.

His eyelids flung open. Adrenalin surged through him.

Bruce is one of the most caring and sensitive people I know... his tone was chirpy.

"What article?"

"She's still alive. You should get it, looks like she's fully recovered."

Bruce's excitement surfed the airwaves, surged through Leo's phone, and ripped off the hope valve in his heart.

48

NOVEMBER 2009

Leo framed his hands over the newspaper photo isolating Aysha's face. Not only was she alive but flourishing. The care in her smile, her eyes.

HER CAMPFIRE EYES.

Aysha and some colleagues had been doing voluntary counseling for Black Saturday bushfire survivors—that tragedy in early February had passed by him and his family while they drowned with grief over Natalie—group talks every Wednesday night, individual sessions on Saturday. Aysha was obviously back to full strength.

But not back in touch. Why?

He looked beyond his dining table to the hill in the distance. Grey and windy, more winter than spring.

Probably so grateful avoiding death, she felt compelled to help others who had lost family, pets, or homes. That's her nature. Compassion is her essence, her DNA.

In the end, it didn't matter why. She was well. Their relationship zoomed to the top of his heart's to-do list.

LEO HAD A THREE TEXT RULE: IF AN EXCHANGE REQUIRES MORE THAN two texts it should be a call.

Hey, Beautiful, so relieved to see you thriving in that newspaper article. Thalassemia never stood a chance against your sweet blood.

Thank you, Leo. Turned out it was a misdiagnosis.

I miss you. Looking forward to catching up.

Yes, must catch up soon.

He stared at Aysha's last message. *This is ridiculous, why are we texting?* She'd opened the door and he wanted to barge right in and hug her, so he called.

Brrr-brr, brrr-brr...

"Hello, thank you for your call. Please leave a detailed message and I'll call you as soon as I can. Bye, Aysha."

She'd let it go to her voicemail. He couldn't believe it.

"Um...hey, Aysha, just thought it would be easier to talk. I really look forward to hearing your voice in person soon. Ciao, Leo."

Kept him waiting four days. Four days and nights. One hundred and three hours.

Aysha responded with another damned text:

Sorry, Leo. With my health early this year and bushfire folk lately I'm emotionally drained. So much sadness. Will call you, Ciao.

But when? Surely, they'd waited long enough.

If the year had taught him anything, it was how precious life was. Every single moment. In the sea of life, you can't catch every wave, but you also can't let them all pass you by or you end up drifting, eventually swallowed by a black shark of death or regret.

He caught his impatience, the tinge of anger.

She had a rough twelve months yet was giving her time, energy, and wisdom to people who had a horrific year. Guilt and compassion overwhelmed him. He closed the files he'd been trying to make sense of from South Korea regarding 8-Crocs. They could wait.

He doodled on his big pad until a poem poured onto the page:

Flowers in the Ashes.
Her soul burns long after the embers
Sadness is all the heart remembers
Decades of wisdom and meditation
Can't digest death's devastation
Seeking peace high up a mountain
Temporary solace from nature's fountain
And that's the harshest irony
Nature delivered this tragedy
I hope I can lighten her heavy load
Help her find a brighter road
Sprinkle laughter in trickles, then splashes
Till her flowers start growing through the ashes

He shook his head when he finished, surprised at what she'd inspired. It wasn't 'art', or an original metaphor, but he was proud of the sentiment. Leo turned on his laptop and sent the poem to Aysha in the body of an email. The only other words were in the subject line:

Whenever you're ready, I'm here for you

OCTOBER WAS A CRAZY MONTH. HE'D EXPERIENCED THE EBBS AND flows of work pressures in a couple of industries—particularly his last day job in sports marketing—but none were as extreme as the independent game business. Months of nothing followed by intense weeks of every nanosecond consuming you with problems screaming for immediate solutions, including intense South Korean distribution partners that never slept. While the marketing and business side consumed him, he felt as far from his creative dream of writing feature magazine articles as ever.

They made their South Korea deadline on the thirtieth of October. Two a.m. next morning he got an email from Pirate Bunnies. Jason and Nicholas had had enough of original games and were ending the partnership. This time it was absolutely FINAL. He couldn't blame them. Creating original content was stressful and taking on the world from Australia was nuts.

He took the first week in November off, sleeping through most of the first three days. By the second week, he was beginning to accept he and Aysha may never happen. Whatever her reasons, she was resisting or avoiding taking their relationship beyond the first date, which was almost a year earlier. Between 8-Crocs, Aysha, and mourning for Natalie, he'd put his heart on hold. Life on hold. He began thinking about hitting salsa nightclubs. If he met someone dancing, it was at least one good piece of compatibility. Plus, there was always a feel-good, party vibe around Latin music.

He couldn't control the situation with Aysha, and he was exhausted with the waiting.

Hello, Leo, do you have time for coffee at Ripe, Sassafras this Friday, 5pm?

LEO'S HEART TURNED INTO A SMILEY FACE. HIS TUMMY RUMBLED WITH love.

This Friday, Seventeen November. Sweet, sweet November.

He'd procrastinated hitting the salsa clubs, not understanding why until the digital doves had delicately dropped her text onto his phone. Fifteenth November, 2009. Exactly two years since his last therapy session with Aysha. Two *official* years. Still in bed, the warm spring sun pushed around the curtain edges and through his veins.

She was waiting for the anti-love regulation to become irrelevant. No need to talk to her supervising therapist or face an ethics committee. Now it's just her heart to my heart.

He could work with that.

The other beautiful sign was the suggested location, the first time she'd been comfortable meeting socially in her home village. He deleted three potential responses, all too mushy. *Plenty of time for mushy romance. Just get in the same space again first. Let it all flow from there.*

His thumbs got back to work.

That would be lovely. See you Friday. Ciao, Leo.

Couldn't help his grin. Sneaking in the word 'love' within lovely, borderline mushy.

He laughed loud, kicking back the duvet so hard it ended up on the floor.

Sorry, have to cancel today.

HE'D JUST FINISHED A CHICKEN, AVOCADO, AND TOMATO SANDWICH FOR lunch when Aysha's text came through. The message was difficult to digest. In all his dating experience, when a woman canceled a date by text without providing an alternative time, it was code for "*Sorry pal, not happening. Ever.*"

But this wasn't any woman. It was Aysha. And it wasn't like they'd just met, traversing a potential first or second date. They had history. A special, deeper-than-ancient-archaeology-digs history. He sent a text back with a sad face emoji and one word.

When?

Maybe Sunday afternoon. Can I confirm that morning?

He could work with Sunday.

Sure. Sunday's good.

Sunday wasn't so good.

By twelve noon, Leo hadn't heard from Aysha.

She couldn't have forgotten.

He sent her a text. *"I'm Ripe for this arvo, what time?"*

Thirty minutes later, no response and the glimpse of Aysha's pattern cooled his anticipation.

Here I am, no you can't have me. Here I am, no you can't have me. Here I am, no you can't have me...

She'd taught him about patterns. Her pattern stared him in the face, but he refused to face it. Shook his head to scrub out the thought. Headed over to his sound system, threw on a salsa CD and slid back to the kitchen floor tiles.

One two three, five six seven. One two three, five six seven...

It was a long, sweaty hour of dancing before Aysha responded.

Sorry, Leo. Anna-Marie's friend's birthday party. Told me last minute.

He'd been there. So many times his boys would dump information on him at the last minute. Birthday invitation and racing through shopping centers for a present on the morning of the party, school camp needs the afternoon before leaving, soccer shin pads gone missing an hour before the game. Parents often joked about never getting a manual on how to be a parent. All they really needed was an army logistics boot-camp.

"Kids!" was his simple reply. He'd waited this long for Aysha, there

was no rush now. Tuesday, he fired off a text seeking a suggestion for an alternative time.

Aysha didn't answer till Thursday.

Definitely this Saturday, 10.15 a.m., if that's okay.

He replied.

Happy face emoji "Okay, beautiful" Happy face emoji.

He'd earned mushy.

49

HONOR YOUR HEART

"Excuse me, what kind of tree is that?" asked Leo.

"Silver Birch. Asked the same thing when I started. Beauty, hey?" said the waiter. "What can I get you?"

"I'm waiting for someone."

"No worries, I'll catch you in a few." The waiter turned away, balancing dirty breakfast dishes.

He wasn't sure if it was the regular trips up the mountain for his sessions with Aysha, the actual therapy making him appreciate more of life's simple gifts, or natural maturing, but in the last year he noticed the beauty of trees. Melbourne was blessed with so many trees with character. This one must've been a hundred years old. Chunky bits of old bark over strong, light-grey limbs spread a peaceful green canopy over the tables on the front decking.

"Hello, Leo."

His soul spun towards Aysha's voice, his heart backflipped and his lungs swallowed all the air in Sassafras before he'd even turned his head.

"Hey, beautiful." He was about to wrap her up in a hug when she pecked him on the cheek and sat down.

Cheek peck? Probably a bit hesitant around her home and work base.

She flipped her sunglasses up onto her hair but clung to her little handbag.

"Great choice," he said.

She nodded. "Homey. In winter there's a fireplace inside with a view of the huge mountain trees out the back."

"I have all the view I need right here." He expected more than her short, controlled smile but hey, it had been a year.

The waiter saved her from more of his cheesy lines. "Ready to order, mademoiselle?"

"A chai latte, please, Ben."

Knew it. "Ginger and lemon grass tea, thanks." He turned to Aysha, "What cake do you feel like sharing?"

"None for me but you should get one. They're all delicious."

Something in Aysha's tone cut through Leo's sugar addiction, killed his appetite. "Maybe later," he said, studying her.

"Actually, Ben, I'll have a piece of your orange flourless cake to go," she said.

To go.

"Done," said the waiter.

Aysha turned back to Leo, "Already had two sessions and have to get back for the next by eleven. Actually, ten-fifty to prepare."

He checked his phone. It was already ten-twenty.

"I thought you'd finished with the bushfire people."

"Christmas," she shrugged her shoulders. "Most clients want to squeeze in extra sessions before I go away."

Away...

She'd triggered so many questions, but he'd driven forty-five minutes to be with her for just thirty. After waiting a year, he didn't want to bog the moment down.

"So...did you sue your doctors?"

Shook her head. "They didn't mean to get it wrong. It was such a relief, there was no point wasting the rest of my life on negative energy."

He nodded. "You're here now, that's the main thing."

She flicked her eyes down to the small timber table with brown slats on top and curved metal base. She looked up, care in her eyes noticeable by its earlier absence. "How's your sister?"

He sat back, throat tightened, squeezing tears into his eyes. "Do you ever recover from losing a child? I don't know how to help her."

Aysha shook her head. "All you can do is be around for her."

He nodded, stared at the tree for a moment. "Working with the bushfire survivors must have been tough."

Her eyes dulled as she nodded gently.

"Here we go," said the waiter. He transferred the cups and pots from the tray to the table. "And your secret affair, mademoiselle, the orange flourless cake." He placed the paper bag near her.

She smiled.

The waiter's energy had brought the vibe back up from the mire of death. Leo caught her up on his work rollercoaster, including the recent trip to Cannes for MIPCOM.

"We have to catch up a few hundred times before you go away."

Aysha always had wonderful posture, but she sat up even straighter in her chair, bag strap already over her shoulder.

"Leo, I wanted to meet because I have something to tell you." Her change in tone as crisp as the mountain air. Long time since she'd resorted to her therapist voice.

His body hairs did their antenna thing.

"I can't do this." She studied his eyes, waiting for a response.

His soul ran up the tree. Heart concrete. Air escaped his lungs, and new air didn't have the courage to replace it. He was all out of responses with Aysha. Half his brain processed the reality of her four words, the other half curious as to how she was going to finish. Were those leaves waving goodbye?

"Leo?"

He turned back from the tree to the eyes he'd loved from the first time. No fire, no tears. Maybe a touch of defiance, or was she bracing herself for anger from him? Her lips sucked in a little, slight movement. Must be her pushing on the inside with her tongue. This wasn't easy for her.

Anger simmered but there was no life to it. Could've come up with a passionate argument for the chance they deserved together, that he deserved with her. He closed his eyes, forced the clean mountain air in deep.

When he opened his eyes, she'd slumped in her seat, posture of a teenage boy at school.

"Why? After everything we've been through. Why can't you do this?"

"After my health scare, I slipped straight into helping the bushfire community as well as supporting my regular clients. I've neglected my kids, I'm out of emotional energy. I don't have anything left for a new relationship. Not even..."

"Not even me."

Aysha, bit her lower lip, shook her head.

She had more make-up than normal yet couldn't hide her exhaustion. Energy usually poured out of her eyes and smile, but without it, she seemed fragile as a newly hatched bird.

"I need to hear my children laughing. Feel sand under my feet. Let salty waves tickle my ankles. I've booked three weeks at Byron Bay."

He nodded. Three weeks would zoom by. What's twenty-one days after their frustrating seven hundred and thirty? The sand and sea might bring her back to a balance, to him.

A large bus parked in front of the café. Chinese tourists poured onto the street. Face masks, designer bags, and black hair under sun hats.

"Anna-Marie is having problems at school. She's always angry now. We never fought before. I keep giving to everyone else. I have to focus the next five years on Anna-Marie and be there for Pauli while he's at uni. This is their time. Precious time."

Five years. On top of the two they'd already wasted. Of all the potential steps he'd projected beyond their catch-up, her clinical axing wasn't one of them. But he couldn't argue with her reasons.

She stood, he stood.

"I'll miss you," he said.

"And me you."

And me you. The first time she'd said it sent his heart into orbit with the moon. This time... this time it was a reverse rocket launch, sucked out every atom of his energy.

She pecked him on the cheek, flipped her sunglasses down then worked her way around the tables, but couldn't enter the street foot-path. Another two buses were now unloading excited tourists. She stepped down onto the path, unable to progress for a while, then her black hair disappeared.

He slumped onto his chair. The woman who taught him to honor his love had become his biggest test. He stared at the tree, a stoic survivor. It was there before the tourists, before the café, before the shops, before the road. No matter the development around it, no matter its age, the essence of the tree was to be a tree.

His essence was to be romantic. The more love that flowed through his heart, the tougher it became through droughts and draining times, the kinder, more giving during relationship. Consciously and subconsciously, he'd explored 'honor your love' through three fascinating women over an intense few years. And he'd learned an important twist on that lesson—honor your heart.

Everything good came from that base. Leo had honored his heart when the universe nudged Zoya, Aysha, and Jade into his path. Had the courage to go on each relationship safari believing in love and romance even when the jungle led him to the same camp, in the same month, with all three women. But he knew deep in his soul he was meant to be with one woman.

Aysha.

Aysha resisted honoring her heart. At every obstacle.

"Please walk this way."

The shrieky voice jerked Leo from his thoughts.

A guy who must've been the tour leader, stood on a bench seat. He had a megaphone and was pointing east. Despite the megaphone, only the tourists closest to him heard. But they couldn't move until the outer group moved.

"Must move now," said the leader, too shy to make the most of the megaphone.

"Must move now, please."

Something moved in Leo. An idea that sparked an electric charge through his core.

Leo squeezed and weaved through the tourists, repeating excuse me, sorry, excuse me, sorry.

He stepped up onto the bench seat and put his hand out towards the tour leader.

"Please," said Leo.

The tour leader gave him the megaphone, probably relieved someone would save his embarrassment and move the masses.

"Aysha!" boomed Leo through the megaphone. "Aysha, I know you're stuck here!"

The café patrons watched him. The tourists all stared at him. Only one head faced down, shaking from side to side, about ten yards away, still within the outer throng.

"There, Aysha!"

All the tourists turned to where he pointed. The crowd magically parted, trying to get a look at who was the troublemaker.

Aysha looked up, still shaking her head but smiling.

He gave the tour leader the megaphone, jumped over the back of the bench seat, and bound over to Aysha.

"You're making a scene," said Aysha.

"I'm not making a scene, I'm making a movie. An epic. Two stars, two directors, two writers, two producers. One never-ending movie."

Her campfire eyes were back.

"If chemistry and compatibility are the engine for a loving rela-tionship, care and kindness are the fuel. We have all of that."

"Timing... timing isn't on our side," she said.

"Enjoy your special time with your kids, but you can't stay on that beach forever. My love is your energy, your escape, during the normal routine of life. We'll cherish as much time together as we can until our kids are independent. And then we'll enjoy more."

If there was a more glorious sight on earth than Aysha's campfire eyes glistening with tears, he hadn't seen it.

"He propose maybe," said one of the tourists behind him. A murmur in English and Mandarin rippled through the crowd.

"You taught me to honor my love. But you can't honor your love unless you first honor your heart. I'm on this planet so that you can honor your heart."

Aysha wiped tears with the back of her delicate hands. He stepped closer. Her eyes studied him, soft yet intense. It would take a million tourists to pull him away from that Aysha magic.

Aysha stepped in, hugged him.

He hugged tight and swung her around. A joyful shriek from Aysha and he lowered her.

"You're crazy," she said.

"You love my crazy."

She nodded. "I do. I love you, Leo, all of you."

"I love you, Aysha, all of you."

They kissed, longer and sweeter than their fist kiss so long ago. How often do you get a chance to drown in the syrupy heaven of a second first-kiss?

In the background, sounds filtered through their passionate bubble, sighs and applause from the tourist, cheers from the café patrons.

This time he was never going to let her go. They were going to honor their hearts and honor their love.

THE END

Writers sweat blood to get stories out into the world and reviews are our super-food.

Every time you leave a kind review, you're doing a wonderful deed for all writers, all stories.

Thanks, Jim.

ALSO BY JIM SHOMOS

Leo's romantic adventure continues in, Kissing Scars

Leads your heart to a festival of love. A romantic comedy novella inspired by a true story.

www.JimShomos.com/kissing-scars

Intoxicating, organic, and simply breathtaking. The Never Ending Bookshelf, 5*

Don't miss Jim's debut novel, Up Here

When you've had two dream marriages, choosing your eternal soulmate in heaven is one hell of a dilemma.

www.JimShomos.com/up-here

The most original romantic-comedy this century. Artisan Book Reviews, 5*

Up Here touched my soul, a beautiful romantic comedy about love, hope and courage. Alli, 5*

Jim Shomos must have written this with a twinkle in his eyes, as moving, as it is funny. Ella, 5*

Jim's latest novel, More Text Than Sex

A relationship comedy-drama drowning in the music biz.

www.JimShomos.com/more-text-than-sex

Deeper than an edgy contemporary romance, More Text Than Sex is a slow dance with the very soul of music. Tanya Doko, award winning singer/songwriter.

What a treat to dive into this insatiable story. Shomos is a literary rock star! Marcelle, singer/songwriter.

Get VIP release news about Jim's coming books at:

www.JimShomos.com/contact

ACKNOWLEDGMENTS

Acknowledgements

To the real women behind Zoya, Aysha and Jade, thank you for passing through my life and touching my heart. None of you have met, nor were you aware of your extraordinary November bond. I have nothing other than fondness for all three of you. And I hope you can forgive me for having to write this story! The only major detour from the true story is the happy ending with Aysha. By the time of that 'scene on the mountain', Aysha's heart had chosen a different path. Please know 'Aysha', I have forgiven you unconditionally and I hope you have found your soulmate.

Angie (and her sons), Effie, and especially, Alli, contributed to elements of this book. Michele R, for your honesty on a dodgy first draft of this story, and your courage to read the last. Ana for your encouragement on this book. Rosalie and Stella for your invaluable feedback on a late draft. Suzanne and Stella for your wonderful insights on Canberra, when I was stuck in the world's most locked down city and could not do my own research. Rochelle, for your information on writing through the potential minefield of a true story.

My lawyer Jenny, for your empathy towards the three women. To my four amigos, who build or slam my ego as needed: Bruce, Chris, Johnny, and Ted.

Carolyn, you are a wonderful editor and I look forward to collaborating on our next book. Lisa, you designed a cover that captures this story beautifully.